CRIMINAL SPIRIT

BY LUCIA T. CHIARELLI

Published by Princess Pipi Publications, Maybrook, NY

ISBN-10: 1484947134

ISBN-13: 978-1484947135

First Edition

For my fiancé Michael,

Thanks for your love and support during the process of this book (and in life in general). You've made me a better, stronger person. I love you.

For Pipi, my "best girlfriend,"

Maybe someday I'll be an accomplished author and be able to stay at home and write all day long with you snuggled up next to me. I love you.

To Dale,
you're one of the
nicest people (and
supervisors) at DSS!
you're wonderful!
Love,
Lucia
☺

Author's Notes

All of the characters in this story are completely fictitious, as is the story, which came to me in a dream. I am not trying to portray any religious belief(s) in a negative light, nor am I providing an endorsement for a life of crime.

I believe all paths eventually lead us to the same destination. But will we all be prepared for our final destination?

Special thanks to Gail Bowe, Gilbert Finesilver, Michelle Hart and Buddy Pace for taking the time to read my first draft and giving me their input, comments and constructive criticism. Thank you also for being such wonderful friends.

CHAPTER ONE – LUCILLE

Guilt is an emerging angel.

That sentence kept running through Lucille's head, for like, forever it seemed. It was what the Mother Superior used to say all the time, although Lucille didn't really understand what it meant until now. Was she going soft (again?) She can't go soft. She worked so hard to be tough and now her family (at least that's what they are to her) needs her to be tough.

Robert is very insistent that the money is here in the warehouse. It seems like they've been searching for too long a time to not find anything. Lucille seems to think that Robert is losing it, becoming unhinged, but Corrine doesn't think so. Corrine thinks Robert is strong, probably the strongest man in the world. That's what love does to you. It makes you delusional sometimes.

Lucille will never fall in love. She knows Dick is in love with her (or at least trying to get into her pants). Who would name a child Dick these days anyway? She tries to call him Richard but he always corrects her. She doesn't care if his feelings are hurt whenever she shows him she doesn't like his name. And anyway, that's why she became a nun. Because she never will, ever will, allow a man to get close to her. Her mother warned her about men, and if anyone knew about men, it was her mother. So Lucille always ignored Dick's little attempts at flirtation, as much as a nerd can flirt. And Dick was a nerd, a total nerd. That's why Robert hired him.

Robert had to have all of his ducks in a row. And we, Lucille thought, are his ducks. He's got his wife Corrine, who is so blindly in love with him, she would probably sky dive off the Empire State Building for him. Also there's Derek, the muscle of the group. While Robert was the brains of the group, Derek was the muscle. And along with Derek came Ben, his little brother (who was very small compared to Derek). Ben was unfortunately a bit slow on the uptake, but he was very sweet and innocent. Derek's life-long responsibility is to take care of Ben, since he's too simple to live on his own. Ben follows Derek's orders to the letter. I guess it couldn't hurt to have a simple duck in our duck gang family, Lucille mused. Ben reminds us of the innocence we all lost once we decided to follow Robert.

And you can't possibly be more innocent than a nun.

But here we are, all of us, Lucille pondered, in this warehouse looking for something that probably isn't here. A pile of money, Robert claimed, that would make us all rich for two lifetimes each. How is that possible? All we've found so far were the paintings, and as far as Lucille was concerned, they weren't worth anything. Who were these artists? She didn't spot any famous paintings from any famous artists. Perhaps someday these particular artists will be famous. It's amazing how some artists don't become famous until after they die; unless these artists died already and their work is just being stored here, sadly, for whatever reason?

Lucille's job was to look through each painting in this particular section of the vast warehouse, take the canvas paintings apart from their respective frames, and look inside for the money. The money could be anywhere, Robert said. And Robert made sure his name was pronounced correctly – RO-BARE. He was French, after all. That was part of his charm for Corrine. He is a real, romantic French man who, being the criminal that he is, stole the pure heart of a nun – a nun who just happened to be her best and only friend in this world.

Is there a safe? If there is, no one has found it yet. Or *has* someone found it, like Robert, and he's too greedy to share it with the rest of us as he promised? After all, there's that old adage, "No honor among thieves." Lucille shook her head. No, that can't be the case. If that were the case, he would be long gone by now. She wondered if he would take Corrine away with him, in his Great Escape? She would follow him to the ends of the earth, for sure. She followed him right out of the convent, after all. The only option for Lucille at that point was to leave the convent too (even though it was her safest haven), in order to follow her best friend, because she knew the convent would never be the same without her.

Now here she was, stuck with a bunch of odd ducks, looking for money that probably wasn't here, all the while trying to skirt the affections of a nerd in the process. Does life get any better than this?

"Hey, come see what I found!" said an excited voice in the distance, echoing in the huge warehouse. The voice was followed by loud thunderous booming footsteps, all running to find where that voice was coming from.

The voice belonged to Ben. What could he have found?

Lucille ran toward the sounds of everyone else's footsteps. Her sense of direction was not very good and she always got lost even just going around a corner. She managed to find the group surrounding Ben, and it looked like they were all waiting for her to catch up before Ben could unveil his discovery.

"Look!" Ben pointed, as everyone strained to see where he was pointing. "It's a rat!"

Sure enough, it was a rat. The poor thing was trapped in a corner under some pallets. What in the world was a rat doing in a warehouse when there was no food to be found? Lucille felt like she hadn't eaten in days and yet strangely enough, she wasn't hungry.

Robert let out an exasperated sigh. "You called us all in here for a RAT?"

"Hey, give him a break," Derek broke in, trying to defend his brother. "He doesn't understand that we're just looking for money. He'll bring your attention to everything he discovers."

"Well," Robert said mock patiently, "the next time Ben hollers that he's found something, I suggest, *DEREK*, that you are the only one who should respond." He strongly emphasized the pronunciation of each of the consonants in Derek's name in order to make his point. Robert was so over-dramatic sometimes.

It's funny how Lucille was so critical of Robert these days. Why? She herself was a trained criminal, expertly trained by Robert. Shouldn't she be inspired by Robert, the master criminal? Shouldn't she aspire to be more like him?

She was feeling guilty. Guilt is an emerging angel. Her nun roots were showing.

Derek shuffled his feet back and forth, sheepishly gazing down at those large shuffling feet of his, shrugging his shoulders. "I'm sorry, dude, but that's just the way he is." It's amazing how small Derek looked at that moment. For a tall muscular man, he suddenly became miniscule next to Robert's huge ego.

"And don't ever call me Dude!" Robert lashed out at him, gritting his teeth, pointing his finger at Derek's nose. "Now, get back to work!"

Corrine put her hand on Robert's shoulder to try to calm him down. Robert's temper was bigger than his ego.

"Come on, honey, he's just a boy." Corrine said while rubbing Robert's back.

"No, he's NOT just a boy! He's a grown man with a tiny little brain!" Robert hissed at her, shaking himself free of her caresses. She was a bit taken aback by his recoil reaction, but she had grown used to his temper by now and just took it in stride. It had nothing to do with her personally. It was just because no one had found the money yet.

Derek didn't overhear the part about Ben being a grown man with a tiny little brain, which was fortunate for Robert. Lucille feared that one of these days, Derek was going to exercise his muscle on Robert. Although Derek didn't seem to be the type of loose cannon that Robert was turning into lately. This hidden money had him obsessed since he overheard that conversation in the bar.

13

They were all at their favorite bar that night, celebrating their latest convenience store victory. They had all fallen into a comfortable pattern, and they operated together like a well-oiled machine. They all knew their jobs so well, each heist was seamless and they left no traces for the police. Robert trained them well. He was the master criminal and they were his tools. He values his tools very much. He chose his tools very carefully. He knows how to use each of his tools to bring out their greatest strengths, to do the job to perfection.

The tools in his toolbox were: Derek, the muscle man (who unfortunately came with the small baggage of Ben); Corrine, his devoted wife and lover, who would die for him; Dick, the computer tech nerd who could hack into any computer known to man, knew how to wire and rewire electrical components, and also had a photographic brain, who could create blueprints by simply walking through a building once; and Lucille, who can best be described as Corrine's best friend (i.e., baggage, as far as Robert was concerned), a convenient ally, and an extra helping hand to find a truckload of money. Lucille was a young woman possessing the gift of an innocent face, which completely threw off convenience store personnel and bank tellers into believing this wasn't a stick-up.

This last job they did, the one they were now just celebrating about, was the smoothest ever. Practice makes perfect, as they say. As usual, it began with Dick entering the store first, walking around to check for the rest room, hidden cameras, phone lines, etc. Once Dick gave the signal via cell phone, Ben and Corrine entered, casually looking through comic books and magazines. Next entered Lucille, who walked straight up to the cashier (after any other customers left) and handed the cashier a note which requested that the cashier please empty out the register.

14

Why a note? Why not just say "Stick 'em up?"

First of all, the term "stick 'em up" was no longer fashionable. That was used in old-time gangster movies. A more appropriate, direct approach was needed these days. Walking up to a convenience store cashier and saying, "Empty out the cash register" was more effective. "Stick 'em up" would just get a chuckle nowadays.

The first time Lucille tried to say "Empty out the cash register," she clumsily blurted out instead, "Can you please......do me a favor......can you please open the cash register and give us all of the money inside of it?"

Needless to say, Robert didn't kill her instantly because this occurred while they were all still in training. Lucille probably needed the most training out of all of them. Lucille wasn't born tough like Robert. Lucille was born to be a nun. So from that point on, Lucille just handed over a note to the cashier or bank teller, and remained completely silent. This was much more effective and ensured them successful jobs and lots of money.

The stunned cashier at this latest convenience store didn't know quite what to make of the innocent face that handed her such a horrible note, and she froze for a few seconds. She smiled at Lucille at first, thinking it was a joke. Lucille smiled back, a little nervously, but continued to remain silent. Her silence showed the cashier that this was not a joke. The cashier quickly reached under the counter to press the panic button, which would alert the police, but that was okay because Dick had already disabled it (among other things). Derek and Robert strolled in quietly, pointing guns at the cashier, and came to stand in place on either side of Lucille. At this point, Corrine and Ben had secured the front door to make sure no one else would enter. Dick, by now, was waiting outside behind the steering wheel of Robert's van, with the engine running, to afford them a prompt getaway.

There was nothing the cashier could do except empty the cash drawer, with a little bit of help from Derek, who was holding open a satchel beside the register. Once the drawer was empty, they all backed away slowly from the cashier. Robert kept his gun trained on the cashier until everyone was safely out of the store and packed into the van. Robert was always the last to leap into the van, which pulled away at a leisurely pace. In movies and television, most or all robberies ended with cars peeling out of parking lots, tires screeching. Since they knew the police were not coming, thanks to Dick disabling the phone lines, they were not in any hurry and didn't want to alert attention to themselves. Any customers about to enter the store would most certainly take note of a van leaving in such a hurry and possibly jot down the license plate number. Regardless, they didn't need to hurry since police wouldn't arrive until they were long gone from the scene. And the cashier never caught sight of the van, since they never parked it in a visible location from the glass front doors.

Lucille was still tossing back the last of her seltzer with cranberry juice (she hated alcohol) when Robert's ears perked up. Everyone knew he was onto something, and he motioned everyone to move a few steps to the right. Let the games begin.

There were two men at a table, and what set them apart from everyone else was that they were not ogling all the women at the bar. These two men were talking softly as if they were conspiring, and their mannerisms arose Robert's suspicions, whereas no one else in the bar would have noticed those two men. To Robert, they stuck out like sore thumbs because he notices the unnoticeable. What seems normal to most people seems out of the ordinary to Robert. He has a real nose for sniffing out trouble, or in this case, opportunity.

Lucille couldn't hear the conversation at all, but Robert put in his special hearing aids (courtesy of Dick, the techno king), and pretended to be nursing his drink, staring down at the table, wearing his best poker face. The rest of the gang scuttled away and spoke in very hushed voices to each other, so they wouldn't drown out what the two men at the table were saying. No one else could hear the men's conversation except Robert.

The men were discussing their latest heist and were quite jubilant, albeit quietly, about all the money they had hidden in an old art warehouse. Robert was listening very carefully and Lucille noticed the throbbing in his neck while he listened. It was his "listening vein," as Corrine called it. Corrine notices everything about Robert and she probably watches him while he sleeps, Lucille thought, annoyed for a fleeting moment. The more excited Robert became, the stronger that vein pulsated. Robert's vein became so huge and purple that Lucille involuntarily stepped aside in case blood started spurting out of his neck.

Robert later said that he heard everything the men said, except of course, for the precise location of where the money was hidden in the warehouse.

After the men left, Robert quickly organized his ducks into a row. Everyone had their usual "following" procedures in order. Lucille liked to call it "The Choreography of Cars." They would take three cars, pairing up, all following the men from the bar until they stopped at the warehouse. They would take turns following them, because the men might become alerted to their presence if they happened to notice the same car trailing behind them all the way to the location.

Once everyone arrives at the location, it gets tricky. That's when the choreography stops and the improvisation begins. That's when the ducks use their trained instincts combined with their mental telepathy. Everyone knows what everyone is thinking, just like those robotic hybrid humans that lived in a box-shaped hive spaceship from a very famous science fiction show.

Lucille really missed watching that show. When she was still living with her mother, that show was her only escape. She was in love with the captain of that spaceship. To her, he was the sexiest man on earth. He was refined, brilliant, courageous, eloquent and handsome all at the same time. He could make split second decisions calmly, barely batting an eyelash.

When Lucille entered the convent, she tried to watch TV whenever possible, after their chores and prayers. She and Corrine would sneak into the library, after everyone had gone to bed, and they happily watched reruns of Lucille's favorite sci-fi show on cable, while sharing a small container of ice cream. Corrine loved the brash alien security officer. She said she adored men with a rough exterior. And you couldn't find someone with more of a rough exterior than Robert, who was tougher than any of that brand of alien. That's pretty tough!

The only time Corrine liked the captain was the episode when he was kidnapped by those robotic hybrid humans and they re-wired him to become one of them. They turned him into one of their soldiers, a killing machine, part of the hive collective mind. Corrine was attracted to a killing machine, it seemed. Lucille used to tease her about her choice of men and told her she was glad she was a nun, since she would probably get killed on her first date, judging from the types of men she was attracted to.

Corrine and Lucille's favorite movie was the one about the young woman who worked in a bookstore and fell in love with a very egotistical writer, yet her mother was trying to match her up with a nice, hard-working man who owned a pickle store. Corrine was in love with the writer, but Lucille said she would have settled for the pickle store guy because he seemed like he was more genuine.

Lucille needed an escape when she lived with her mother, so she gravitated towards books and television. While her mother was upstairs in her bedroom with whichever boyfriend she happened to bring home that night, Lucille was downstairs in the living room blasting the television to drown out the noises coming from the bedroom. At least those noises were better than the sounds of her father beating her mother until she collapsed on the hard tile floor. The sounds of beating were always followed by the noise of her father's footsteps leaving the kitchen. She always found it amazing that the tiles didn't break from all that abuse the floor took from her father's heavy boots and her mother's unconscious, dead-weight body falling on it.

Lucille would break into her usual protocol at that point. She grabbed the smelling salts to rouse her mother out of her unconscious state, and then she would help her mother drag herself to the couch. After tending to her mother's wounds, Lucille would leave her on the couch to recuperate from all the blows she received, and resume her next chore in the kitchen, which was cleaning up the blood. One time, her mother's nose was broken but she refused to have Lucille call the ambulance to come take her to the hospital. Instead she called her uncle, her mother's brother, who re-set her nose and gave her some illegal pain medicine to take. Uncle Charlie was a medical school drop-out, who at least had some tiny clue about re-setting bones and diagnosing ailments. He left medical school to go to pharmacy school, so he could become a pharmacist and steal all the drugs he wanted.

When her father finally left for good (or perhaps Uncle Charlie killed him and buried his body in some hidden location, Lucille wasn't quite sure what happened, since her father just never came home), her mother decided she was very lonely and never had enough money to pay bills. So she brought home men that Lucille's mother called "Sugar Daddies" that would provide for them as long as Lucille's mother provided for their needs.

By the time Lucille escaped at 18 years old to join a convent, her mother must have gone through at least 20 sugar daddies. Lucille couldn't take it anymore, and she had no place to turn (especially when one or two of the sugar daddies took an interest in *her*). She learned how to fight from watching television, and she would attack any vulnerable spot she could find on a man. It was pretty easy, actually. Men's eyeballs and Adam's apples were very susceptible to sudden and steady pressure. She also learned quickly that her elbows were the sharpest parts of her body and she used them repeatedly in battle against her mother's suitors whenever they turned their attention to her instead of her mother. She managed, miraculously, to escape without any of her body parts being infiltrated.

Lucille felt her mother should have just gotten a job, like she herself did, working at a library after school. The pay wasn't much, but at least it afforded her some dignity. She was a Page – a person who restocked books on shelves. She loved working at the library and hated coming back home in the evenings after work. She never knew what she was going to find once she got there.

Lucille knew instantly she would be happy in the convent. She knew she wouldn't ever have to worry about men groping her, for one thing. She was very content to have a life of peace, prayer, good meals and the occasional episode of her favorite science fiction show on television.

Corrine was the nun that answered the door the night that Lucille escaped.

When the Final Straw occurred, Lucille ran out of the house. She didn't take any clothes or any other belongings with her because she hadn't prepared for her Great Escape. She didn't have any plans on where to go. When yet another man started groping her, she yelled for her mother at first. Her mother came out of her bedroom, with blood-shot eyes fixed accusingly on her daughter. Her mother thought Lucille was seducing her boyfriend.

"GET OUT!" her mother yelled, as if it were Lucille's fault that she was being groped.

Lucille didn't think twice and didn't even look back at her mother as she propelled herself out the front door.

Lucille ran and ran blindly, not knowing where she was going. It was pouring rain, raining so hard that it was like the heavens opened. The water was pounding her body, cleansing her. She ran through bushes, she ran through streets, she ran through neighborhoods with mansions and she ran through neighborhoods with shacks. She finally came to rest on the steps of a church (which was closed). While trying to catch her breath, she noticed the door to the convent across the street. That door shone like a beacon of light to her. She gathered up her courage, ran over and tentatively knocked. She knocked softly at first. Then she knocked a bit louder. Lucille knocked more urgently, until it became a steady, loud pounding. With each knock, Lucille rehashed in her mind all the events of the night, the past week, the past month, and her entire miserable life. She sobbed violently with each knock, pounding for all she was worth, her knuckles practically bleeding. Finally, the door opened and she fell through it, onto the floor, at a nun's feet.

"Oh, my!" Corrine gasped in surprise, as other nuns rushed to the door to help her.

Lucille was in tears and near hysteria. She could not speak coherently. More nuns approached the door and they ushered Lucille into the warm convent (practically carried her in). They grabbed some towels and blankets, set her on a couch and brought her hot tea.

The aroma of cinnamon and apples tickled her nose and calmed her down as she sipped at the tea. She had trouble swallowing at first because she was still choking on her tears. The nuns' sympathetic faces made her feel at home. She took several deep breaths as she stared into the dancing flames in the fireplace. Corrine sat beside her on the couch and put her hand on her shoulder, comforting her.

When Lucille had finally calmed down, she blurted out her story. She felt at first like she wasn't making much sense, but the nuns understood her. She pleaded for refuge. More than that, she spoke truthfully that based on the events in her life, she really wanted to become a nun. She was ready and willing to give up her life to serve God.

They gave her a room to stay for the night while the nuns discussed her case with the Mother Superior. Corrine took Lucille by the hand and led her to an empty bedroom, helping her turn down the bed. She handed her a very plain cotton nightgown. Corrine sat on the bed and listened patiently as Lucille poured out more of her heart's miseries. Corrine was ten years older than Lucille, but she sincerely empathized with Lucille's story.

They became fast friends and were soon inseparable. Lucille took to her religious studies and lessons whole-heartedly and became a full-fledged nun at the ripe old age of 20. She loved wearing her habit, loved the way she looked in it (when they were allowed to look in a mirror, which wasn't often). She loved the fact that only her face showed, the rest of her was covered up so that you couldn't see her shape, couldn't even see her hair, not even her hairline. She felt like a mystery woman, only God knew who she was and what she looked like. Well, Corrine and God.....and the other nuns knew what she looked like too. But that was it. She was happy to exist in her new world, her new home. The convent meant the world to her and so did her friendship with Corrine.

Little did she know her safe little world would be torn asunder by a man.

A man named Robert.

CHAPTER TWO – CORRINE

Sister Celia had done a very bad thing.

She had taken the very vow most precious and broke it. And now there was no more concealing it. She couldn't cover it up any longer. Her secret would be revealed soon, in just a few months.

Why did nuns have to take vows of chastity? It did not make any sense. Priests and nuns should have the option to marry, if they so choose. What did having a wife or husband matter to God? God would not be jealous of His servants having a mate, as long as they continued to serve Him in the fashion they promised to. A woman can still be a woman, function as a woman needs to, with all her wants and desires, and still be able to serve God wholeheartedly. And priests, well, maybe if they were allowed to marry, there wouldn't be all those scandals with altar boys.

But this was Celia's problem now. She would have to confess her sin to a priest. Would it matter that a certain priest already knew her sin? That he was part of her sin? That their sin together would be made manifest soon?

Celia's whole life came crashing down on her. How would she live? Who would take care of her? Where would she go? What would she do? The sisters would never forgive her once they knew what she had done. She would have to leave the convent immediately. And he would have to leave the priesthood.

Celia had not told Father Harris the news yet. She didn't know how to break this kind of news to him. She was afraid of how he would take it. She knew he was an honorable man, after all, he was a priest. He was honest, caring, giving, loving, kind, generous... and he would take care of her. Celia had nothing to fear.

Celia was on her way to morning Mass, along with the other sisters, all walking in unison, heading for the church across the street. She wondered if Father Harris was going to be leading the Mass.

She broke away from the others before they were all seated. Mother Superior watched her enter the Sacristy, wondering why she was going in there, since it wasn't her turn to help with the sacraments. Perhaps Sister Berta had fallen ill and Sister Celia was taking her place this morning. That would be her way, Mother Superior thought fondly. Sister Celia was a great help to the other sisters and a wonderful asset to the convent.

Sister Celia crept silently into the Sacristy and almost ran full force into Father Harris.

"Whoa, there, Sister Celia!" Father Harris laughed gently as he gave her head a little pat. "What are you doing in here? I was just putting on my vestments. You shouldn't see me like this!"

Sister Celia took a step back and caught her breath.

"Oh, Harris!" she cried and fell into his arms. Harris was taken aback and looked around, hoping no one saw her display of emotional affection.

"Sister Celia," he stated firmly, "you must get a hold of yourself. There are others nearby and they might see us."

Celia pulled away and gazed at him intently. "Perhaps this isn't the proper time to tell you. I just didn't know when I would see you again."

"The other priests and I will be joining you for dinner this evening, don't you remember? We can then escape to the library and speak privately. Will that work for you?" Harris searched her face. "I hope there's nothing wrong."

"Oh, Harris," Celia tried to wipe some tears off her cheeks, "There's something terribly wrong! I must confess!"

"Sister Celia, now is not the time to confess. I'm about to lead a Mass." Harris looked around and tossed his hands helplessly in the air for a moment. "I wish there was more I could do for you. Is it something Mother Superior can help you with?"

"Mother Superior will be so ashamed of me......" Celia paused. "Of us."

Harris was startled by that comment, but as he gazed into Celia's eyes, his breath caught. She was so beautiful and only he knew just how beautiful she really was. He loved her deeply, but he loved being a priest too.

Celia's gaze went down to her stomach and she unconsciously rubbed it gently. Harris turned pale.

"You don't mean......?" he choked out.

She looked up at him and the tears sprang fiercely out of her eyes, like a dam had just burst.

"Yes." Celia said quietly and put her head down, looking at the tips of her black shoes poking out from under her long black habit. "I've been late for three months now."

Harris drew in a sharp breath. "How could you not tell me until now?"

"I......." Celia was finding it hard to speak while tears were running down her face quickly and sliding into her mouth. "I wasn't sure. But three months is a long time and I feel........something alive inside of me."

"Oh, dear God!" Harris sat down on a nearby bench, looking like he was going to faint. "Oh, dear God, forgive us!"

An altar boy came in at that moment and became both confused and concerned to find Father Harris with his head in his hands and Sister Celia crying over him. He started to approach them but backed away suddenly. Something was not right here. He left the room but stayed within eavesdropping distance, even though he knew it was not the right thing to do.

"What are we going to do?" Father Harris sobbed into his hands. "Our lives are over!"

Sister Celia straightened up. "Our lives are not over, Harris. We will have to leave the Church and raise this child together, as honorably as we can, as man and wife."

Harris grew quiet. He wiped his face on a cloth from under his robe and sat up. He gazed at Celia for a long moment, looking deeply into her eyes. He did not speak for several minutes.

"We cannot." Harris finally said.

Sister Celia felt the panic rising in her stomach. When she finally had the courage to speak, she said, "Why not? We have to. It's the only way."

"No."

"You don't love me?" She got on her knees and beseeched him. "I know you love me. You have to take care of me and our child."

"I will do no such thing!" Father Harris leapt up from the bench and angrily pointed a finger at the door. "You need to leave me, the only thing I *have* to do...... am *obligated* to do right now....... is to conduct a Mass this morning."

Sister Celia was flabbergasted. She stoically walked to the door he was pointing at and stopped before she left, taking one last look back at him.

"Will we talk later?" she asked meekly.

"Perhaps," Father Harris replied, staring her down without emotion. "We will see what the day brings."

As Sister Celia left, the altar boy came out of hiding and entered the Sacristy, awaiting his instructions from Father Harris.

Sister Celia walked on trembling legs back into the church and found her seat. Mother Superior watched her in confusion, wondering why she didn't stay in the Sacristy with Father Harris. Wasn't she helping with the sacraments?

The altar boy came out and put the sacraments on a little table near the altar. Then he waited by the altar for Father Harris to come out.

The minutes ticked by. Before long, the Mass was fifteen minutes overdue. The sisters were beginning to murmur among themselves, wondering what was happening. Mass was never late.

Mother Superior got up and marched into the Sacristy. She was worried that something was wrong, that something terrible had happened. She had not seen Sister Celia's face when she came back, or she would have noticed her red, blotchy, tear-streaked skin. Yet, she knew somehow that something was wrong.

The Sacristy was empty. There wasn't a single priest there.

Mother Superior walked over to the altar boy, who was sitting alone on a bench, and asked him quietly who was supposed to be leading the Mass that morning. The altar boy told her he was waiting for Father Harris to finish getting dressed and come out to start the Mass.

They went together to check all of the small rooms in the Sacristy. No one was there.

The altar boy struggled with telling the Mother Superior what he had witnessed only a few short minutes ago, but he decided not to. He was a little afraid of her, all of the altar boys were. She was a formidable woman, not given to any kind of nonsense. He wasn't sure if he heard right, after all, it didn't make sense. Nuns and priests were not supposed to have children together. Since he was only eight years old, he didn't know the facts of life and didn't understand what was happening. He decided he would go to the Pastor later and speak to him privately about what he had heard and seen.

Mother Superior went to the phone and called the Pastor. There was no answer. Where was everyone?

Sister Celia sat on the bench quietly, holding back her tears. She was numb with shock at this point. She hadn't expected Harris to react so coldly with her. She knew he would be shocked and dismayed, but she had not expected that cold, harsh reaction. She expected him to step up and tell her that they would find a way to be together, no matter what, and raise their child. Yes, they committed a great sin, but wouldn't it be an even greater sin to abort the child? Wouldn't it be better to leave the Church and surrender to their love for each other, a love that had created a life? God would forgive them, she knew He would. He was a loving God and what stronger love was there than a parent's love for their child? Weren't they all God's children and God was their Father? Wouldn't He understand that people are imperfect, nuns and priests included, and that it was a part of life to make mistakes as long as you could fix the mistakes? Wouldn't it be a big mistake, a huge mistake, to not raise a child conceived in love together?

Mother Superior came out onto the altar and announced to the sisters that there would not be a Mass that morning. She said she wasn't sure what was happening, but for everyone to file out of the benches and return to the convent immediately. The sisters got up in unison and marched quietly out of the church and back to the convent.

Later on that evening, when dinner was ready, the priests were all there except for one. Father Harris was missing. When Sister Celia entered the dining room and found him missing, she fainted.

The next day, the Pastor called Sister Celia into his chambers. Mother Superior was already there when she arrived, as well as the altar boy from yesterday's Mass.

Shaking, Sister Celia took her seat.

"My child," the Pastor began, "do you know anything about the whereabouts of Father Harris?"

"No Father, I do not." Celia answered truthfully.

"When was the last time you saw him?"

"Yesterday morning, before Mass," she answered meekly, her heart thudding so powerfully that she was afraid everyone in that room could hear it.

"And what transpired between you two at that time? Please....." the Pastor paused, giving Celia a look that was both concerned and expectant. "Please do not leave out any details."

Celia opened her mouth to speak but no sound came out. She felt a heat rising up from her chest, going into her esophagus, growing hotter and hotter until she felt like her throat was on fire. Yet her tongue was frozen in place. It was a strange sensation.

"Sister Celia?" Mother Superior asked gently. "Are you all right?"

Celia still had her mouth open and began to make gurgling sounds. She was fighting to breathe, it seemed like a fire was consuming her whole body.

"SISTER??" Mother Superior rose from her chair and walked over to Celia, shaking her by the shoulders. "Please, sister, say something!"

Celia looked up at the Mother Superior and their eyes locked. There was power in their eyes, different kinds of power in both women. There was the power of truth in Mother Superior's eyes, truth and righteousness. There was the power of shame in Celia's eyes. They both recognized the different kinds of power in each other.

"Perhaps," Mother Superior gulped, "it would be better if Sister Celia and I speak privately. Will that be acceptable?"

The Pastor nodded his agreement. "Please take her back to the convent, and when you are ready to meet again, please give me a call."

But Sister Celia was rooted to her chair, like a statue. Suddenly, the gurgling sounds became words.

"It was not his fault." Sister Celia croaked out. "The child is mine only."

Mother Superior's eyes widened. It was indeed what she feared, based on what the altar boy told the Pastor.

"What do you mean, the child is yours only? Are you with child, Sister Celia?" Mother Superior asked firmly, but gently.

"I was confessing my sin to Father Harris. " Sister Celia suddenly came out of her numb state. "I was in love with him and did not know what to do with my love for an earthly man. So I........"

They waited. The silence seemed to go on forever.

"So you what?" The Pastor and Mother Superior finally spoke together.

"I went outside the convent, found a man and.....had relations with him." Sister Celia finished her lie, hoping they would believe her.

Celia never wanted to hurt Father Harris or to destroy his calling as a priest. She decided to protect him, even though he had hurt her deeply by running away. She wanted to make sure he wasn't brought into this mess. Her love for him was that great.

Celia began to spin a tale to the Pastor and the Mother Superior about meeting someone when she went food shopping and something evil within her took over and she had relations with a man in the back of a car. She wanted to atone for her sin and doubled up on her rosary and all of her devotions. She was afraid when she missed her first period, but then decided it was just because of the stress of her guilt, that her period didn't come. She decided that was the same reason for the next month's period not coming as well, so great was her guilt. But now that almost four months had gone by with no menstruation, she had to fear the worst.

"I will do whatever you ask me to do," Sister Celia finished, bowing her head. "I am the Lord's handmaiden and I have gravely sinned and disappointed Him and everyone. I will bear whatever punishment you bestow on me and will do whatever you ask of me."

The Pastor cleared his throat after a silence that lasted a few minutes. He was at a loss as to what to say. Finally, Mother Superior spoke.

"I will take Sister Celia back to the convent with me, where she will stay in confinement until we make our decision. Is that acceptable to you, Father?"

"Yes, Mother Superior, that would be acceptable." The Pastor let out a sigh and rose from his chair.

The altar boy was already dismissed before Celia told her story, so Mother Superior and Celia walked silently back to the convent. Celia was happy to be back in her room, happy to be confined for a short period of time. She could not face anyone.

She wanted to remember everything about Harris, every detail of his face, his body, his scent, his smile, his laugh. She wanted to picture the look in his eyes when he was filled with desire for her. Her body was filled with a physical ache for him just from the memories of their lovemaking. It only happened three times, but she would remember every detail of those three glorious moments for the rest of her life.

She gradually became exhausted and dozed off. She was awakened by Mother Superior entering her room. She sat up in bed expectantly and waited for the Mother to speak.

"Celia, my dear child," Mother Superior began, "I think it's best we take things one step at a time. The first thing that must be done is to atone for your sin. I know you said you already spent time atoning, but there is more that you must do. We will arrange for your penance after we are finished speaking this evening. It was a grave sin you committed, you violated the sacred vow of chastity. However, now you are with child, and to abort the child for the sake of preserving the convent's reputation is unthinkable. One option would be giving up the child for adoption."

Celia started to protest and Mother Superior put up her hand to quiet her.

"Please, sister, let me continue," Mother Superior gently chided her. "I am a woman too, and I understand women's needs. I am 40 years old and I've been a nun since I was barely 20. I went through all of the physical temptations, just like you and every other woman that enters the convent has. So I am speaking to you as a woman and not as your superior. Understand?"

Celia nodded, tears beginning to form in her eyes, as the Mother continued.

"I know you are attached to this child because it was conceived in love."

Celia's eyes widened in shock. "What do you mean? I....I....told you it was a stranger."

35

Mother Superior shook her head gently and smiled a sympathetic smile.

"My dear, I know it was Father Harris."

"But.....how could you possibly know that?" Celia asked, wiping away a tear.

"Because I've seen how you look at him, my dear. I know love when I see it."

Celia bowed her head and the tears continued falling.

"Sister Celia, I will make a confession to you." Mother Superior said as Celia looked up at her. "I, once, believe it or not, felt the very same way about our Pastor."

"No!" Celia gasped. "Seriously?"

"Seriously." Mother Superior sat on the bed next to Celia and grasped her hand. "But the difference is that I did not take it to the level that you did. I have continued to love him in my heart silently for all these years."

"How do you do it?" Celia asked, seeing the Mother in a whole new light.

"It's not easy. Many years have gone by and time makes it a little easier. I've accepted the love I feel for him in my heart and I've also accepted that I will never have him."

"Does he feel the same way about you?" Celia had a newfound respect for the Mother.

"No," Mother Superior shook her head. "Well, actually, he doesn't know how I feel, and if he loves me in return, he hides it pretty well."

"Aren't you curious? At all?" Celia pressed herself closer to the Mother, feeling almost like they were co-conspirators.

"No, not at all curious." Mother Superior let go of Celia's hand and leaned in closer to her. "The reason I'm not curious is because knowing he loved me in return would be positively dangerous."

Mother Superior got up from the bed and turned her back to Celia for a moment while she continued speaking.

"If I knew he loved me in return, it would be too tempting to leave the Church. For me, at least. I don't know what he would do, what decision he would make, if he loved me."

She turned back to Celia and sat back down on the bed.

"Father Harris," she said. "Does he love you?"

"He claimed to, Mother." Celia answered. "He told me many times. That's why I can't believe he........." Celia began to break down and choked out the next few words. "I can't believe he RAN away! He ran away from me!"

Mother Superior let Celia cry on her shoulder, and she patted her head while she cried, even kissed the top of her head.

"My child, you must get a hold of yourself. I know you are hurting deeply. This is why I understand that you want to keep the child."

Celia looked up at Mother Superior in shock. "What do you mean? What......"

"I mean," Mother Superior said gently, moving Celia away from her so she could look at her. "I mean that you have a choice to make. You can leave the Church and raise the child on your own, or you can raise the child here with all of our help."

Celia's heart soared at that news. Of course she would stay here and raise the child with the help of her Mother and all of her Sisters. She never dreamed that would ever be an option. She thought they would all be ashamed of her, especially the Mother.

"Oh Mother!" Celia cried and hugged her. "I want to raise the child with you and all of my sisters!"

Mother Superior had tears in her eyes. "I was hoping you would say that. A child here would refresh all of our souls. Of course, this must never get out, the child must never leave the convent and she will be raised to be a sister. She will be sheltered from the outside world. No one on the outside must ever know about her, understood?"

Celia looked up surprised, and Mother Superior smiled at the perplexed look in her eyes.

"How do you know it will be a girl?" Celia asked.

"When I left you earlier, after our meeting," Mother explained, "I went into my room and closed my eyes to meditate and pray on the situation. God told me the child would be a girl."

Celia's eyes widened. "How come I never get messages from God when I pray and meditate?"

Mother Superior chuckled. "Perhaps I've been more in tune with The Divine Source since I've been a nun for 22 years. And with all the guilt I carry around myself, being in love with our Pastor........guilt is an emerging angel."

"What do you mean?" Celia had never heard that expression before.

"When you feel guilty, that's your conscience speaking. And the voice of your conscience is really one of God's angels whispering guidance to you. That's what I've always believed. So if an angel can whisper guidance, an angel can also whisper God's wisdom and insights to you as well."

"You're that sure it will be a girl?" Celia couldn't believe what she was hearing.

"Yes," Mother Superior grasped both of Celia's hands and shook them up and down. "I'm that sure. Her name will be Corrine."

Mother Superior didn't mention to Celia the rest of her vision. Mother Superior tried to forget the part of the vision that went terribly wrong. She decided instead that God could change His mind, or perhaps she didn't see the vision correctly all the way through. Time will tell and faith will see them all through.

Corrine was born healthy and beautiful. She was an angel from the beginning. She slept all the way through the night. She was a very happy baby that gladly accepted attention from everyone. She hardly ever cried, only if something was wrong, like if she woke up with a very heavy diaper. Otherwise, the sisters all marveled at what a wonderful baby she was.

As she grew, the sisters had more to be proud of. Celia, especially, was very proud of her daughter and how smart she was. Corrine took to all of her lessons eagerly, learning quickly. She was quiet when she needed to be, helpful with all of the chores, and raised everyone's spirits with one of her smiles. She was as beautiful inside as she was outside.

She didn't really have curiosity about the outside world. The sisters told her how terrible the world was, so why would she ever want to leave the convent? She watched television occasionally, mostly wholesome family programs. She had many questions about why they were sisters and didn't marry and have families. She understood that God's service was more important than service to a human husband and children. She was curious as to why she was born in the convent, since they weren't allowed to have husbands, but they only told her that she was an orphan and was brought to them as a baby.

Celia had a hard time when Mother Superior told her that her penance would be that her child must never be told she was her mother. She said that would complicate things; Corrine would become confused as to how she could have been born to a celibate nun, and the Mother Superior was right. Corrine always had a plentiful supply of questions on hand, such was her great curiosity about life, and she kept all of the sisters on their toes.

Corrine would look out the windows of the convent and sometimes wonder if the world was as terrible a place as they said it was. After all, in the television shows she watched, all of the people were pretty honorable and respectable. But those were times long past, the sisters would tell her. The shows she was watching were very old. Those were very different times, when men were farmers and women were housewives. The world was evil now, filled with evil people who could not be trusted.

Corrine's world was impacted by the arrival of Lucille. The sight of this young woman in such horrible shape, all due to abuse at the hands of a foolish, weak mother with lustful boyfriends, just confirmed to Corrine all of the things that Mother Superior and all of the sisters have been telling her.

The only men that she knew and came into actual physical contact with everyday were the priests, and they were men of God. They were respectable and they could be trusted implicitly. She was especially close to Father Harris.

Father Harris had been gone from the parish for ten years. It was told to her that he left because he got a calling to go to another church that needed his special talents and gifts. Father Harris told her that during those ten years, he missed his home church and had to return. He was quite fond of her and spent a lot of time with her. She absolutely adored him.

She didn't understand why Sister Celia had such an adverse reaction to Father Harris returning. In fact, Sister Celia hardly ever spoke to him. She overheard a conversation one day, when he first returned, but she didn't understand it at all. Something about his running away when he was needed most. Sister Celia asked him why he returned now and he simply told her that God wanted him to know the love of all of his children, especially his own. She kept asking him if he returned for any other reason and he told her that if there were any other reason, it would be a sin to admit it. She told him that love in all forms was holy and pure, that God Himself, after all, created love. He told her that God also taught restraint, and though he lost that restraint once in his life, he would never lose it again.

After that conversation, Sister Celia and Father Harris never spoke again.

Corrine and Lucille became fast friends. Corrine felt like an older sister to Lucille, since she was basically now an orphan too. The two women had that in common. Corrine had no more curiosity about the outside world after seeing what it did to poor Lucille. She spent all of her free time with Lucille, ensuring that she would be happy in the convent. They were best of friends.

She never dreamed that she would one day become a victim of love at first sight. She never dreamed that in only a few short years after the arrival of Lucille, another arrival would lure her directly into the evil world that she had been sheltered from.

CHAPTER THREE – DICK

Dick watched his life play out like a film noir. He knew his friends viewed him as some kind of geek but he envisioned himself as brilliant with a debonair style.

His father never thought of him as brilliant and debonair. His father thought of him as a grave disappointment.

Instead of bringing home football trophies, he brought home fantastic grades. But that wasn't good enough for his father.

Dick was considered the "runt of the litter," in his father's eyes. He was the youngest of five boys, and his older brothers all picked on him constantly. They made fun of him, they poked him in his skinny ribs, they threw him up against walls while laughing their heads off, and they even had creative abuse contests.

For instance, they would place their bets, before the contest, to see who could scare him the most. They all won some contest at one time or another. But their best method of scaring him was when they all conspired together. One day, when Dick was around eight years old, they collectively (and very successfully) scared him more than he's ever been scared in his whole life.

The basement was the family's recreation area. They had a full bar, a pool table, a television, stereo, even books and magazines, with two oversize sofas and coffee tables, complete with a plush carpet. There were French doors leading out to a deck overlooking a large backyard. His father felt that installing a full bathroom as well would complete the effect of total comfort and convenience for everyone.

The first problem with the bathroom was that it had no windows (which kept it nice and dark if the light bulb ever went out), and the other problem was that the room was always either freezing cold in the winter or swelteringly hot in the summer. Dick always believed this was the case because his father was too cheap to pay the extra expense of having the bathroom walls properly insulated. After all, they wouldn't be using that bathroom much, would they? It was there only for convenience purposes. Just for "show" or "emergencies." That was his father's logic.

Dick's brothers dubbed the bathroom "Antarctica" during the winter season and "The Equator" during the summer season. Dick was surprised they had that much geographic knowledge in the first place, since they were all muscle-heads like their father.

One day, his brothers thought it would be very funny to lock Dick in that bathroom. It happened to be during the Antarctic season, and ten year old Dick was vulnerable – easy prey indeed – while he stood outside on the deck for a few moments, watching their dog do his business in the back yard. When Dick walked back inside, he was suddenly grabbed from behind and viciously pushed into that bathroom. They slammed the door shut while he struggled to try to reopen it. He groped around for the light switch in the total blackness, but when he finally found it, the light did not turn on.

A small moan rose up from the depths of his heart. He hated being in the dark and he hated closed-in spaces. He felt his throat close up in panic and he struggled to breathe. He also felt sure that if he was indeed able to breathe normally, (and if it wasn't so dark), he would have been able to see his breath coming out as a white, foggy mist. It was so cold in there! He thanked God that he at least had the sense to put on a light jacket, which he wore only as a precaution against the winter air, because he knew his dog never took longer than a couple of minutes to do his business outside. After all, why wear full winter gear consisting of a heavy down jacket, hat and gloves, just to be outside watching his dog for such a short duration?

Here he was, trapped inside a frozen and dark confined space. He was so scared and cold that his teeth started to chatter. His moaning quickly turned into screaming. He started to pound on the bathroom door.

"LET ME OUT! LET ME OUT, YOU *FREAKS*!!!"

He heard laughter coming from the outside of the door. Suddenly, one of his brothers banged on it harshly, to startle him further.

"HEY!" his oldest brother yelled out. "Pipe down in there! You don't want anyone to hear you, do you?"

Dick screamed even louder. Of course he wanted someone to hear him.

"MOM!!! MOOOOOOM!!! HELP ME, MOM! MOMMEEE!!! HEEEELP!!!"

His older brother banged on the door again.

"Mommy's not home, you little nerd weasel," one of his other brothers sneered contemptuously while the others laughed. "Pipe down, or we'll put a rat in there with you."

Dick instantly quieted down, mostly from the shock of hearing the word "rat." Where did they find a rat? Was it already in the bathroom with him?

As if on cue, he heard scratching on the door. He could almost see the rat's little feet pawing at the door. He knew rats had no bones and could slide through the smallest cracks. The rat could easily slide under the door and make his way in. Suddenly, the scratching sounds seemed to be coming from somewhere else. That was the thing about total darkness, it played tricks with your mind and threw off your perception. Maybe the rat wasn't scratching at the door. Maybe it was already inside the bathroom? Maybe it was in the toilet, scratching under the toilet seat lid, wanting to get out? Dick reached over to make sure the lid was closed – yes, thank God. He was about to start screaming again, but thought better of it. After all, sharing a dark, cold confined space with a rat was much worse than being completely alone in that dark, cold confined space. Poor little Dick never imagined for one second that there was no rat. He never thought that his brothers would only just *tease* him about it in order to make Dick's experience more terrifying (and also to just get him to stop screaming so their mother wouldn't hear him). He knew how evil they all were, and since they were so very evil, they would be quite capable of securing a rat from someplace.

Dick was so scared that he peed in his pants. He knew he had to pee before he let the dog out. He figured he would let the dog do his business first, and then he would take care of his own business after that. But Dick was too afraid to open the toilet seat lid and release the possible rat. After a couple of hours, he pooped in his pants as well. He could no longer hold in his bodily urges, he had lost control due to his total panic.

At some point, he fell asleep. He didn't know if it was daytime or nighttime. He didn't hear his brothers anymore, only silence. The smell of his urine and defecation ceased to bother him after a while. He had nightmares which startled him awake – and then he woke and found himself in the actual nightmare - the reality of being locked in a dark, cold, confined space.

He began to weep. It started out as mere trickles of tears running down his face. Then his whole body started to shake as he sobbed and sobbed. He moaned while sobbing, and then he started to hiccup. He was freezing cold, he was starving, and he was soiled. He was never more humiliated and scared in his entire life.

His mother finally rescued him that evening. She had been stuck at work a little later than usual, so she wasn't home when the incident happened in the early afternoon. She worked as a waitress in a diner, and her boss asked her to stay an extra hour until he could find a replacement waitress to take over for the usual woman that came on duty after she left. She didn't even know Dick was missing when she came home from work. She figured he was in his room reading as usual. She cooked dinner and when everyone showed up to the table except Dick, she asked her sons and her husband where he was.

"Beats me, mom," her oldest son replied. "I haven't seen him all day."

There was a chorus of "Me neither" going around the table. Her husband shook his head and said, "I haven't seen him either. Maybe he finally ran away from home?"

Her husband threw back his head and laughed, and Dick's brothers all "hi-fived" each other around the table. Dick's mother immediately left the table and went looking for her son.

"Hey, what about our dinner?" Dick's father called out, while the boys started chanting, "WE WANT TO EAT! WE WANT TO EAT!" with their forks and knives in hand, pounding them on the table.

First, Dick's mother checked his bedroom. She checked under his bed and in the closet. Then she went into each of the other boys' rooms, doing the same. The next thing she did was go down to the basement. When she saw the bookcase up against the bathroom door, she surmised immediately where he was. A sick feeling enveloped her as she began pushing the bookcase out of the way.

"Richard? Richard, honey, are you all right?" she cried out, pushing with all her might, but that bookcase wouldn't move. It was loaded down with heavy books.

There was no answer. She started pulling books off the shelves, flinging them to the floor. She hoped the bookshelf would be light enough to move without all those heavy books.

"RICHARD! RICHARD! Are you in there?" she cried frantically.

A small muffled, "Mom?" finally came from the other side of the door. She heaved the remaining books to the floor violently, sweeping them off the shelves. She didn't care that she was making a huge mess. She didn't stop until the bookshelf was completely empty, and she was now able to shove it away from the door.

"RICHARD!" she cried out as she opened the door. The room was dark and her nostrils were instantly assailed by the smell of urine and feces. "Oh honey, what did they do to you?"

She went to turn on the light but it didn't work. She opened the door wide and then ran around to turn on all the other lights in the basement. When light illuminated the bathroom, she was absolutely horrified.

The first thing she did was remove all of his clothes and throw them into the tub. She grabbed a heavy blanket from the couch and wrapped it around him. He was limp in her arms. She had to carry him up the stairs. She didn't bother to call for help from her husband or sons because she knew they were the ones who had locked him in there in the first place. She was well aware of their torturous games.

She had the strength of an ox carrying her 60 pound son up the stairs. A mother's love gave you that kind of strength. She brought him into the upstairs bathroom and ran a nice hot shower for him. She bathed him until he was squeaky clean, and when he finally was able to speak, all he whispered was, "Thanks Mom."

Then she put him into bed and he fell asleep. She knew he should eat something, but after that kind of ordeal, she figured a nice warm bed and some rest would do him more good than food.

She would bring him up some hot soup later, after he slept for a while.

She marched back into the dining room, where the "WE WANT TO EAT!" song tirade was still being sung. She went into the kitchen and began to serve her family dinner. She didn't say one word to any of them. What was the point? She knew they were all evil. She didn't speak a word to them all through dinner, and when it was finally over, she breathed a sigh of relief when they all left the table and clamored into the living room to watch TV. She cleared the table, and did the dishes. She went down to the basement and moved the empty bookshelf back where it belonged. She reset all the books, then rinsed out Dick's soiled clothes in the bathtub and put them in the washing machine. When all her chores were done, she tiredly walked back upstairs and made some soup. She then headed to Dick's room and checked to see if he was awake. He was still sound asleep, poor baby. She crawled into bed with him and hugged his limp little body against hers. She cried quietly into his pillow and kissed him softly on his head. She slept in his room all night with him and he felt greatly comforted by her presence.

She knew there would be more abuse of her youngest son from his older brothers, but this time she kept a more watchful eye on him. There was nothing else she could do. Her husband was a brute and her older sons were his evil spawn. She prayed for the day to come when she could gather up the courage to leave all of them and take Dick with her. But that day never came. Instead, something else entirely happened.

Dick's escape was reading books. He read everything he could get his hands on. Whenever the teachers at school gave their students reading assignments so they could write book reports,

Dick's world was wonderful and complete. The other students grumbled and complained about having to be stuck in the house reading instead of playing outside, but Dick reveled in his book assignments. He finally had an excuse to not have to be outside roughing it up with his brothers (or rather, outside while his brothers roughed him up). He would much rather spend time in his room, instead of being outside with them playing football or hitting on girls that walked by. It seemed that his brothers were chasing after girls since they were born.

Dick couldn't care less about girls when he was younger. In fact, he couldn't care less about any female as he got older, either. That is, until he met Lucille.

Lucille was different. She was innocent. She didn't have those phony airs that other girls had. She wasn't self conscious about her appearance either, like other women.

He remembered one particular girl in high school who always used to check her hair and face in a mirror, putting on lipstick (or some other type of lip balm to make her lips shiny). She had blond hair and green eyes. She was the most popular girl in school and all the boys (except him), were after her. She would just tease all the boys and leave them hanging. Or so it seemed. He found out later that she had slept with half the boys in the class. He also found out much later that after high school, she went to work for an up-and-coming clothing line and basically slept her way to becoming president of that company. She married the owner of the company, and as far as he knows, she's still running the now-famous designer clothing company. Go figure.

Lucille would never do that. In fact, he didn't think Lucille would ever sleep with anyone.

That must be why he was so crazy, madly in love with her.

When he graduated high school with a full scholarship to a very prestigious college, his father was still not proud of him. All of his brothers went to college on football scholarships and they took out student loans for the rest. Only Dick himself got the full scholarship. But that still wasn't good enough for his father. His father told him that at least his brothers had the reality of working their way to the top, while Dick seemed to have things handed to him on a silver platter.

Well, Dick didn't believe things actually were handed to him on a silver platter. Dick felt he had to work harder at things than his brothers did. Like, for instance, he had to constantly work for his father's approval. His brothers all became police officers because their father was a police officer. Dick became a computer tech engineer.

But his father was still not proud of him. Dick's mother, on the other hand, was extremely proud of him.

Dick's birth certificate read: Richard Carl Hanning. But his father called him Dick, his brothers called him Dick, and his mother was the only one who called him Richard. He knew his mother loved him. But he so desperately wanted to be loved by his father and brothers too. They called him Dick.

Growing up, people used to laugh at his name. He refused to change it to Richard. As much as they laughed at him, he felt the laughter just made him stronger. He would never give in to the name Richard, even though that was his real name. He knew his fathers and brothers called him Dick for a reason....a not-so-good reason. But he decided he was strong enough to cling to that name since it was the name his father gave him. And one day, he would turn around and find a way to please his father.

Where was his father now? Dead. His father was dead. His father died of a heart attack, watching a football game, while eating a large stick of pepperoni. His brothers were all sitting around his father, watching the game, while Dick was in the kitchen with his mother, washing the dishes. When one of his brothers came running into the kitchen to tell them their dad was having a heart attack, Dick stayed in the kitchen while his mother ran to her husband's side. She yelled out, "CALL 911!" but Dick decided not to. He finished washing the dishes instead. When he was done, his mother and brothers came in to tell him that his father had died.

Dick picked up a glass and threw it at the wall. It was his fault that his father died. His fault, because he didn't dial 911 like he was supposed to.

From somewhere in the great beyond, he could hear his father laugh and say, "Now I'm proud of you. You finally got one over on me, son."

Dick secured a great job after college. Dick found a job that most men only dream about. He had his own office in one of the best computer firms. He was always on call to fix customer problems, which he could do over the phone. Once they gave him a certain code, he could link to their computer and solve all of their problems. His boss and co-workers were totally amazed at his level of knowledge and skills which far surpassed his usual work duties.

But until Robert came along, Dick was never amazed with himself. Dick always took his skills in stride, just chalking them up to good education and intelligence. He never felt really, truly challenged......until Robert gave him some assignments.

Dick didn't need the extra money. No, it was not the money that motivated him about Robert's plans. It was the challenge, the danger, the intrigue. It was trying to win Lucille's love. His life was, in essence, turning into a film noir.

"Tell me about yourself," he imagined Lucille would say, while puffing on a cigarette.

No, scratch that, he thought. Lucille was too pure to smoke. Okay, how about this?

Lucille sat in a chair, her long dark hair swept up loosely into a sexy French braid. She was wearing a smart blouse and a tight skirt, which rode up when she sat down, and rode up even more when she crossed her legs. She was wearing dark grey stockings and heels. She was sipping a cranberry and seltzer, gazing lovingly at him with wide, inquisitive eyes.

"Please, Dick," she beseeched him. "Please tell me all about yourself."

"Well, sweetie," Dick began, "I had the usual life. Four older brothers who beat me up, a mother who adored me, and a father who hated me. And I killed him."

Lucille's chocolate brown eyes widened. "What do you mean, you killed him?"

"I killed him," Dick licked his lips as he remembered the night, "by not calling 911 when he was having a heart attack."

"Why didn't you call 911?" Lucille asked breathlessly, searching his face.

"I wanted him to die."

"Why?"

"I wanted him to die because he hated me; because no matter what I did, he was never proud of me. I wanted him to die because he loved all my brothers more than he loved me."

"Oh Dick," Lucille moaned seductively. "Is there anything I can do for you, any way I can be of comfort to you?"

"Yes," Dick replied. "Please give me a hug. I can really use a hug."

Lucille came over and straddled his lap. She brushed her lips against his, gently teasing him. Then she threw her arms around his neck and enveloped him in a passionate kiss that took his breath away. That kiss knocked his socks off. Yes, Ladies and Gentlemen, his shoes *and* socks suddenly swept themselves off and shot off across the room.

Well, Dick thought, that's how I wish it would play out someday. Maybe someday she'll melt into my arms, be taken by my charms, our heat will set off some alarms..........

"DICK!"

Robert's voice was loud and angry. Dick looked up, shaken out of his reverie.

"Have you found anything yet?" Robert asked in a stern, impatient manner. "You've been staring at that particular painting forever! Unless you plan to sell it, we're not going to make any money. Will you please stop daydreaming and actually look for the money?"

"Robert, I'm sorry," Dick said softly. "I don't know what I was thinking. I guess I was daydreaming. Do you have any ideas where else I should look?"

"Any ideas? ANY IDEAS? Are you KIDDING me?" Robert shook his head in frustration and disgust. "You're the brains here! That's why I hired you! Be creative! Look in the walls, in the floorboards! Maybe there are some loose bricks somewhere! USE YOUR HEAD!"

"Sorry, Robert, I'll try harder." Dick said, and left the room.

Look in the walls, the floorboards. See if there are loose bricks. Dick shook his head. Robert was definitely losing it.

He entered another room in the warehouse, and watched Lucille and Corrine talking. They were sitting on the floor looking through paintings as well, removing them from their frames and looking inside for money.

"Any luck yet, ladies?" Dick asked them, his heart skipping a beat when Lucille glanced at him.

"No, not yet." Corrine said, and smirked at Lucille, who just rolled her eyes. Dick tried not to be offended, knowing the eye-rolling was for his benefit.

"Luci, I think I hear Robert calling me!" Corrine said playfully and got up, hitting Dick in the arm lightly before she left. It was like she was saying, "Go Slugger! Step up to the bat!"

Dick approached Lucille shyly and squatted down next to her. "How long have you been looking through these paintings?"

"Forever," Lucille answered without looking at him, seemingly absorbed in her work, "just like you have been."

"What are we doing here?" Dick asked, running his hand through his short, light brown hair. He took off his glasses and blew on them to remove dust clinging to the lenses.

"The question is," Lucille stopped looking through the paintings and turned to face him. "Why are you here?"

Dick looked blankly at her, and his heart stopped; he was completely taken aback by her strong gaze into his eyes.

"What do you mean?" he asked weakly. Were his knees knocking together? His thighs were shaking from his squatted position, so he tried to shift his position in order to gracefully and nonchalantly sit next to her. Unfortunately, nothing was graceful and nonchalant about his movements; he plopped down on his butt while his feet went out from under him.

"I mean," Lucille ran a tongue around her lips self consciously, while completely and unknowingly arousing Dick. "What's a smart guy like you doing here?"

"The same as you," Dick said, faltering in his response. His mind went completely blank as another part of his anatomy rose to attention. How he hoped she would not notice!

"What do you mean, 'the same as me'?" Lucille scoffed, looking away. "You know nothing about me!"

"But I want to know everything about you!" Dick exclaimed passionately. "I wish you would open up to me!"

"I'm asking YOU a question, smarty pants!" Lucille turned back to look at him, hands on her hips. "Don't try to turn the conversation to me! It's not about me! I'm asking about you!"

Dick took in a sharp breath and tried to calm down his nerves. He was always so nervous when he talked to Lucille.

"What do you want to know about me?" Dick asked her shakily, clearing his throat.

"Are you daft?" Lucille shook her head. "I'm asking you, why are you here, working for RO-BARE......when you have a great job already and don't need the money?"

Dick thought for a moment. He wanted to provide a good answer to her good question.

"It's challenging." Dick finally said.

"Challenging? Yeah, that's for sure! We've been digging around in this warehouse for money that's probably not even here. Any other reasons?"

Dick felt like she was baiting him. He would happily take the bait, if it pleased his lady.

"How else can I get to hang around with you?" Dick said debonairly, and he even managed a demure smile.

"Hang around with me?" Lucille spat out, disgusted. "What's your problem, anyway?"

Dick was totally taken aback.

"Why does it surprise you so much that I like you?" he asked her point blank.

"Oh, please!" Lucille rolled her eyes. "All men like all women! There's no surprise there!"

"That's not true!" Dick said passionately. "All my life, I haven't been attracted to anyone except you."

"You expect me to believe that?" Lucille laughed coldly. "Come on, Dick, do I look like I was born yesterday? How old are you, anyway?"

"I'm 31 years old." Dick replied. "And I swear to you, that you are the first woman I've ever been interested in."

"Interested in getting into my pants!" Lucille turned away from him.

"NO!" Dick grabbed her arm and spun her around to face him. Their faces were inches from each other.

"I'm interested in YOU." Dick said softly. "Everything about you. Y-O-U. Not your pants or what's inside your pants. You."

Their eyes were locked together. Neither one of them could look away. All of a sudden, Lucille took a sharp breath and her eyes filled with tears.

"Luci?" Dick pulled her into his arms and she fell into them hard. Suddenly he felt her body drop to the floor. He dropped with her and they lay on the floor together, holding each other, her face buried in his chest. He hoped she couldn't hear the hammering of his heartbeat.

"No one's ever said that to me before." Lucille sobbed uncontrollably.

"Well," Dick rocked her gently. "Then you've never been truly loved before."

Lucille looked up at him with her tear-streaked face. "You love me? How can you love me?"

"I don't know," Dick replied, wishing he had a better reply. "I'm new at this too, you know!"

She laughed. She laughed and laughed and she made him laugh. Before they knew it, they were rolling around on the floor laughing so hard that their stomachs started to hurt. Next thing they knew, they were gasping in pain, trying to breathe normally again.

Corrine walked in at that moment. Lucille guiltily looked up at her and quickly extricated herself from Dick's arms. She jumped up and was on her feet in an instant.

"I know, I know," Lucille said. "Back to work."

Lucille walked away and sat down next to another set of paintings across the room, with her back to Dick, completely ignoring him, as if nothing had just happened between them. Dick looked at Corrine, astonished at Lucille's dramatic change of mood. Corrine shook her shoulders at him and smiled gently.

Dick got up off the floor, shook some dust off his pants, and walked out of the room. He hoped Corrine and Lucille didn't notice his trembling legs.

CHAPTER FOUR – DEREK AND BEN

Derek wished all the time that he didn't run. Correction – that *they* didn't run.

After all, they had a nice life, didn't they? Until Lee had to come along and ruin it. Lee ruined everything. But then......at least Derek has Ben. Ben is good. Ben is everything that Lee was not.

But the nosy neighbors didn't think Ben was good. They all thought Ben was stupid. Ben was far from stupid. Ben was good. So what if Ben wasn't smart? That didn't automatically make a person stupid, right? Is that all there is in life, only two kinds of people, stupid or smart?

He knew a lot of stupid people, but Ben wasn't one of them.

Derek and Ben were the children of two doctors. Their father was an orthopedic surgeon and their mother was a psychiatrist. Life was good, it really was. Derek and Ben had everything they needed in life. Until.

Until life became not so good anymore.

Why did their father have to die before he could retire? Their parents talked often of retiring early and traveling the world together. *Together*, of course, meant just the two of them, without the children.

If you could call them children. Derek was 40 and Ben was 30. Those aren't children anymore, Mom and Pop. Derek would have welcomed the privacy he and Ben would have shared if their parents were retired and traveling the world. They could have stayed in their luxurious mansion with their feet up, watching a big screen TV, having a wonderful time of their lives. But instead....a different sort of life happened.

Derek was a very popular boy in school. He was a great team player. He played football, baseball and soccer. He was the king of the prom, with Susanna Doyle as his queen. Susanna was the most popular girl in school. All the boys wanted to be with her and all the girls were jealous of her. They had planned to get married and have babies when they grew up. They promised each other. They didn't know at that time that those kinds of promises were meant to be broken.

Ben would always be Derek's baby. Even though he was his little brother, ten years his junior, Derek always felt like he was the only real father figure that Ben ever had. Even his own father behaved coldly towards Ben; his own father didn't understand his "special" son.

Derek always got everything he wanted. He won a scholarship to a great football college. But he decided not to go. He didn't know what would happen to his little brother if he went away to college. Susanna, on the other hand, went to college. She wanted to be a forensic investigator. She probably was very successful right now, Derek thought. They probably had a character based on her on one of the many crime drama shows.

Derek was always a big boy, with big bones, resembling a large breed puppy that has yet to grow into his huge paws. Once he grew up, he was huge in stature. People generally were afraid of him until they realized what a gentle giant he was. But you couldn't call him gentle if you messed with his little brother.

When Ben was in school, all the teachers and all the students realized he was "different" at a very early age. He wasn't autistic or severely mentally challenged. Derek could only best describe him as "simple." Everyone considered him to be stupid. He wasn't the most eloquent speaker in the world, but whatever he said had meaning if you read between the lines. Even though his words weren't profound in any way, shape or form, sometimes you couldn't help but take a step back and gaze at him in surprise after realizing the insight of something he just said to you. It was like he could read your soul.

He was always a simple boy who grew into a simple man. He had goodness in him. He could never be devious. He was always honest and wore his heart on his sleeve. Whatever he saw, wherever they went, whatever they did, everything was always an adventure to him. He appreciated everything in life. What adult these days could say the same thing? He was a happy person, no matter what people said about him.

Ben had no friends in school. Everyone made fun of him and he didn't know why. Whenever he heard the children laughing at him, he would simply laugh too. One day, someone put a tack on his chair and he almost jumped three feet in the air when it made contact with his butt. Everyone in the class laughed, especially the bully that put it there. But all Ben did was remove the tack from his butt and laugh. The teacher asked him if he was okay and he told her he was just fine, thanks. Unfortunately, he wasn't just fine, since the tack broke through his skin and he bled right through his pants. Granted it wasn't a lot of blood, but his favorite pants were ruined. Yet still he laughed.

He loved peanut butter and jelly sandwiches. Derek and Ben's mother never packed them peanut butter and jelly sandwiches for lunch, though. They always had the best cold cut sandwiches, or grilled veggies, or meatloaf sandwiches. Ben didn't even know what peanut butter and jelly was, since Derek was allergic to peanuts, so there were never any peanut products in the house.

One day, a new girl in school brought a peanut butter and jelly sandwich for lunch. Ben was outside on a picnic bench sitting alone. It was a beautiful warm day in late September. Ben was around 10 years old. The new girl came and sat with him on that bench, not knowing yet that it was a stone cold fact all the other children in the class stayed away from him. They all basically treated him like he had the plague. But she thought Ben was cute.

"Hi." Ben said shyly, when she asked if anyone was sitting with him. "You can sit here, sure!"

He beamed at her and she smiled back at him. She opened up her lunch box and took out her sandwich. He made a face when he saw brown and purple stuff squishing out of the white bread.

"What's that?" he asked, pointing at her sandwich.

"Peanut butter and jelly," she answered, looking at him quizzically. "Haven't you ever seen peanut butter and jelly before?"

"No. What is that?" he asked, laughing. "It looks yucky!"

"Well, it's yummy!" the little girl retorted, as she tore off half of one half of her sandwich and handed it to him. "Here, try it."

He made a face like he was going to gag as he took it from her. He kept giggling as he smelled it, then he licked at it. When he got his first taste, it was as if his eyes were opening for the first time and he could see the sky, the trees, the flowers and the birds all at once. His eyes widened in surprise as he tentatively took a small bite. It was the most delicious thing he ever ate in his whole life.

"Wow!" Ben said, laughing as he gulped the rest of the quarter sandwich down. "That was the best thing I ever had!"

"I thought you would like it," the little girl said smartly. "I can't believe you've never had it before."

"Do you want a piece of my sandwich? It's corned beef on rye bread." Ben offered.

"No thanks," she declined and continued eating her sandwich. Ben kept eyeing her while she ate and it made her a little uncomfortable. She was about to take another bite, but then hesitated.

"Do you want to trade?" Ben asked, hopefully. "My sandwich is delicious too! It's got mustard on it!"

The little girl realized how much Ben wanted her sandwich, so she just shrugged her shoulders and handed it over to him. He handed her his corned beef sandwich, which he had only taken one bite out of.

"My name is Jessica. What's yours?"

"Ben."

"Hello, Benjamin. Nice to meet you."

"Not Benjamin. Just Ben."

"Okay, Just Ben. Nice to meet you, Just Ben."

They both laughed. It was the beginning of Ben's first friendship.

Ben and Jessica ate lunch together every day. The children made fun of Jessica because she was friends with the stupid boy. Jessica would stand up for him and tell the children that he wasn't stupid, they were stupid. But they kept on teasing and taunting her. Ben didn't understand what was happening, so one day he saw them teasing her and he laughed too, not knowing, as usual, what they were laughing about. Jessica saw him laugh and thought he was laughing at her too, so she threw her lunch pail at him. It hit him squarely in the jaw.

He said "Ouch!" and rubbed his jaw while watching Jessica run away. He was puzzled. Why did she hit him? She looked like she was crying. He ran after her.

"Jessica, why did you hit me?" he asked, running alongside her when he finally caught up with her.

"GO AWAY, you *STUPID* boy!" she cried and ran away from him.

That stopped him dead in his tracks. She called him stupid. The other kids called him stupid too. What did stupid mean, anyway?

So he went home and asked Derek what stupid meant. Derek said that only stupid people knew what stupid meant, and if anyone called him stupid, it was because they themselves were stupid.

So the next day, Ben went to school and told Jessica that she was stupid. She took one of her books and threw it at him while the class laughed. The teacher ran over to prevent Jessica from throwing anything else at Ben. Jessica went to the principal's office and got detention. She went home and told her parents that some stupid boy called her stupid. Jessica's parents met with the principal and asked to be told what this was all about. The principal explained about the simple boy named Ben who was in Jessica's class. They suggested that he be taken out of her class, possibly be left back, if he was such a slow learner. The principal told Jessica's parents that he had already been left back. So Jessica's parents advised Jessica to stay away from him, to not even look in his direction.

Sadly, that was the end of Ben's only friendship, which lasted only long enough to give him a craving for peanut butter and jelly for the rest of his life.

Derek, on the other hand, had a craving for the finer things in life. Except when life turned everything topsy-turvy, he had to adjust his cravings for only what was absolutely necessary.

Their parents did not retire together. A few months before his dad's retirement, he was involved in a fatal car accident.

Their parents were driving to a party one Saturday evening in November. It was during the twilight hours when deer were the most active. Their father always drove very slowly and cautiously, always on the alert for deer. There was an SUV just in front of them on the windy, country road. That SUV hit a deer.

But it didn't end there.

The deer flew up over the SUV and plowed right into their parent's car, right through the windshield. It was a buck, a magnificent 12 point buck with the most beautiful rack of antlers anyone had ever seen. Those antlers went straight through the windshield and into their father's face. He was dead within seconds. Their mother could not stop screaming.

It was a sight that would stay with her for the rest of her life.

Derek and Ben were devastated when they found out. Ben was especially devastated, because he always wanted to get closer to his father, but for some reason, his father always kept him at arm's length. Derek couldn't figure out the underlying reason for his father's detached behavior toward Ben, because his father always treated Derek warmly. Why was he so aloof with Ben?

Derek thought maybe his father was ashamed of Ben because he was simple. Here he was, the son of a prestigious orthopedic surgeon, and he was.....simple. How can that be? Derek was a football star, after all. Derek was the most popular boy in school. But Derek too, became a disappointment to his father when he decided not to go to college.

Derek, instead, trained to become a security guard. What else could such a large, burly man become? He didn't want to become a police officer because he didn't want to be in such a dangerous occupation. In case something bad happened to him, who would take care of Ben? Derek was Ben's only friend, he had to be there for him no matter what.

After their father's funeral, an obnoxious man named Lee started coming around. At first, he brought flowers to their mother, offering his condolences for her loss. But then, he kept on coming whether she wanted him to or not. He seemed to be bullying her and Derek tried to confront him one day.

"My mother doesn't want you here!" Derek said, blocking him from entering the doorway.

"Derek, it's okay, honey, you can let him in." his mother said, weakly.

His mother seemed to lose all signs of life after her husband died so tragically. It was like her spirit was broken. She wasn't the same woman anymore.

"Why, mom? You know you don't want him here." Derek said, giving Lee the once-over.

"Just let him in." his mom answered, sounding defeated.

Lee smugly pushed past Derek and went into the kitchen where his mother was waiting. Derek followed him to the doorway and watched the two of them. They didn't know he was there.

"What do you want, Lee?" she looked up from her cup of tea.

"You know what I want, Gloria." Lee said, sitting down opposite her at the table. "I want my son to know his father. His real father."

"Why, Lee? It's been so many years. What do you want with him?"

Lee slammed his fist on the table. "Damn it, Gloria, he's my son! I've stayed away all of his life, I never told your husband, as promised. I've enjoyed taking your money all these years, but now.....I just want to get to know my son."

Who was his son? Derek asked himself. Surely not............?

Gloria looked at Lee, and for the first time since his father died, Derek thought he saw a spark of life in her eyes.

"How much?" Gloria asked Lee, her gaze not wavering from his face.

"How much what?" Lee smirked. "How much to keep me away from him, or how much do you want to pay me to take him away from you?"

"He's my son!" Gloria screeched. "You were just a one-night stand! You were a lowly cab driver thirty years ago, driving me home because I had too much to drink! If I was sober, I never would have given you a second look! As far as I'm concerned, it was rape! You took advantage of an impaired woman!"

Derek stepped into the doorway and waited for his mother to look up and see him.

She gasped.

"Don't tell your brother." she pleaded with him. "Please Derek, don't tell your brother Ben what you just heard."

Derek rubbed his chin, and tears started to fall down his strong, hard face. It was as if his face didn't realize tears were falling, as if the tears had a will of their own, without him realizing they were there. The tears were infiltrating his strength.

"Don't you care that I JUST HEARD WHAT YOU SAID?" he spat at her. "Ben is Lee's son?"

"Derek, didn't you wonder why he was so simple? That's because of his genes. Lee's his father. Lee is……." She trailed off.

"Lee is….." Lee decided to finish her sentence. "Lee is a low-down, no good cab driving rapist that never would have amounted to anything without Gloria's payoff to keep my mouth shut about my son."

Derek looked at him, questions filling the tears in his eyes.

"I didn't just let it go that night." Lee said quietly. "I thought your mother was something special. I knew where she lived, after all, I drove her home. I tried to contact her—"

"YOU STALKED ME!" Gloria shrieked.

"Okay, I stalked you. Until you offered me money to stay away from you. And I did, Gloria, didn't I? That didn't mean I didn't run into you now and then, right? Hey, I was living the high life too, now that I had some money to burn. When I saw you with that baby in your arms, only ten months after we had been together.....I knew he was mine."

"And you wanted even more money to stay away!" Gloria got up and slapped Lee across the table.

Lee rubbed his cheek and looked thoughtfully at Gloria, then up at Derek.

"I didn't want the money, Gloria. I wanted my son. It was you who insisted on giving me the money."

"But you took the money anyway, didn't you, you bastard?" Derek was fighting back both tears and the urge to slam his fist into Lee's jaw.

"Your mother pleaded with me that this would ruin her marriage. She wanted her husband to believe that Ben was his. But he never did accept Ben as his son, did he, Gloria?" Lee turned back to Derek's mother.

Gloria sighed and dejectedly looked down into her teacup. "I just wanted my boys to have a nice, normal life. I didn't want to bring any problems into my marriage. It was bad enough, my indiscretion. It was a huge mistake. I should have never gone out with the girls that night, never should have had so much to drink."

She looked up at Derek then. "Your father and I were having some problems. You see, he cheated on me and I found out about it. He promised it would never happen again. I believed him. Now how would it have looked if he found out about my one-time affair? Do you think he would have forgiven me? Do you think he would have even thought of raising Ben if he knew Ben wasn't his son?"

Derek looked from Lee to Gloria, then back again to Lee.

"What do you want with Ben now?" Derek asked. "He's thirty years old. He won't understand that you're his real father. He can't grasp that kind of concept. It will shatter his life."

"Okay, then don't tell him I'm his father. I just want to be in his life, get to know him a little, play baseball with him, that sort of thing." Lee said, shrugging his shoulders.

Derek shook his head and forced out a bitter laugh. "Baseball? You're got to be kidding. He doesn't play sports. He's a runt!"

"Don't call my son a runt!" Lee got up forcefully and faced Derek, as big as he was.

"I didn't mean he's a runt," Derek said, regretting what he said because he loves his brother. He just couldn't understand why someone who had been out of his life for so long, needs to be in it now?

"I love my brother." Derek stated flatly. "I will do anything for him. I've given up my career for him. I want him to be properly taken care of, always. I'm the only one in this world that he trusts."

"So what would it hurt if he had one more person in his life to care for him and love him as you do?" Lee asked, in what seemed like a sincere tone of voice.

Derek shuffled his feet and looked down. He was so torn. On the one hand, he knew it would probably destroy Ben if he knew that the only father he had ever known was not indeed his father. That's why it was so important to not tell him. Derek didn't even think Ben could grasp the concept anyway, of how another man could be his father.

The only way this would work is if Ben never found out Lee was his father. Perhaps they could just tell Ben that Lee was a friend of the family that wanted to spend some time with him. Ben might be happy to have another friend in his life.

But would Lee indeed be a friend to Ben, be a father to him? That was the question. Derek would be watching Lee like a hawk whenever he was near Ben; that was for certain.

"Well, mom, what do you think?" Derek finally said. "Do you think it would be all right to introduce Lee to Ben, just not as his father, since we both don't feel that he'd be able to handle it, or understand in the first place?"

"Yeah, mom," Lee smiled at her smugly. "What do you think? Can Ben come out and play with me?"

Derek gave Lee a warning look and Lee shrugged his shoulders.

"Just making a joke, son," Lee said, smiling like a Cheshire cat.

"Don't call me son." Derek warned, looking like a cobra about to spring on that Cheshire cat Lee. "I'm not your son."

Gloria looked at Derek and Lee, feeling defeated.

"If it means you'll get off my back so I can actually keep some of my income to live on now that my husband is dead......then fine." Gloria said, sighing. "You can get to know your son, if you want to. You won't get a penny more from me."

Lee looked at Derek. "Where is he?"

"He's up in his room. I'll bring him downstairs." Derek said, slowly walking upstairs, feeling like the weight of the world was on his shoulders.

CHAPTER FIVE – LUCILLE

Living with Robert and Corrine was not easy. She wished she hadn't ever left the convent, her safe haven. From the moment she first walked through the door of the convent, it felt like home. Even in her sad state of affairs at her arrival, she could smell the wonderful kitchen aromas of cinnamon apple tea and baked chicken. Just the scent of the convent alone made her feel welcome. All of the wonderful sisters who tended to her that first evening, especially Corrine, were the peace and comfort she was looking for her entire life.

She wished she could have talked Corrine out of leaving. But at that point, Corrine was madly in love and couldn't be reasoned with.

When they left the convent, Robert invited them both to live in his modest little house on the outskirts of the city. It was a very charming little home. Lucille had her own bedroom and could come and go as she pleased. She even had her own TV in her room. So why wasn't Lucille happy?

Corrine had Robert. Lucille had no one. She felt like she had lost her best friend in the world. Just when she thought she had the world under her feet, now she felt like the rug had been pulled out from under her. But she would adapt. She always adapted.

The nights were always very long for her. Even though the bedrooms were far apart from each other, Corrine's rapturous moans could be heard quite clearly. For someone who had been born and raised in a convent, Corrine adapted to a man's affections quite easily. Lucille guessed that's what usually happens when someone leads such a sheltered life. The sheltered-but-now-free person would want to run out and explore the world as much they could when they got the chance, opening themselves to every human experience possible.

Lucille thought Corrine was happy in the convent. Lucille, had in fact, adapted to the convent better than anything else in her life. She had finally been happy for once in her life. Now that happy life was gone.

She decided to look for a job. She wanted a job where she could be of service to humankind, to be able to help people who were in need. That way, she felt that she could extend her sisterly virtues outside of the convent.

She looked for jobs in customer service. Unfortunately, as it turned out, she wasn't any good at customer service.

She answered an ad to work as a customer service agent at a very popular credit card company. She worked the night shift so she wouldn't have to be at home to listen to the sounds of Robert and Corrine making love.

Lucille wasn't at all prepared for the customer service world. She was especially not prepared for how to deal with the kinds of people that called late at night. There were all kinds of people up at all hours in the dead of night, it seemed, besides just your regular run-of-the-mill insomniacs.

Lucille thought the night shift would be an easy way (that paid well – shift differential) to get her out of Robert's house and that uncomfortable situation. She didn't realize the call volume would be so.......volumous (for lack of a better word – was that even a word at all?) Volumous was the only way she could describe her call volume. Very volumous.

"Good evening," Lucille answered the phone, as she had a hundred times before, with a smile on her face so the customers could "hear" the smile. "My name is Lucille, how could I help you?"

"Yes, Lucille, I'm having a problem paying my credit card this month," the caller stated.

If Lucille had a dollar for every time she heard that statement, she would be rich. She would be so rich that she would buy the convent and fund it for the rest of its life.

"What seems to be the problem?" Lucille asked, after she entered the caller's account number into the computer.

"Well, I only get paid twice a month and your bill always comes between my checks. I need to pay all my utilities first, then buy food, car insurance, you know, that sort of thing. Then when my second check comes, I need to pay my rent. I have no money to pay my credit card."

"WELL THEN, STOP USING YOUR DAMN CREDIT CARD ALL THE TIME!" Lucille wanted to scream at the customer. Instead she said politely, "Well, perhaps you need to budget your money a little bit better. Let's see, I notice you use your credit card to buy groceries, is that right?"

"Yes," the customer answered warily.

"Well, if you're using the money from your first paycheck for groceries, as you just told me, then why are you using your credit card for groceries as well?" Lucille asked pleasantly, genuinely trying to help.

"It's none of your business what I use to buy groceries!" the customer said, her voice starting to take on a nasty tone.

"Well, ma'am, it is my business when you call to tell me you have no money to pay for your credit card because you used up your paycheck to buy groceries and pay your utilities. Which, by the way, the activity shows you also pay the utilities with your credit card." Lucille tried to keep her voice pleasant, on an even keel.

"Well, my paycheck isn't that big!" the customer said, raising her voice. "Sometimes I need to charge my groceries and my utilities!"

"But ma'am, don't you see? You're just digging yourself into a hole that way. If you stop using your credit card for groceries and utilities, then your outstanding balance will be smaller and more manageable."

"Don't you tell me how to spend my money!" the customer yelled. "I work very hard for a living and earn just a little bit of money! I need to get by, pay my rent, my electricity, water. I need to eat, know what I mean? I don't need you telling me how to live my life and spend my money!"

"Ma'am, I'm not telling you how to spend your money. I'm just trying to help you create some sort of a budget that can help you manage your money better so you'll have more on hand for paying bills, and eliminate or decrease the credit card debt. Do you understand what I'm saying?" Lucille asked kindly. The customer calmed down a little bit. Lucille took a deep breath and went on.

"Are you ready to let me help you create a budget?" Lucille asked.

"Okay." The customer sounded resigned.

"How much is your gross income per month?" Lucille asked.

"THAT'S NONE OF YOUR BUSINESS!" the customer screamed at her.

"Ma'am," Lucille tried so hard not to scream back at her. "I'm trying to help you. You gave me your permission to let me help you create a budget. We can't create a budget unless you tell me how much money you earn and how much your bills are each month. Do you understand that?"

"Okay.......I guess so."

"All right then, what is your gross income per month?"

"What's gross income mean?" the customer asked.

Lucille took another deep breath. "Your gross income is the amount of money you make before they take the taxes and deductions out."

"I don't know what that is," the customer stated flatly.

"Okay, then, how about your net income?"

"What's net income mean?"

Lucille wanted to let out a primal scream.

"Net income is the amount of your take home pay. How much money do you take home?" Lucille was trying very hard to keep her voice sounding pleasant.

"I don't know how much money I take home," the customer said. "First I go to the store and buy my lottery tickets."

Lucille took out a tissue and wiped her face.

"Okay, how much do you spend per week on lottery tickets?" Lucille asked.

"Damn if I know! I keep buying them until I win something!"

"And do you ever win anything?"

"Hardly ever. Twenty dollars here, ten dollars there, never what I need, like the big jackpot."

"Ma'am, I think I see your problem right here." Lucille said. "You're spending most of your money on lottery tickets and not enough money on groceries and utilities. Does that sound right?"

"Are you telling me I can't buy lottery tickets anymore?" The customer's voice was rising again.

"No, I would never tell you what to do. But perhaps if you had a better handle on what you spent on lottery tickets, maybe cut back a bit, then you'd have more money for groceries and expenses."

"How do I do that?"

"Well," Lucille thought she was finally getting somewhere. "How about setting a limit on your lottery purchases, like ten dollars a week?"

"TEN DOLLARS A WEEK?" the customer shrieked. "How can I win anything if I only spend ten dollars a week? I need to spend at least fifty dollars to have a good chance to win something!"

"But you said you only win twenty dollars here, ten dollars there, didn't you? That's not getting you ahead, don't you see? You're falling way behind that way! And winning lotteries are strictly dependent on luck and not actually on how much you spend."

"If I spend more, I'll have more tickets and my luck odds go up because I have a better chance of winning that way."

Lucille slapped her forehead.

"Okay, let's move on.   How much do you spend on groceries each week?"

"Don't you know that? It's on the credit card statement, miss-know-it-all, since you said I use my credit card to buy groceries."

Miss Know-It-All? Lucille smiled sarcastically to herself. I've been called a lot of things, but never that, she thought.

"Well, I'll need to know how much income you earn as a starting point. Do you have your paystub handy?" Lucille asked.

"I don't get a paystub," the customer stated, "on account that I work off the books."

"If you don't mind, may I ask what you do for a living?" Lucille thought maybe she could get a job doing what the customer does; only she wouldn't spend it all on lottery tickets.

"I clean houses," the customer answered.

"Okay, then, how much do you charge per hour or per job?"

"I don't charge a set amount. I work for someone else who pays me my wages twice a month. It's different every time."

Lucille felt like she was running into a brick wall. "Okay, then how much did you get paid this last time?"

"I don't know. I got robbed."

"You got.......robbed?" Lucille shook her head, not sure if she heard right. "Where did you get robbed?"

"When I was at the liquor store."

"And how much money do you spend on liquor each week?" Lucille was beginning to see a pattern here – liquor and lotteries could suck up all of a person's money.

"I don't know, depending on how much I feel like drinking every night." The customer's voice started to sound a little slurry. Lucille wondered if she was drinking right now.

"Ma'am, I can see it will be difficult to help you set up a budget if you don't monitor your spending. This is what you need to do. The next time you get paid, instead of going first to buy lotteries and to the liquor store –"

"I buy my lotteries at the liquor store," the customer interrupted.

"Okay, and do you buy liquor as well?"

"I buy both. I already told you that! It's like one-stop shopping! I buy my cigarettes there too. If I shop all in one place, I save money on gas that way!"

"Hold please!" Lucille pressed the hold button and then banged her forehead lightly on her desk. One of the cleaning people walked by at that moment and witnessed her head banging. She gave Lucille a puzzled look.

"Are you okay, Lucille?" the cleaning lady asked, concerned.

"Yes, Millie, I'm fine. I'm just dealing with a very difficult customer."

Lucille smiled at her. Millie was the Monday through Friday cleaning lady - an honest woman making an honest living. She liked and respected people like that.

"They're all difficult, right?" Millie smiled back, giggling a little bit. "You hang in there, Lucille."

After Millie passed by her desk and was out of sight, Lucille took a deep breath, made the sign of the cross, and picked up the phone again.

"I'm sorry to keep you waiting, ma'am." Lucille said. "Okay, where were we?"

"Stop calling me ma'am." The customer said flatly. "I'm only 30 years old, I don't need to be called ma'am."

"Well, you're older than I am, but I do apologize for calling you ma'am." Lucille said, suddenly putting her hand over her mouth. She shouldn't have said that. Now the customer got even testier.

"Oh, you're younger than me, huh, big shot?" the customer spat out. "You must be sitting over there on your high horse, judging me and calling me ma'am like I'm an old lady or something. What gives you the right, anyway? What's your name again?"

"Rebecca," Lucille lied. She didn't want to get into trouble and there was no one in the company, (that she knew of), named Rebecca.

"Well, Rebecca, Righty-Tighty Uptighty Rebecca," the customer said in a sing-song voice. "You get off that high horse of yours and help me!"

"How do you expect me to help you," Lucille said through gritted teeth, "when you don't answer my questions? You don't know how much money you make, you take whatever money you make and spend it on liquor, cigarettes and lotteries, and then you use your credit card to pay for your groceries and utilities."

"I forgot to tell you, they're shutting off my electric if I don't pay my bill this month, I'm three months behind. So I'm going to need you to increase my credit line."

"ARE YOU KIDDING ME?" Lucille screamed, and then quickly regretted her slip. "HOLD PLEASE!"

She didn't know what to do. This female customer had testicles bigger than a male gorilla. Bigger than a male elephant! Why the heck was she thinking about testicles anyway? She's a nun! Well, she used to be. She shouldn't be thinking about big testicles. Why did she have testicles, big or small, on her mind in the first place? Oh yeah, the customer had them! How on earth was she going to get out of this one?

She got back on the phone. "Hold please, I'm checking with my supervisor about your credit line increase." She pressed the hold button again.

Lucille got up and began to walk around. She walked over to her co-worker, the only other person besides herself who worked the night shift.

"Madeline, I've got someone on the phone and don't know how to handle it."

Madeline looked up from her cubicle. She was in the middle of painting her nails and blowing them dry. She painted them purple. Purple nail polish, of all things. Wouldn't that clash with her fake flame-red hair? Lucille was busy plucking out her own genuine brown hair by the roots while her only co-worker was painting her fingernails purple.

"Lucille, honey, you just get on over there and give that customer what for!" Madeline answered in her southern accent.

Everyone loved Madeline and her southern accent. Everyone, that is, except Lucille. She saw right through that innocent southern accent and fake southern hospitality attitude. Madeline was a slacker, but she charmed everyone into thinking she was a hard worker.

Lucille suddenly decided what she was going to do. It hit her with a sudden clarity and she felt absolutely calm.

"Thanks Madeline, you're a doll!" she said, smiling at her.

"I know, honey!" Madeline smiled back. Of course she knew that.

Lucille walked back to her cubicle, whistling the theme from her favorite science fiction show.

"Hello, ma'am?" Lucille said sweetly.

"I warned you not to call me ma'am," the customer said flatly.

"Sorry about that, ma'am," Lucille laughed. "Oops! Sorry again!"

Lucille heard the customer grunt on the other end of the line.

"I spoke with my supervisor," Lucille said. "And she told me we could give you a credit line increase when Sodom and Gomorrah return from vacation."

"Who are Sod Em and Go More Uh?" the customer asked. "And why do I need to wait for them to get back from vacation?"

"Because they're the ones that handle the credit line increases. They're also experts on creating budgets for customers. You'll have to forgive me for all the mistakes I've made in trying to help you with your budget, I have no experience, I'm new at this job and I hope you'll forgive me and call back during the hours of nine am and five pm."

"Should I ask for either one of them by name?" the customer asked, totally perplexed. "When will they be back from vacation?"

"Not sure, really, they're in the Holy Land right now. Their plane was hijacked and they're being held hostage."

"Oh my God, really!" the customer gasped while Lucille was holding back giggles.

"Yes, can you believe it? So right now, it's just little ol' me working the night shift, hoping I don't screw things up so much. I've got my own bills too, lots of them, and I'm having trouble paying them too. I know exactly how you feel!"

"Oh Rebecca, I'm so sorry!" the customer said. "Should I wait a week and call back then?"

"No, ma'am, you're in desperate need of help right now! You shouldn't have to wait a week to be helped. Just call between 9 a.m. and 5 p.m. tomorrow and the more experienced customer service agents will help you. Okay?"

"Okay, I'll do that. Good luck, Rebecca!"

"Good luck to you too, ma'am!"

Lucille waited for the customer to hang up before she let loose with loud guffaws and screechy little giggles. She almost lost her breath, she was laughing so hard.

The phone rang again. Lucille answered it with a smile.

"Is this Rebecca?" the caller asked, but it wasn't the same voice, it was a man.

"Um," Lucille said, not sure of what to say. "Yes, this is Rebecca."

"Well, Rebecca, this is Lucille's boss speaking. Can you please tell her that we monitor the phone calls periodically, and can you also please tell her that she handled her last customer in a deplorable, unprofessional manner."

Lucille gasped. "Mr. Manning?" Mr. Manning was the vice president of the company.

"Lucille," he said patiently, "I understand your frustration with the customer, but we have to be very patient, no matter how testy they get, and we need to solve their problems while they're still on the phone. If you ask them to call back, you're just passing the buck to someone else and showing that you're not capable of doing your job. Plus, you actually made up a story, lied to the customer!"

"I'm sorry, sir. Please give me another chance and I'll....." Lucille started, flustered.

"You're fired. We'll mail you your final check. Good night." Click.

Lucille then tried her hand at waitressing. That was another way she could be of service to people. What better way to serve humankind than by giving them nourishment for their bodies and beverages for their thirst? So she applied for work at a nearby diner.

The diner owner told her she needed to wear sneakers, she had to buy her own apron and wear a white shirt with black jeans. She had to tie her long dark hair back in a ponytail or just put it up altogether. The other two waitresses taught her how to balance plates, but she didn't get the hang of it immediately, so they asked her to just get the beverages for the tables for their orders. They also asked her to bus the tables until she learned how to balance the plates properly.

That first evening, she squirted a lemon in her eye while placing it on the rim of a diet cola. She tried to ignore the stinging in her eye while she brought the drink to the table. Her lemon eye was blinking so badly that the gentleman who ordered the diet cola thought she was winking at him, so he winked back.

She was told she wouldn't be collecting her own tips that first night, but she would be given a portion of the final tip jar. She was okay with that for the time being. She would learn to juggle the plates like a pro!

The first time she poured out hot coffee from a spout into a coffee cup, she scalded her hand when the hot liquid didn't stop pouring immediately after she shut off the lever. She quietly ran into the kitchen to muffle her scream and asked the cook for some butter to put on her burnt hand. He incredulously shook his head, looking at her like she was from another planet, and gave her a pat of butter. She started to rub the butter on her hand, but her hands were shaking so much that she dropped the butter on the floor. In her haste to pick up the butter, she bent down in a quick, fluid motion while her long ponytail braid whipped up behind her, trailing across the gas burner (which was on high) and almost set her hair on fire, if it wasn't for the quick reflexes of the cook wielding a dish towel.

Startled, she thanked him and when she turned around to get out of the kitchen, she collided with another waitress, who dropped all of the dishes she was carrying. A few of the dishes broke and the owner muttered something in Greek.

One of the waitresses asked her to practice taking orders, and she must have used up at least ten guest checks trying to write the orders correctly. She was told to abbreviate chicken as "chix" and hamburgers as "HBG" or cheeseburgers as "CHBG" and things like that. The cook still didn't understand her writing.

When she was cleaning one of the tables, she put the tip money in her apron and was fully intending to put it in the tip bucket, but she slipped on some spilled soup residue on the tile floor and temporarily forgot about the money in her apron while flailing around, trying to not drop her own dishes and/or fall on the floor. One of the waitresses was watching her and accused her of trying to steal her tips.

That was only her first night.

After about a week, she was still not good at balancing plates. She frequently dropped silverware in people's laps when she was setting the tables. Lucille did discover that her best bet was to move quickly back and forth from kitchen to table, carrying only one or two plates at a time. This system worked well for her and the customers received their food hot *and* without mishap. She did, however, burn her thumbnail on the eggplant parmigiana dish. It was a hot metal dish that was placed over a regular dinner plate, and when she was rushing quickly to the table, the hot metal dish slid back on the dinner plate and landed securely on her thumbnail. She smiled at the customer while setting the plate down on the table in front of him, and managed to suppress her scream until she got to the kitchen again.

The rules were: all meals came with soup and salad, potato and vegetable, except for hot open sandwiches, which only came with potato and vegetable. The customers gave their dinner entrée orders, and then you asked them what kind of soup they wanted, what kind of salad dressing, what kind of potato and which vegetable.

But that was a little confusing to Lucille at first.

A handsome man with curly brown hair and deep green eyes walked in. He smiled at Lucille, then came and sat at the counter. He was really very handsome. Lucille's breath caught in her throat as their eyes met. For the first time in her life, Lucille got a little flustered by a man's charms.

"What can I get for you?" she asked shyly.

"How about a menu?" he teased, cocking his head and smiling mischievously at her. She wanted to slap her forehead. But instead, she handed him a menu with shaking hands and almost knocked over the beverages that one of the waitresses had set out on the counter.

When he was ready to order, she was waiting with baited breath and pen hovering over the guest check properly placed with the cardboard between the carbons. She wanted to make sure she didn't ruin any more guest checks. Sometimes she had the cardboard in the wrong place and made the carbon run onto the next guest check. That's when the cooks in the kitchen had even more trouble deciphering her orders.

"I'll have a hot open roast beef sandwich with fries," the cute man said, smiling at her.

"What kind of soup?" she asked out of habit.

"It doesn't come with soup!" the waitress with the drinks on the counter said. "Hot open sandwiches only come with potato and vegetable. Got it?"

Lucille thanked her. Regardless of the correction, she was about to ask what kind of salad dressing he wanted, even though it didn't come with salad. She stopped herself before she could ask, but she was still flustered from the waitress correcting her. She would have paid for his soup and salad if she had to, he was so cute!

So instead of asking him what kind of salad dressing, even though it didn't come with salad, she gazed into his eyes and blurted out instead, "Bleu Cheese?"

He tilted his head at her again, looking at her the way a dog does when it's trying to understand what you're saying. The waitress shot her a look again, rolling her eyes.

"I'm sorry," Lucille said breathlessly. "No salad for you. What kind of potato?"

"I said fries!" he answered, getting a little bit impatient.

"Okay, sorry!" Her hands were shaking while writing the order down. "What kind of vegetable?" She knew it had to come with a vegetable, after all, right? Lucille was insecure enough to glance at the other waitress for approval. The other waitress nodded. Hurray! She was right about the vegetable! Score!

"No vegetable, thanks anyway." Cutie Pie said, as Lucille's heart sank in disappointment. Lucille felt like the biggest idiot that ever walked the earth. She took his drink order and poured it out, almost knocking it over as she brought it to him.

She went into the kitchen to place the order and then occupied herself with other tables until his order was ready. She brought him his food, thankfully without dropping it on the floor first, and asked him if he needed anything else.

"I'm fine, thanks." Handsome Harry said, winking at her. Her heart fluttered.

She was suddenly at a loss as to what to do, since all she wanted to do was stand there and stare at him while he ate his food. She realized now how Corrine must have felt about Robert the first time she laid eyes on him.

Alas, he was a fairly quick eater and finished his food in no time, much too quickly for Lucille. She was already panicking, wondering if she would ever see him again. She realized it was silly to feel this way about a stranger.

But he was SO CUTE!!! And she was completely unaccustomed to feeling this way.

When she took his plate away, she asked him if he wanted anything else. She was really hoping he would say, "Yes, your phone number please."

"The check please." Gorgeous George said instead.

Lucille's heart sank as she gave him his check. He took money out of his wallet and walked to the register. He didn't even say goodbye or leave her a tip. She felt stupid, so stupid. That's what she gets for screwing up his order in the first place. How could she possibly think she could hold down a job? She wasn't good at anything, she had no skills, couldn't even wait tables. She couldn't remember who gets soup, salad, potatoes and vegetables. After all, waiting tables was the ultimate in service to people.

Bringing them food was a noble thing and she couldn't even get that right! She was useless.

As she was cleaning the counter, The Beautiful One walked over to her. She looked up and was startled to see him standing in front of her. He placed a ten dollar bill on the counter. Was he giving her a ten dollar tip on a seven dollar meal??

"Thank you," Wonderful Wally said. "What's your name?"

"Lucille," she answered breathlessly.

"I'm Jeff. It's nice to meet you." He extended his hand. "I think you have a very pretty face and a nice smile. I'd really love to take you out to dinner sometime. Please give me a call if you're interested."

His business card was on the counter, on top of the ten dollar bill. She looked down at the money and the card, and then she looked back up at him, in total shock. He was asking her out? She almost got his meal order wrong and he wanted to take her out to dinner?

"Thanks!" she said, feeling the heat rise into her cheeks as she shook his outstretched hand. She felt heat rise into her cheeks and hoped he didn't notice she was blushing. He did notice – and he smiled broadly at her.

CHAPTER SIX – CORRINE

The convent was so cold. There was something wrong with the heating system. Mother Superior finally decided to make those inevitable phone calls to try to find a reputable company to repair it. The convent didn't have much stashed away in emergency funding for heating repairs, but the church would help provide them with the rest. They would need to ask their congregation to be a little more generous with their tithes and offerings.

Mother Superior needed to get a few quotes from different companies to secure an inexpensive but efficient job. The Pastor recommended a couple of companies that he had dealt with in the past. Several people from different companies arrived to look at their heating system until she finally settled on one company. She felt the representative from that company gave her good "vibes." She wanted someone she could trust as well as being inexpensive and efficient.

The doorbell rang and Sister Celia answered the door to greet the two men who would be working on the heating system. She ushered them in and led them to the basement so they could start working on the furnace. While they were all heading for the basement door, Corrine happened to be strolling toward them.

Corrine glanced at the two men and smiled politely, then demurely lowered her eyes to the floor. Suddenly, she felt an electric shock in her stomach. She looked back up at one of the men.

He was the most beautiful man she had ever seen. His eyes locked with hers and she was suddenly frozen in place.

"Sister Corrine?" Sister Celia looked at her daughter, concerned. Corrine's face appeared transfixed, as if she had either seen a ghost or was having a major revelation. Either way, it was a bit disconcerting seeing her daughter with that expression on her face.

"Sister Corrine, dear, are you all right?" she asked again.

Corrine's eyes took him in fully from his head down to his toes. She wanted to inhale him into her soul. He was tall, muscular, with medium brown hair and hazel eyes. His hair fell like a mop around his head, playfully framing his gorgeous features. He had high cheekbones, an upturned nose and sensuous full lips.

"Sister Corrine!" Sister Celia raised her voice and almost had to reach out to shake her daughter. "Speak to me! What's wrong, child?"

Corrine's gaze finally shifted to Celia as she slowly came back to her senses. Corrine felt like the world was moving in slow motion and for a moment, time had stopped for her.

"I'm fine, Sister Celia. I'm......sorry if I scared you. I just........" she trailed off, glancing at the gorgeous man again. "I just felt a little faint for a moment. I'm fine now."

"Would you like me to get you a glass of water or some tea?" Sister Celia asked.

"No Sister, I will be fine." Corrine quickly glanced at him again before walking briskly away. She waited two seconds and boldly turned around to steal one more glance at him before they were out of sight.

Corrine gasped.

He was looking back at her as well!

Corrine quickly turned away from him and bumped full force into Lucille.

"What the........?" Lucille said as they collided. "Are you okay?"

"Oh, Luci!" Corrine said breathlessly. "I don't know......oh, my dear Lord in Heaven!"

"What's the matter with you?" Lucille asked, concerned. "What happened? What??"

Corrine pulled Lucille into the kitchen. Thankfully no one was in there. Corrine went to the sink and poured herself a glass of water. Lucille sat down at the table, expectantly waiting to hear why Corrine was in such a tizzy.

Corrine drank down the water in full, long gulps. With shaking fingers, she set the empty glass down onto the table. She then sat down and faced Lucille across the table.

"Oh, Luci," she began. "I don't feel too well."

"What's wrong?" Lucille was really concerned now, her heart beating fast in fear for her friend's well being.

"I just saw........the most beautiful man in the world!" Corrine said breathlessly.

"WHAT?" Lucille said, shocked. She rose up out of her seat and towered over Corrine. "Corrine! We're nuns, for God's sake! You're not supposed to be looking at men! You're not supposed to be attracted to any man except Jesus!"

Lucille had already seen the two men enter the convent, so she knew Corrine was talking about one of them. Neither one of them looked particularly beautiful to Lucille, though.

"Luci, I'm so scared!" Corrine said, trembling. "I've never felt like this before!"

"Well, you'd better stop feeling this way, if you know what's good for you! You're a nun! You've been a nun practically all of your life! Get a grip, Sister!" Lucille said, heat rising throughout her whole body. She couldn't understand why, but she suddenly felt threatened.

"I'm not just a nun!" Corrine shot up from her chair and faced Lucille at eye level. "I'm a woman! I have feelings! I don't know about life outside of this place! All I know and all I've ever known, is this convent! You yourself have experienced the outside world, so you know what it's like. You're lucky in that way!"

"Lucky?" Lucille screeched. "LUCKY? Are you kidding me? Don't you remember what I've been through? You call that lucky?"

Corrine quieted down for a moment, and as if on cue, Lucille calmed down as well. They both sat down and stared quietly at each other, breathing heavily. Lucille reached out a hand to Corrine across the table.

"Okay, think about this for a moment." Lucille said gently. "What's so special about this man? He's just a man. He's going to fix the heating system and then he's going to leave. He'll be out of our lives. You'll never see him again. You're getting yourself into a tizzy over nothing, right?"

Corrine released a heavy sigh. "Right."

"So, then what's the problem?" asked Lucille, the voice of reason.

"The problem is.....the thought of never seeing him again......the thought of him walking out of my life........scares me." Corrine answered in a small voice.

"But......you just met him!" Lucille said frantically. "You don't even know him!"

Sister Celia walked into the kitchen at that moment.

"My child!" Celia said, pulling out a chair next to Corrine. Celia sat down and placed her hand on Corrine's shoulder, searching her face. "Are you all right?"

"I was feeling.....faint." Corrine said, looking away. "I'm feeling better now."

"You don't look any better." Sister Celia said worriedly. "You look like the devil just drained your soul."

Corrine laughed to herself. "I think he did."

It was really hard for Celia to continue to pretend that Corrine was not her daughter. As the years went by, it got even more difficult. Corrine blossomed into quite a smart and beautiful woman, and Celia was so proud of her. She was so mature, so caring, and intelligent. Celia longed to open her heart and confess everything to her. She wanted to be recognized as her mother. They resembled each other strongly, with their golden blonde hair and sea green eyes. It was frustrating to Celia that Corrine didn't notice their resemblance at all. But Celia had promised the Mother Superior that she would never tell Corrine that she was her mother. That was the promise she had to make in order to not lose her daughter to adoption. Every single day, she thanked God that she was blessed with such a wonderful daughter. Yes, she was a blessing as far as she was concerned, even though this blessing was conceived in sin -- the worst sin possible for a nun, excluding committing murder.

As much as Celia wrestled with her feelings toward wanting to bond further with her daughter, Father Harris, on the other hand, was not wrestling at all. He visited with Corrine every day and they seemed to always have a jolly old time together. They had quite a bond, and Corrine confessed to him once that she thought of him as a father figure to her. Celia had walked into the room at that moment and it felt like a dagger went through her heart when she heard those words come out of her daughter. She always wished secretly that Corrine would feel that way about her, that she would recognize their mother/daughter bond on some spiritual level. Celia noticed the expression of complete bliss and peace on his face when their daughter told him how she felt about him. There was no guilt, no longing, or struggle for him. He was completely happy with his relationship with his daughter. He was totally fine with the fact that he didn't have to admit he was her father.

It was probably because he was really the only man in Corrine's life and that made him special. After all, Celia had to share Corrine with all the other sisters. How could Corrine feel a special bond to Celia when she wasn't allowed to spend any kind of quality one-on-one time with her? Celia tried many times to have a private word alone with her daughter, but it seemed that there was always some sort of interruption. Mother Superior might walk in at a crucial bonding moment, or one of the other sisters would need something from her.

Once Lucille entered their lives, Corrine was consumed with her. They became best friends and were inseparable. In some ways, Celia was more jealous of Lucille than she was of Harris.

"Would you like a beverage?" Corrine asked the two men, who turned to look at her.

Corrine had boldly sneaked down to the basement after she convinced Celia and Lucille that she was fine.

The two men exchanged glances and one of them smirked and asked, "Well, what are you offering?"

The other man, the beautiful man, shot him a punch in the arm and said quietly, "What's the matter with you? Show some respect! We're in a convent!"

The not-so-beautiful man replied, "Sorry, miss. I mean, Sister. What I meant to say was, what's on tap?"

The beautiful man shook his head again, punching his co-worker in the arm again. He was upset despite the fact that the innocent, beautiful sister had no inkling as to what he was referring to.

"Do you have water?" the beautiful man asked. "We would both love a cold glass of water."

"Well, we do have several kinds of juices as well." Corrine offered, which made the not-so-beautiful man double over in laughter.

"The water will do just fine, Sister, thank you," the beautiful man answered, shooting his co-worker a stern look. Celia had no clue why he was being so cross with him.

"Water it is, then." Corrine said and turned her back, gently swishing her habit in a graceful turn.

Corrine ran up the stairs to the kitchen, hurriedly poured water over ice into two glasses, and quickly walked back down the stairs, trying not to spill the water. She was trying to be quick about doing this naughty, dirty deed without being seen by the other sisters. When she reached the bottom of the stairs, both men shook some dirt off their pants and walked over to her to take the glasses from her.

As they sipped the water, the beautiful man's eyes never left Corrine's eyes. Her eyes were locked with his, frozen. She couldn't look away from him if she tried. Her feet were cemented in place.

As he finished the last drop of water, he brought the glass to Corrine and his fingers lightly touched hers when the glass exchanged hands, their eyes still locked together. Corrine felt a warming sensation in her private place at the feel of their hands making contact. She didn't understand what was happening; it was like an electric current was going through her entire body.

"What's your name?" The Beautiful Man asked her.

"Corrine." She answered, but her voice came out in a squeak. She cleared her throat and said again, more distinctly and clearly, "Corrine. My name is Corrine."

"Don't you mean Sister Corrine?" The man of beauty asked her gently.

"Yes." Corrine answered. "I suppose so. Sister Corrine."

The beautiful man chuckled. "My name is Robert. Robert DuBois."

Oh dear Lord, be still my heart! Corrine thought to herself. He spoke with a French accent and pronounced his name Ro-Bare.

Robert extended his hand to her while their eyes were still locked. It was like they were trying to set a record in the Guinness Book of World Records for eye locking.

The other man cleared his throat and said, "I'm Danny, but who cares, right?"

Robert and Corrine were still holding hands, looking into each other's eyes. Neither one spoke.

Suddenly there were footsteps on the stairs. The footsteps were very soft, but Corrine heard them and she reluctantly released Robert's hand. She suddenly looked away and turned toward the stairs to see Mother Superior. The Mother was startled to see Corrine there and was even more startled when she saw Robert's face.

It was the man. The man in her vision. The man who would destroy everything.

"Sister Corrine, child!" Mother Superior said sternly, her voice trying to mask the frantic beating of her heart. "What are you doing down here?"

"I was just getting water for the workers, Mother." Corrine bowed her head and curtseyed respectfully. "I didn't mean to upset you. I should have asked permission and I'm sorry. Please forgive me."

"Go back up to your room, child!" Mother Superior said, a little more forcefully than she should have. She was speaking out of pure fear, she realized that. Corrine looked at her, completely perplexed, not knowing why she was being so stern with her.

Corrine quickly backed away from her and ran up the stairs holding Robert's glass. Danny still had his glass, which he sheepishly held out to the Mother Superior.

"Thank you, Mother Superior," Robert said, turning on the charm. "Sister Corrine was very kind to us, no doubt, reflecting all the love and purity of your sacred convent. She was merely offering us some water, knowing that we're working quite diligently down here. We want to do the best job possible for you."

Mother Superior softened somewhat, but her vision returned to her quite vividly. She sighed and felt a sense of resignation. If it is God's Will.......how can she stand in His Way?

By God, she certainly would try!

"Thank you, sir." Mother Superior answered curtly. "I trust that you will behave in a most professional manner at all times."

Robert knew exactly what she meant. "Yes, Mother Superior, you can count on us."

She nodded to them and went back up the stairs.

Corrine couldn't sleep that night. She knew the men would be coming back the next day; more specifically, that *Robert* would be coming back the next day. She knew she had to act quickly, had to find a way to spend some more time with him. She didn't know why she needed to spend time with him, only that she needed to see him like she needed to breathe air and drink water in order to survive. She never felt this way before.

She had her share of guilt. She knew she was a nun, knew that she had taken vows, knew that she was married to Jesus for life. What would happen to her if she decided to divorce Jesus and marry someone else?

Marry! That was crazy! What was she thinking? She was an adult woman in her early thirties, why was she thinking such crazy thoughts? She was a nun, for God's sake! She's not supposed to be thinking such thoughts about any mortal men.

But he was so beautiful! Corrine sighed. He was the most beautiful man she had ever laid eyes on. She never believed that any man in the world could possibly be so beautiful.

And what was going on inside of her body? She was feeling electricity, and her heart was racing just at the thought of his face. And she had a burning, yearning feeling in her private area. This was not natural to her; she didn't understand what was going on. There seemed to be a sensation of wetness, almost like she had her period, but the fluid appeared clear. What was happening to her?

Lucille was absolutely right. She should not feel this way about any man. It was wrong to feel this way. She was married to the Lord, she had pledged her life to Him. Or had she?

As far as she knew, she was born in this convent. She had no memories of any life outside of the convent. She was told someone dropped her off, as a baby just a few weeks old, at the convent doorstep. They had no choice but to take her in. Or didn't they have a choice? They could have given her up for adoption. Why did they take her in?

She would speak to Father Harris in the morning about it. She hoped her curiosity about where she came from would not arouse suspicion. No, then again.......perhaps she shouldn't speak of it. But if she didn't speak to someone about it, she would never know where she came from.

Curiosity killed the cat, as they say. But she wasn't a cat. She was a grown woman and she deserved to know where she came from. She was born and raised in the convent. She did not have a choice, she couldn't choose whether or not she wanted to go out in the world or become a nun. She had to become a nun because she was raised by nuns and it was all that she knew. And that wasn't fair. That wasn't fair at all. Was it?

Didn't everyone have a right to choose their own life, to choose their own destiny? Just because she was practically born a nun, did that mean she had to be a nun forever?

Being a nun meant she took vows that she would be a nun forever. It would displease God if she turned her back on the convent and ran away. She would go straight to Hell when she died, she knew she would. It was a sin for a nun to feel the way she did about any flesh and blood man. Especially about a man that she just met.

But he wasn't just *any* man. He was special. Robert was the most beautiful man she had ever seen. She imagined herself married to him. She imagined herself in a kitchen, wearing an apron, cooking dinner for him. She imagined herself kissing him. As she imagined herself kissing him, she had that moist sensation deep down inside again.

She watched movies; she knew men and women kissed each other. But they were not allowed to watch any movies or television shows that showed anything beyond kissing. She knew about sexual intercourse, she was taught about that. It was a very sterile, pure thing that happened between a husband and wife in order to have children. That was the sole purpose of copulation, no other reason.

She decided she wanted to try sex. Can't she just try sex once, just to see what it felt like? Would that make her a terrible nun?

Yes, it would. She would go straight to Hell if she had sex with a man. Straight to Hell.

Was Hell really so bad? And what was so great about Heaven anyway? Floating around on clouds and stuff like that?

Was it worth it? Was it worth playing with her soul like this? Flirting with fire?

No. It wasn't worth it. This was just temporary insanity, a temporary life glitch. This was the devil tempting her, nothing more. She must not give in to the devil. She suddenly implored God to give her the strength to resist this man, this beautiful Robert. How could any man be more beautiful than God, after all? God Himself was the most Beautiful One.

But she had never seen God. She believed in Someone whom she has never seen. And she has seen Robert. And she thought he was beautiful. Did she dare think that he might find her beautiful too? She couldn't deny the way their eyes locked. Just the memory of their eyes locking, the intensity of his eyes looking right into her soul, shot another volt of electricity through her. She was falling helplessly in love with Robert and she knew it.

What sort of folly is this? Love is more than just a feeling, isn't it? Corrine tried so hard to reason with herself. This is pure unadulterated infatuation. That's what this is, right? After all, she thought, she only just met him. He was, for all intent and purposes, like someone she saw on television. Could she fall in love with someone on television? Of course not. Folly, pure folly.

Go to sleep, she demanded to herself. Go to sleep and forget about this. Forget about him. Forget about Robert!

As much as she tried to forget about him, he filled her dreams. She slept fitfully, not knowing where she was or who she was. The only thing she knew for sure, the only thing she saw, the only thing she breathed, and drank, and ate, and felt, and longed for, all night long, was Robert.

The next day, she tried to hide when they arrived to work. She occupied herself in the kitchen, she peeled potatoes and carrots. She prepared the chickens for dinner. She washed all the dishes. Mother Superior was really impressed with her zeal for cooking and cleaning. Mother Superior was keeping a close eye on her since yesterday when she caught her in the basement. She breathed a sigh of relief when she saw how hard Corrine was keeping busy, staying away from the men in the basement. Most importantly, she was staying away from "him."

The only one Corrine wasn't fooling was Lucille. Lucille was keeping an even closer eye on her than Mother Superior. Lucille stayed with her in the kitchen and helped with all the cooking and cleaning duties. They were just about done cleaning the counters, playfully throwing sponges at each other, giggling.

To their surprise, they heard a man's voice behind them, clearing his throat. They spun around and saw Robert standing there.

"I was wondering," Robert asked, looking at Corrine intensely, "if I could have a glass of water? Well, two glasses, actually, one for my co-worker as well. Please?"

Lucille went to the fridge, took out two bottles of water, and walked over to him. She looked over at Corrine and saw that her eyes were locked on Robert.

"Here you go!" Lucille said, waving the bottles at him, trying to get him to take the bottles and leave. But Robert would not be dismissed so easily.

"Thank you, Sister." he replied, his eyes never leaving Corrine's eyes, even though he was addressing Lucille with his thanks. "I appreciate your hospitality."

Robert quickly shifted his eyes from Corrine briefly enough to nod at Lucille, and then glanced back at Corrine once more before he turned and walked out of the room. Lucille could feel the burning heat, the electricity between them. And it scared the daylights out of her.

Lucille turned to Corrine, who was frozen in place. Corrine's cheeks were flushed and her hands were shaking. Lucille knew Corrine was in deep trouble. Lucille also felt like the rug was being pulled out from under her.

The men worked a long day, to try to get the work done as fast as possible. They were still working while the sisters were having their dinner. Mother Superior went downstairs to ask the men if they would like something to eat. They said yes, thank you. Mother Superior invited them to eat in the kitchen after the sisters were done with dinner.

It was the Mother Superior's idea for them to work longer days. In that way, she reasoned, they would finish the job that much faster. And they – him mostly – would be out of their lives forever and Corrine would be safe.

Father Harris dropped by that evening, at Mother Superior's request. She felt a male presence in the kitchen with the workers would take some of the pressure off her and she could occupy herself elsewhere while the workers were being watched by someone else. Father Harris sat down at the table with them and they shared an enjoyable meal together. Robert really impressed Father Harris with his knowledge of the priesthood and he wondered if Robert had once tried to enter the priesthood himself. He was very taken with Robert.

After the meal, the men went back down to the basement. Father Harris retired to the den, where he was asked to remain so he could let the men out when they were done for the night. All the sisters had gone to their rooms and were expected to stay there until morning. Everyone was indeed in their rooms, except for Lucille and Corrine who were in the library, having some private television time there as usual. Father Harris had no idea they were there, and as the hours grew long into the night, he dozed off.

Lucille and Corrine were wearing their pajamas, watching a marathon of an old classic television show. Lucille was tired from all their chores of the day and she soon fell sound asleep on the couch. Corrine looked over at her friend and was about to wake her, when all of a sudden, a thought occurred to her. A very naughty thought.

Corrine crept into the den to talk to Father Harris for a private moment. When she entered the den and found him asleep, she knew.

This was fate. God made both of her guardians fall asleep so she could talk to Robert.

Corrine knew he was still in the house. What would she do? What excuse could she use to sneak down to the basement again? They already had their dinner, she was sure they didn't want any water. Should she just wait here until they left?

Her question was answered when Robert came up the stairs. He stopped when he saw her and Corrine's breath was frozen in mid-air when she saw him.

"Hello....." Robert said tentatively. "I'm sorry, I thought everyone was asleep."

Corrine didn't say a word. She just gazed at him, frozen. She almost felt naked without her habit. Her blonde hair flowed wildly around her shoulders and her eyes were wide and bright with excitement. Robert already thought she was beautiful before, but the sight of her without her habit was startling. She looked pure and vulnerable.

"I....uh.....was just going to the rest room. I'm sorry to disturb you, Sister Corrine."

Robert turned abruptly and walked briskly to the rest room. He was in there only for a few moments and came out fairly quickly. Corrine was still frozen in place when he came out. She felt she should be ashamed of herself, waiting for a man to come out of the rest room, but she couldn't help herself.

"Hi again," Robert greeted her when he saw her still standing where he had just left her. "We're going to be leaving now, so I guess I'll just say goodnight then?"

The disappointment on Corrine's face was plain to see. And Robert was a great reader of faces.

"Corrine?" he said softly as he walked toward her. "May I call you Corrine?"

"Robert." She breathed his name softly, like she was saying a prayer.

Robert could read desire on a woman's face a mile away. Even though this woman was a nun, D-E-S-I-R-E was written all over her face. He held his hand out to her.

Corrine didn't know what came over her. She was in his arms in what seemed to be one millisecond. She didn't know how she got there; she didn't remember anything, except the feel of his arms around her, the feel of his lips on hers, the feel of his tongue parting her lips and the electricity of their tongues blending together.

Time and space ceased to exist. All she knew was Robert, the feel of him, the taste of him, and the scent of him. Their kiss went on forever. When they finally pulled away, they looked breathlessly at each other. Her lips were tingling, her tongue was burning. In fact, her whole body was burning. They kissed again, even more urgently than before.

Robert was the one to pull away from the kiss first. Corrine tried to kiss him again, but he held her at arm's length.

"What are we doing, my darling?" he said tenderly, stirring that longing in her private area again, which was now soaking wet. "This is wrong, is it not?"

"Please," Corrine whispered, "please don't stop. I've never felt this way before. I feel like I'm alive for the first time in my life. Please…..just kiss me one more time."

His lips descended on hers again and she was caught up in rapturous bliss. She didn't care if anyone caught them; she knew in that instant that her life in the convent was over. She didn't want to be a nun any longer. She couldn't be a nun now that she knew she could feel like this.

"Please meet me again tomorrow," she pleaded when they pulled away again. "I need to see you again, to kiss you again."

Robert kissed her on the nose. "As you wish, my sweet Corrine. I would love to see you again. Tomorrow then?"

"No." Corrine said suddenly, fiercely. "Now."

Robert chuckled gently. "What do you mean, now?"

"Please take me away from here. Just for a few hours. I can sneak back into my room later, everyone will be asleep and nobody will even know I'm gone." Corrine pleaded.

"I don't want to put you in any danger of getting in trouble," Robert said. "I will just see you tomorrow, then, Corrine."

"NO!" Corrine pulled at him vehemently. "Now! I will meet you outside!"

She broke away from his arms and ran quietly to get her coat. She crept quietly past the sleeping Father Harris and out the door. Robert shook his head, called down to the basement to Danny, and he woke Father Harris as they left.

"Father Harris?" Robert shook him gently. "We are leaving now. We'll see you tomorrow, then. Thank you for your hospitality, I enjoyed talking with you at dinner."

Harris sat up and tried to shake the sleepiness off. He shook Robert and Danny's hands and walked them to the door. He didn't even notice that Corrine was standing, shivering, outside behind the door hiding.

"See you tomorrow, gentlemen. May God be with you." Harris said as he closed the door and locked it. By the time Father Harris retrieved his coat to go back home across the street, Corrine was already in Robert's van, which was driving away.

CHAPTER SEVEN – DICK

After Dick's father died, life at home didn't get any better for Dick. His brothers held him responsible for their father's death, since he was the one delegated to call 911 and didn't. His mother, on the other hand, didn't hold that against him. She seemed.....what was the word? Relieved? She was relieved that her husband died. She was now no longer under his rule.

Unfortunately, she still had her other sons to contend with. Her oldest son Jason seemed to be the "ringleader" of the group. He corralled his brothers together after their father died and convinced them to force their mother into giving them their inheritance early. Jeremy, Jerard and Jasper all wholeheartedly agreed to this; of course they would think that was a great idea. Since their mother was still alive and did not have to give her sons any of their inheritance yet by law, they threatened to kill her.

Well, they didn't outright threaten her; they were too clever for that. Instead, they staged a plan to let Dick overhear their evil plan to kill their mother.

The night of his father's death was a night just like all of the others in his life. His mother cooked dinner for them all. They all sat at the table and ate together. His father and brothers dominated the conversation, sometimes speaking all at once, with food in their mouths, and sometimes even spitting the food at each other across the table. Dick was the only one who had any table manners, it seemed, besides his mother. He used to ask his mother why she fell in love with and married his father. Was his father always so uncouth, brutish and abrasive?

His mother told him that he was a wonderful man when they met. She was working as a waitress in a diner and he used to come in every morning for a cup of coffee and a toasted corn muffin before heading out to work. She said he was very handsome in his policeman's uniform. He used to always leave her a huge tip, too.

One day, after about a month of seeing her at the diner every day, he asked her out to dinner. She, of course, accepted. She always thought of herself as a Plain Jane, thought no one would ever be interested in her. In high school, no one ever asked her to go to the prom and none of the boys ever asked her out to go on a date. In fact, even the girls didn't like her. She wasn't pretty enough, wasn't popular enough. She had very low self esteem and generally kept to herself.

That's why she was so shocked that this handsome young police officer could possibly be interested in her.

Their first date was wonderful. He took her to an elegant restaurant for dinner and they went to the movies after dinner. The movie they saw was about a young woman whose mother was trying to match her up with a man she wasn't interested in. The young woman was already in love with someone else. Little did she know that the man she was in love with was a cheating snake and the man her mother was trying to match her up with was a genuine, loving fellow. The young woman figured it all out in the end and happily married the man her mother matched her up with.

120

Dick's mother absolutely treasured the story and kept it in her heart. It was very special to her; so special that when it came out on video, Dick's father bought it for her as an anniversary present.

Their courtship was very smooth and he did all the right things. He never tried any moves on her and was always the perfect gentlemen. After a three-month courtship, he proposed marriage. Dick's mother was thrilled that this wonderful man wanted to marry her and spend the rest of his life with her. The fact that a man loved her enough to marry her, (even though she herself felt she was not worthy of such a wonderful man), made her feel special for the first time in her life. She had finally accomplished something in life she could be proud of.

She wanted to be a good wife to him. He asked her to quit her job and take care of him and the house. She was happy to do so, since waitressing was very hard work. She became pregnant almost immediately; in fact, probably became pregnant on their honeymoon in the Catskills. When Jason was born, that's when she noticed things started to change with their relationship. He spent all of his time with Jason and hardly ever spoke to her except at dinner. Of course, at night, in bed, he always wanted her attention. But otherwise, he hardly ever spent any quality time with her any longer, only with the baby.

When Jeremy was born, he was as proud as can be. He was so happy to have two sons. It made him feel very virile and he used to brag about his strong, healthy sons every day at work. Jeremy was born less than a year after Jason, and Jerard and Jasper, twins, quickly followed less than a year thereafter. It seemed he just wanted to keep her pregnant all the time. But now, with four sons under his belt, he decided his wife could take a little break from being pregnant.

Dick was born four years after the twins were born.

He wasn't big and strong like his brothers were. Instead he was small, pale and sickly. He had to stay in the hospital for two weeks, in the neo-natal unit, until he was strong enough to come home.

His father was ashamed of him. All of his other sons were strong and robust, yet here was this little runt. Where did he come from? Did his wife have an affair when he wasn't paying attention? This could not possibly be his son, after all.

Dick's brothers were all very big, strong athletes. Dick preferred books and television.

Dick's brothers all wanted to become police officers, just like their father. Dick was more interested in computer science and technical studies. His father used to call him The Bookworm Nerd.

Dick's brothers all thought Dick was a weakling because he didn't want to become a cop like all of them. They would lord it over him all the time, about what a "girlie-man" he was.

The night of his father's death, Dick was in the kitchen helping his mother wash the dishes, as usual. His father was in the living room, snacking on a big stick of pepperoni. His stomach had gotten huge, between his beer drinking and eating all kinds of junk food. Here he was, after dinner, (after dessert, in fact), gnawing on a large stick of pepperoni. Dick's mother would cook big, wonderful meals, practically soup to nuts, and it still wasn't enough to satisfy him.

His father and brothers were all watching a football game when suddenly, his father started to choke and sputter. They ignored it at first, since their father always made all sorts of grunting sounds when he ate. But when the sputtering persisted, and especially when his father flung the pepperoni across the room, was when they realized something was wrong.

"Dad, are you all right?" Jasper, who was sitting the closest to him, asked.

Their father didn't answer. He was clutching his chest, trying to breathe. He was turning an odd shade of blue.

Jason ran into the kitchen. "Dad's having a heart attack! Call 911!"

Dick's mother stopped washing the dishes and ran into the living room. Dick stopped drying the dishes for a moment, uncertain of what to do. Should he be the one to call 911? He knew the ambulance would be here instantly if he called, since his father was a retired police officer. Everyone in town knew him and respected him. Dick thought the townspeople's respect was more out of fear of him, than actual respect. Dick always suspected his father may have been a "dirty cop" but he couldn't prove it. His neighbors always said what a wonderful man he was, but there were times when he saw things that he knew he probably shouldn't have seen.

Like the time he saw his father getting out of the car that belonged to an attractive young widow whose husband had just died the week before.

They were both laughing and he saw his father give her a full kiss on the lips before he walked away from the car. She didn't appear to be grief-stricken that she had just lost her husband only a week ago.

In fact, she looked like a woman who might have paid someone, like a cop, to murder her husband for whatever reason. Dick saw the woman driving around in fancy cars after her husband died. Perhaps her husband left her a large sum of money. Perhaps she knew he would leave her a large sum of money. Perhaps she speeded the process along so she could finally get that large sum of money.

Perhaps she was so indebted to someone for his services that she would buy him a fancy car too.

His father came home with a fancy car a week or so after Dick witnessed that exchange between the widow and his father.

Perhaps Dick had an overactive imagination. Or perhaps Dick had good instincts about people, especially people like his father and his brothers.

So Dick was thinking to himself, I'm sure one of the others must have called 911 already (even though their only phone was hanging in the kitchen, only a few feet away from his head, while he was still drying the dishes).

What would happen if he didn't dial 911? Would his father die? Should he go to him and stay with him, with his brothers and mother, while he died?

Dick decided not to. He figured his father would not want to see the runt of his litter in front of his face only moments before he died.

His father was a strong man. He was probably not having a heart attack. He was probably just choking on the pepperoni. His brothers were all police officers. Didn't they have training on how to do the Heimlich maneuver and other life-saving procedures?

Dick decided to finish the dishes that his mother had stopped washing once she ran out to the living room to see about being with his father. Yes, he would be more useful in that way, wouldn't he be? His father wouldn't want to see him while he was choking. Heck, his brothers already probably dislodged the pepperoni from his gullet and they were all probably laughing their heads off about it. His father probably picked up the dislodged pepperoni from the carpet and had probably eaten it, carpet lint fuzz and all.

It was awfully quiet in the living room, Dick thought to himself as he shut off the water and picked up the dish towel to dry his hands. He pictured his father sitting there, hugging his sons and thanking them for saving his life. He pictured his mother on the floor, just watching this scenario, apart from it all. She was always apart from him and his sons. All he cared about, once his first son was born, was having even more sons. He wanted to train them to be tough and strong police officers. Sons he could be proud of. Sons that would serve the community and the community would look up to them and respect them.

Not sons who would work on computers and be useless in everything Dick's father held dear, like watching football while drinking beer and eating pepperoni after a big meal including dessert. Not girlie-men sons who would help their mother clean up after dinner.

His mother walked into the kitchen and put her arms around Dick.

"He's gone." She whispered into Dick's ear and laid her head on his shoulder. "He's gone."

Jerard stomped into the kitchen next.

"HEY YOU!" he yelled to Dick. "When's the ambulance coming?"

Dick and his mother pulled apart from their embrace and she looked at him questioningly.

"Did you call 911?" she asked softly.

"No, I didn't." Dick answered quietly.

"WHAT'S THAT?" Jerard yelled again. "Didn't you call 911, you son of a bitch?"

Dick picked up a glass and threw it at the wall. Then he turned back to his brother, fuming.

"NO, I DIDN'T CALL 911!" Dick yelled, his face turning red. "I thought since you were all in there with him, the brotherhood of cops, that one of you might have called 911 from your cell phones or your police radios! Why did I have to be the one to call 911?"

"YOU SON OF A BITCH!" Jeremy yelled, walking into the kitchen and just catching that exchange. Jason and Jasper were right behind Jeremy and Jerard, who also lunged at Dick, ready to kill him.

"STOP!" their mother yelled. "I HAVE HAD ENOUGH!"

Their mother put herself in front of Dick to protect him.

"DO NOT lay a hand on my son!" she said fiercely. "He did nothing wrong! He's absolutely right, one of you should have gotten on your police radios and called the ambulance! That would have been much quicker than Dick calling from the house phone! Don't blame your brother, it wasn't his fault!"

"Well, why didn't you come out to be with the rest of us?" Jasper asked accusingly. "Didn't you even want to be with Dad while he was having the heart attack?"

Dick was quiet for a moment while he collected his thoughts. He finally asked, "How do you know I wasn't there?"

They all looked blankly at him.

"While Dad was having his heart attack, you were all busy looking at him and tending to him. You wouldn't notice whether or not I was in the room, would you?" Dick said, strangely calm all of a sudden. He couldn't believe the calm feeling that had settled over him.

"I didn't see him." Jason said quietly. "I guess he's right, we were all busy trying to revive Dad."

"Did you see me?" their mother asked. "I was there too. You four brutes wouldn't let me near my husband, your father. You were all in a football huddle around him, I couldn't get anywhere near him. Even though I was," she stopped and looked at Dick, squeezing his hand, "even though WE were there, we couldn't get anywhere near him."

Jasper burst into tears. The rest of his brothers started to cry too. Dick had never seen his brothers blubber like that before. They must have all really loved their father.

"I know it was your fault, somehow!" Jeremy sputtered, looking accusingly at Dick while wiping his eyes. "I don't think you were really in there. I didn't hear your voice, but I did hear Mom's voice."

"Dick was quiet as a mouse," Dick's mother cut in. "He was too shocked to say anything, too shocked to move."

"Yeah, right!" Jason said. "Dick's probably glad Dad died!"

Dick didn't say a word. He stayed quiet as a mouse. He kept picturing his father looking down at him from wherever his spirit was floating. His father would have a big smile on his face and he would say, if Dick could hear him, "You got me, son! You got me, Dickie boy! You really pulled one over on everyone, didn't you? Well, it's about time you grew some balls, son! You really killed me good, didn't you?"

He pictured his father throwing back his head and laughing that loud laugh that was more like a guffaw. He pictured his brothers laughing right along with him, as they so often did, at Dick's expense.

A week after the funeral, Dick was in the kitchen alone while his mother had gone upstairs to her bedroom after dinner. Dick had just finished the last of the dishes when he heard something strange from the living room. His brothers were in there all together, without the TV on, sounding like they were conspiring about something together.

"We could make it look like an accident!" Jasper said in a loud whisper, as if they wanted Dick to hear what they were saying.

"It would be easy! We could put something in her tea at dinner. Then when she falls over choking, none of us will call 911, right?" Jared said triumphantly, in a stage whisper.

"It would serve her right, not giving us our inheritance!" Jason said, also in a stage whisper. "If she would only give us that money that Dad left for us, she wouldn't have to die!"

A horrible dread came over Dick, more horrible than when he was locked in that bathroom. They were planning to kill his mother over money? Dad's money? He had to warn her, he had to do something!

He couldn't call the police, because, well, they were the police, after all. Everyone knew them. No one ever would suspect them of killing their mother. If anyone ever did suspect that, someone at the police station would squash it down to protect them. All these police officer brothers always protected each other, no matter what.

They never protected Dick, though, ever. One time he got a speeding ticket and tried to give it to his brothers, asking them to somehow absolve it as they absolved all the speeding tickets of their friends. They wouldn't do it.

One time, one of Jason's girlfriends broke up with him. He responded by stalking her, terrorizing her, following her everywhere, threatening her, and just basically scaring the crap out of her. She called the police. Funny thing, the police didn't do a thing. They let her file a report but then........funny thing again...... when she called the station once more to file another complaint and she referenced her original complaint report number, that number didn't exist. Wasn't that strange?

The reason Dick knew about this was because she worked with Dick at the same office where he worked. And Dick felt completely powerless to protect her and defend her from his brother. She told everyone in the office what a wimp Dick was. So everyone at the office, willing to believe anything that could stir up some drama, started treating him as such; except for his boss, and all of the "higher-ups" who valued Dick's work performance and ethics. But unfortunately, his co-workers all treated him terribly and he had to fight the harassment daily. He was the office wimp. He tried to file a complaint against them, but nothing was ever done. It seemed the "higher-ups" didn't like any kind of drama and didn't want to deal with any unpleasantness. So it was Dick's burden to carry. And he did carry that burden every day, day in and day out. He was happy he had his own office, so he could lock himself away from their negative comments.

He crept upstairs to his mother's room and knocked softly. She was asleep. He gently nudged her awake and she woke up with a start.

"Richard! Honey! Are you all right? What's happened?"

"I'm fine, Mom, please lower your voice!" he hushed. "I have something to tell you."

So within a week, Dick's brothers had their inheritance. They also had the house. Dick's mother decided to give them the house, and she and Dick moved out and rented an apartment together. They were finally happy, finally at peace. What a relief.

Except that the problems at work made his ulcer come back. As if matters couldn't get any worse, his co-workers started calling him a "Mama's Boy" now because he moved in with his mother. They didn't understand that she was living with him so he could protect her from her other sons, they just figured he lived with her because he was too attached to her and couldn't cut the apron strings. Truth is, he knew his mother was quite capable of living on her own, as was he. But at this point, his mother was his best friend, and didn't people sometimes become roommates with their best friends? He didn't see anything wrong with it. They each had their own lives. They both came and went as they pleased.

In fact, his mother decided to go to college to study fashion. She confessed to him one evening after dinner that fashion had been a dream of hers until she met his father. Once she met him, her dreams had to go right out the window so she could raise her sons. Previously, before meeting Dick's father, she had been working two waitressing jobs so she could afford to go to college.

Now thanks to her husband's retirement funds, she could finally go to college and pursue her dream. Dick was really happy for her.

Dick's reverie was interrupted again by Robert entering the room. While Dick was daydreaming, he was still indeed very hard at work trying to find the money.

"How's it going in here, Dicky boy?" Robert said in a gentle and kind tone of voice. Robert could see how hard Dick was working.

"Fine, Robert, just fine. Nothing yet, though. I'll keep you posted." Dick replied back, as respectfully as he could.

"Dick, I know I can count on you."

Robert walked toward Dick and placed a hand on his shoulder.

"Dick, I realize how much time this is taking and I know you have other things to do, other places to go to, other people to see." Robert began as Dick stopped what he was doing and turned to face him. "Dick, I guess what I'm saying is …….thank you. I really respect you and your skills and I just wanted you to know that."

Dick was really touched by Robert's statement. It was very rare that Robert had such tender moments with any of them. He praised them all for their good work quite often and treated them all extremely well normally, but never with such *tenderness*, for lack of a better word. Dick had never seen this side of Robert before. He was sure Corrine did, otherwise why would she be with him? She loved him through thick and thin, through both his joy and his anger.

"Thank you, Robert, I really appreciate that." Dick smiled at him.

132

Robert seemed uncomfortable and awkward all of a sudden, perhaps the tenderness was too much for him.

"Okay," Robert said, "I'm going to get back to work. Whoever finds the money first gets to pick the restaurant we'll be celebrating at for dinner!"

Robert flashed him a huge smile, from his heart, and walked out of the room. Dick saluted him as he was leaving.

Dick thought of Robert and Corrine's relationship and wished he could have one with Lucille. Out of all the women he's ever known in his life, he felt such strong feelings for her. In his heart, he knew without a shadow of a doubt that she was a woman he could be happy with until the end of his life. He felt like he could protect her, would protect her fiercely, if it ever came down to it.

Suddenly, a scenario passed through Dick's mind. He wasn't daydreaming, it was almost like it was a memory, even though he didn't understand where it came from.

Dick and Lucille were outside of the warehouse. They were surrounded by cops. Four of the cops approached him and Lucille, sneering at them. Two of them were wielding clubs and the other two were carrying guns.

The four cops were his brothers.

They descended on Lucille. Jasper was tearing at her clothes and Jeremy was trying to lick her face. Dick ran over to try to stop them. He knew he would get beaten up severely in the process, but he didn't care. He would die for her.

As Dick jumped angrily on top of Jasper, he was hit from behind by someone. It was Jason and Jared. They were beating him senseless. He was trying to fight back but he was blinded from the pain. They were kicking him, they were spitting on him. He looked over at Lucille and helplessly watched her try to fight back. She was kicking them, biting them, whatever she could do. They laughed at her efforts. Lucille was on the ground and Jasper now had his club on Lucille's neck, cutting off her air supply. Jeremy was using his club to open Lucille's legs. He heard a gunshot and felt something burning in his stomach. His ulcer felt like it was exploding.

Suddenly the scenario went black. Dick shook his head, not knowing what just happened. Was it a premonition? He never had premonitions before. It seemed like it was a vision of some sort, even though he was not subject to visions either.

It all seemed so real, like it actually happened. Dick started to shake like a leaf. Suddenly, he heard a sound like a door creaking open. The room he was in did not have a door, but he turned in the direction of the sound. There was a bright light coming from the doorway and he heard his mother's voice calling him.

CHAPTER EIGHT – DEREK AND BEN

It was with a heavy heart that Derek knocked on Ben's door. When he heard Ben sing out, "Come in!" in that cheerful voice of his, he entered.

"Hi bro!" Ben said with a smile. Ben was watching cartoons on his television.

"Hi bro!" Derek smiled back at him, then sat on the bed next to Ben and involuntarily let out a huge sigh.

"Derry, what's the matter?" Ben asked him. "Does your stomach hurt?"

"No." Derek answered, trying to find the right words to begin telling Ben that his life was going to take a different turn than they all expected.

"You have a headache?" Ben asked.

Derek shook his head. "There's nothing physically wrong with me, Ben. There's something I have to tell you and I'm not sure how to."

Ben searched Derek's face.

"Is it something bad? Did Mom die too?" Ben asked, springing up from the bed in a panic.

"No Ben, relax, calm down, Mom's just fine, she's downstairs."

Derek put a hand on Ben's shoulder, getting him to sit back down.

"Is dinner ready?" Ben asked.

"No, it's not about dinner. There's a......visitor downstairs."

"What kind of visitor?" Ben cocked his head, like a dog does when he's trying to understand what you're saying.

"Do you remember that man that keeps coming around the house to talk to Mom?" Derek waited for Ben's reaction.

"That creepy guy?" Ben asked. "Yeah, I remember him. He's downstairs?"

"Yes, Ben, he's downstairs. Why do you think he's a creepy guy?"

"Because he always makes Mom sad when he comes over."

Ben may be simple but he had good instincts and noticed everything.

"Well, Ben, maybe he's not a creep, we're not sure about that yet."

"Anyone who makes Mom sad is a creep." Ben said, crossing his arms over his chest, which usually indicates that the case is closed.

"Well, he wants you to come down and talk to him. He said he really likes you and wants to be your……friend." Derek said, a queasy feeling coming over him.

Ben eyed him warily. "What do you mean, he wants to be my friend? You're my friend, Derry. That's all I need."

Ben's warm statement eased the queasy feeling in Derek's stomach somewhat, but the queasiness still won over the warmth.

"Well, Ben," Derek tried again. "Sometimes in life we get to have more than just one friend. Lee really likes you and wants to get to know you better."

"How can he like me? He doesn't even know me."

For a simple man, Ben can sure be smart sometimes.

"Well, I think you're right about that, bro." Derek started, choosing his words very carefully, "That was a very smart thing to say. But I think because he knows Mom, and Mom tells him all about you all the time, well, that's how he likes you."

"What does Mom tell him about me?" Ben was making it harder for Derek than ever.

"Well, she tells him about proud she is of you working at your job at the hardware store, keeping the shelves stocked and all. How much all the customers there like you. That kind of stuff."

"Does he want to give me a job?" Ben asked, cocking his head. "Will he pay me more?"

A light bulb went off in Derek's head. "Maybe that's it, Ben! Maybe he wants to give you a job! Would you like another job, making more money?"

Ben eyed Derek critically for a few minutes then finally answered. "No thank you."

Derek was about to reach the end of his rope. "Why not?"

"Because I like my job. Don't you like your job, Derry?"

"Yes, I like my job, but.....he's not offering *me* a job."

"What kind of job is he offering me anyway?" Ben asked.

"Benny bro, I didn't actually say he was offering you a job. I said *maybe* he was offering you a job. You see, buddy, there's a difference."

"Well, why else would he want to see me?" Ben asked, driving Derek crazy.

"I don't know exactly, so why don't we go downstairs and ask him?" Derek asked, hopeful that this would finally coax him into going downstairs. "Maybe it's a surprise!"

"I don't like surprises."

In that moment, Derek felt like growing his hair long just to make it easier to grab. He would pull out one strand at a time, by the roots, until it was all gone and he was completely bald.

"Well, I didn't actually say it was a sur--" Derek started but Ben cut in.

"Yeah, I know. M-A-Y-B-E it's a surprise."

"Right." Derek said, looking at his brother, smiling sheepishly.

Ben was quiet for a few moments, looking at Derek thoughtfully. Derek just waited until Ben finally spoke.

"Derry, do you like him?"

Derek didn't know how to answer that. As it was, he would prefer to keep Ben out of the situation and not introduce him to Lee because he didn't trust Lee and didn't know what his motives were. But at the same time, he thought it might be good, if Lee's motives were sincere, that Ben should have another friend in his life. He didn't have to know that Lee's his father (as long as Lee kept to his end of the bargain). All Ben needed to know was that he could have a possible new friend in his life.

"Well Benny bro, how about this? I'm not sure if I like him. I'm waiting for you to tell me whether or not we should both like him. What do you think of that?"

Ben looked at Derek dubiously. "You don't like him, do you? Then I don't like him."

Ben was amazingly perceptive.

"I just told you I'm not sure if I like him or not." Derek attempted to salvage the situation, but it didn't seem to be working. "How could you say that I don't like him?"

"It's all over your face, Derry. I know when you don't like someone. Why do I have to like him?"

"You don't have to like him, Ben. I'm not going to force you to meet him. But at the same time, there's a MAYBE here, a BIG MAYBE, that tells me maybe you might like him. If you don't, then end of story. Okay bro? Can we go downstairs and just say hello to the guy and see what he has to say?"

"I want Dad back. If Daddy was here, that creepy guy wouldn't be coming around. Would he, Derry?" Ben said suddenly.

Derek was really taken aback. "No, Ben, I guess he wouldn't be."

"I know he likes Mom. What if he wants to marry Mom and be our new Dad?"

Derek was amazed at how Ben was starting to put the pieces of the puzzle together.

"He doesn't want to marry Mom." Derek answered truthfully. "He just wants to get to know you."

"What about you? Doesn't he want to get to know you?"

"Sure he does. He wants to get to know both of us. I've already formally met him, but you haven't. Come on downstairs and meet him, won't you buddy?" Derek beseeched him. "Please? Do it for me?"

Ben finally uncrossed his arms and looked down at his lap. Derek could see the wheels in Ben's brain spinning.

"Okay." Ben finally said. "But if I don't like him, I don't want to see him ever again."

"You got it!" Derek was jubilant and jumped up, opening Ben's bedroom door. "Let's go, bro!"

They walked down the stairs, Derek leading the way. Lee was sitting at the table across from Gloria, still drinking her tea. Derek noticed she never did offer Lee a cup of tea.

"Ben, this is Lee." Derek swept his hand in a grand gesture toward Lee, nudging Ben in front of him to enter the kitchen.

Lee got up and put out his hand to Ben. Ben took his hand and solemnly shook it, his eyes never leaving Lee's face. Derek sometimes thought that Ben could search people's souls.

"Why don't you have a seat, Ben, next to me?" Lee said, pulling out the chair and motioning for him to sit next to him.

Instead, Ben walked over and sat next to his mother, directly across from Lee. Derek decided to sit next to Lee so he could subdue him, if necessary.

Lee seemed dejected that Ben didn't want to sit next to him.

"So, what do you want?" Ben asked. Ben could be very direct sometimes. That's how a simple, honest man operates. Get to the point or get out.

Lee was taken aback by Ben's directness. He stuttered a little bit, not knowing what to say.

"Ben, I'm an old friend of your mother's. I've known her about 30 years now." Lee began.

"I'm thirty years old." Ben said. "That's funny."

Derek's stomach started to get queasy again. It looked like Lee was about to reveal that he was Ben's father, since Ben gave him such a great lead-in. Derek placed a warning hand on Lee's arm just in case. Lee looked down at Derek's large hand and swallowed hard.

"Well, I know you're thirty years old. I'm proud of you." Lee said, trying to figure out what to say next.

"How can you be proud of me when you don't know me? Mom's proud of me because I work at the hardware store. Do you want to give me a new job? With more money? Because I make pretty good money where I am and I like it there. I'm going to be getting a raise soon anyway, so why should I come work for you?" Ben said, still looking Lee directly in his eyes.

"Well, I wasn't offering you a job, exactly……" Lee sputtered. "I just want to….. hang out with you sometime. Take you places you're never been to before."

Ben cocked his head and looked at him. "Are you some kind of pervert?"

Lee gasped and Derek chuckled. Gloria just sighed and then laughed to herself, shaking her head. Gloria was thinking of what Lee was, remembering what Lee was.

"NO!" Lee almost shouted. "Why would you think that?"

"You're a grown man my Dad's age that wants to be my friend." Ben said, reasonably calm. "Why don't you find friends your own age?"

Good point, Derek thought to himself. Ben was protecting himself pretty well.

"Funny you should say I'm your Dad's age, Ben……" Lee started as Derek squeezed his hand on Lee's arm. Lee shook off Derek's hand quickly and shouted, "BECAUSE I'M YOUR REAL FATHER, BEN!"

Gloria and Derek rose up from the table in an uproar. Lee tried to reach out to Ben but Derek pulled his arm away and put it behind Lee's back, holding it securely. At that moment, he was happy he was a security guard; his training came in quite handy in this situation.

"WHAT DO YOU MEAN?" Ben shouted, his fingers rubbing his eyes. "WHAT DO YOU MEAN? YOU'RE NOT MY FATHER! DAD WAS MY FATHER!"

"NO HE WASN'T!" Lee shouted back, trying to be heard over Gloria's moans and Derek's threatening growls. "I'M YOUR FATHER, BEN! I'M YOUR REAL FATHER!"

"This wasn't part of the deal!" Derek hissed in Lee's ear. "What the hell are you trying to pull here?"

Ben started screaming. He put his hands over his ears and started screaming. His feet started pounding the floor. He was having a tantrum. Ben hadn't had a tantrum for a long, long time.

One time, Ben had a tantrum when he was twelve years old. He was at the park with Derek. Ben was sitting on a park bench eating a peanut butter and jelly sandwich while watching the other kids skateboard and play basketball, or swing on the swings and play on the monkey bars. A young girl came running out of nowhere and quickly approached them.

"What are you eating?" she asked, giggling. "Is that peanut butter and jelly?"

"Yep." Ben answered and kept on eating. Usually he would offer to share, but he decided not to. Perhaps he could tell that she wasn't nice enough to make him want to share half of his peanut butter and jelly sandwich with her. Perhaps, in his own perceptive way, he knew what was going to happen next.

"I like peanut butter and jelly sandwiches." The young girl said, twisting her hair in her fingers playfully. "Can I please have some?"

Derek watched Ben to see what he would do. He wasn't about to tell him one way or the other what to do with his sandwich.

"Nope," Ben said flatly and kept on eating.

"Well, that's rude." the young girl said. "Didn't your mommy ever teach you any manners?"

Derek decided to speak then. "Didn't your mommy ever teach you not to speak to strangers?"

"Or not to ask strangers for their sandwiches?" Ben added.

The young girl started to shriek. At first, it was a low, growling sound. Ben and Derek watched her, perplexed, while her face started to turn blue. They were wondering what was going to happen next. Then the low sound slowly, very slowly, edged its way up the musical scale and the note she must have finally hit was higher than the highest C. She then suddenly lunged at Ben and ripped the sandwich out of his hands. Ben was so transfixed by her strangled blue face and high notes that he didn't even see that coming. When he suddenly realized that she had taken his sandwich and ran away with it, *he* started turning blue.

Derek watched him as he started to moan and cover his ears. Derek knew what was coming. Ben started to scream, jumping up and pounding the cement ground with his feet. He was pummeling his ears with his fists. Derek was on his feet, trying to

145

calm him down, but Ben was having none of it. Derek had to physically pick him up and remove him from the park, while stunned men, women and children watched. The boys stopped skateboarding and playing basketball. The girls stopped swinging on the swings and playing on the monkey bars. Everyone's eyes were transfixed on Ben and Derek until they were out of sight.

Derek brought him out of the park and walked quickly with Ben heavy in his arms, until his screams turned into sobs. Then Derek gently put him down and hugged him. Derek hugged him until the sobbing subsided. Then they walked home, hand in hand, Ben still sniffling now and then.

When they got home, Derek made Ben a double-decker peanut butter and jelly sandwich.

"Why are little girls so mean?" Ben asked Derek before he took a large bite out of his sandwich.

"They were just built that way, I guess." Derek answered. Derek knew that most girls and women were mean to them, so he didn't even try to sway Ben into thinking any differently about the female species.

"Oh." Ben replied and continued eating his sandwich.

But a peanut butter and jelly sandwich could not console him now. Derek wasn't sure what to do. His first instinct was to shove Lee's face into the table, which he did. Lee yelled out, but didn't fight it. Derek had him pinned down on the table.

Ben suddenly stopped his tantrum and watched Lee pinned down on the table.

"You're my father? How could you be my father?" Ben asked, rubbing his red, tear-soaked eyes.

Gloria put a hand on Ben's shoulder. She guided him gently into a chair. Ben sat down. Derek released his grip on Lee and forced him into the seat next to him again. Derek kept one hand on Lee's arm. He did not want to let go of Lee.

Derek looked at Gloria. "What do we do now?" he asked her.

"I guess we should tell Ben the truth." Gloria sighed, tears coming out of her eyes as she looked at Ben. Ben noticed his mother was crying and he reached out and pulled her head to his chest.

"Don't cry, Mommy." Ben said and stroked her hair.

"Oh Ben, honey, I'm so sorry I never told you." Gloria began. "I just wanted us to have a normal life."

"How could Lee be my father, Mommy?" Ben asked. "I thought Daddy was my father."

"Daddy was your father, Ben, in many ways. He just wasn't your father in the....." Gloria searched for a word that Ben would understand. "He wasn't your father in the physical sense."

"You mean we don't have the same genes?" Ben asked, surprising everyone by his knowledge of genes.

"That's exactly, right, honey." Gloria told him. "Your mommy made a mistake and Lee was the one who helped with your genes, not your Daddy."

"What kind of mistake?" Ben asked.

Ben did not understand the facts of life. He thought it was completely gross when Derek tried to explain sex to him. Ben decided he preferred to hear that men put eggs in women's bellies and made them pregnant that way. Where he got this idea was beyond Derek, but Ben was adamant that this approach was the actual way it happened, not that yucky penis and vagina story that Derek tried to sell to him. A man (married) uses his penis to insert his eggs into the woman's (his wife's) belly through her belly button. That was that.

"Mommy was sleeping one day and didn't know that Lee put eggs in my belly. Lee was a cab driver and Mommy fell asleep in the cab by mistake. So Lee pulled the car over and put eggs in my belly. One of those eggs hatched and Mommy gave birth to you." Gloria explained.

Ben believed that -- hook, line and sinker. Ben turned to glare at Lee.

"Why did you do that?" Ben demanded.

"Because I wanted my own son." Lee said, finding courage again, whipping Derek's hand off his arm. "But your mommy kept you from me. She just wanted you to have a normal life with her, but not with me."

"Did you love my mommy?" Ben asked him.

148

"Yes, I did! Very much!" Lee lied, but Ben didn't believe him.

"No you didn't." Ben shook his head.

"I loved you, though Ben. I always have." Lee looked at him, crocodile tears forming in his eyes. "But they kept you from me. And now I want you to be with me. You don't have to be with me every day, just come and stay with me for a little while. It will be like you're on vacation."

"What do you mean, 'come and stay with me for a little while'?" Gloria asked Lee, while Derek squeezed his large hand on Lee's skinny arm.

"Well, how can I get to know my son if I don't spend any time with him?" Lee asked. "Why can't I take him home with me? Just for a week, how does that sound?"

Derek shook his head and Gloria just stared dumbfounded at Lee.

"How else can a man get to know his own son, if they don't spend any quality time together? Quantity is important too. I can't just pick him up for one day and bring him to the zoo, after all! He's thirty years old!" Lee said, looking at Ben. "Look at him! He's a grown man! We could watch sports together and have meals together and just share some quality time together!"

"I don't like sports." Ben said quietly. "I like cartoons."

"Okay, then!" Lee said. "I like cartoons too! They are my favorite shows on TV!"

Ben's eyes widened. "They're my favorite too!" Ben actually smiled at Lee and Derek's stomach started to churn a little more.

"Mom, can I spend some time with Lee?" Ben asked Gloria. "If he likes cartoons, he can't be all bad, can he?"

"Let me think about it." Gloria replied. She looked at Lee. "Can I have one day to think about this? Please?"

"Of course." Lee said, and put his hand across the table to Gloria. She wouldn't take it.

"One day." Gloria said firmly. "I will call you tomorrow. Please leave us now."

Lee was surprised he was being dismissed like this; Gloria never dismissed him. But it seemed that there was a glimmer of hope for him to be able to take Ben for a little while.

"Okay." Lee stood up and turned to Ben. "I look forward to seeing you again, son."

"Bye, Lee." Ben said. Ben didn't want to call him Dad. Not just yet, anyway.

Derek was relieved when Lee left as he was asked to.

"Can I go to my room now?" Ben asked, surprising Gloria and Derek. They expected him to have a million questions for them, but he just needed some quiet time. Derek knew he would be thinking about this all night and would probably not get any sleep.

"Sure, my Benny boy," Gloria said, giving him a kiss on the cheek. "You go on upstairs and rest. I love you. Please remember that always."

"I love you too, Mom." Ben replied and walked away from her. "You too, Derry."

Ben gave Derek one last look before going up the stairs. Derek and Gloria slumped back down in their chairs and just looked at each other. They both felt as if they had just survived a train wreck.

Over the course of the rest of the day and evening, they discussed what to do about Ben and Lee. In the morning it was decided that Ben could spend a week with Lee. Derek helped Ben pack his things and drove him to Lee's house that Sunday.

Derek was surprised to find that Lee lived on a farm with horses and cattle. Lee explained that he bought the place with the money that Gloria had provided him with all these years. Lee had men running the farm and taking care of the animals so that he wouldn't get his hands dirty. Lee enjoyed riding horses and he said he would teach Ben to ride.

Ben was like a kid in a candy store when he saw the animals. He immediately gravitated toward the horses, petting them on the neck and whispering into their ears. The horses seemed to like Ben very much too. One horse nuzzled Ben while Ben giggled. Derek breathed a sigh of relief, and his fear of Ben being away from home dissolved a bit.

It was agreed that Ben would call them every evening to let them know how his day was. Derek went to the hardware store and told them that Ben would be taking one week's vacation. Derek just told the owner of the hardware store that a family friend came into town and took Ben back to his ranch with him. The owner of the hardware store was very happy to hear that Ben was doing something different, exploring new things, because he needed some new adventures in his life.

Ben called each night, as promised. He was having the time of his life riding horses and helping to feed the cattle. Ben didn't know that Lee was raising cattle for slaughter, or he would have been very sad and possibly thrown another tantrum. Gloria and Derek were relieved to hear that Ben was having a great time.

When Friday night rolled around, there was no call from Ben. Gloria tried to call Lee's house but there was no answer. Derek decided to drive over there and find out what was going on.

The farm was dark when Derek arrived. There were no lights on in the house and all of the animals were in the barn for the night. Derek rang the doorbell but no one answered. He pounded on the door but no one answered. Suddenly Derek's cell phone rang. It was his mother.

"DEREK! Oh my God!" Gloria was sobbing. "Oh my God, what did we do? We should have never agreed to have Ben stay with Lee."

"MOM!" Derek's heart was in his mouth once he heard the tone of his mother's voice. "What happened?"

"They've taken us hostage!" Gloria gurgled through her tears. "They've taken us hostage!"

"Who's 'they,' Mom?" Derek asked, heart pounding as he ran back towards his car. "Do you mean Lee?"

"No! Lee's dead!" Gloria gasped out in a raspy voice. "They killed him!"

A sense of dread bigger than the planet Jupiter enveloped Derek.

"What do you mean, Lee's dead?" Derek asked Gloria in a steely voice, even though he felt his legs were about to collapse.

"They're here now! With me!" Gloria gasped. Suddenly there were sounds of a struggle on the end of the line and a man's voice came on the telephone.

"You'd better come home, boy." the man said. "You'd better come home and tell us where the money is. Don't call the cops. You hear me, boy? If you call the cops or get anyone else involved, your brother and mother are dead."

Click.

CHAPTER NINE – LUCILLE

"So……are you going to call him?" Corrine asked her.

Lucille was at the kitchen counter drinking a cup of tea, staring off into space.

"Lucille?"

Lucille looked at Corrine then. "What?"

Corrine laughed. "Are you going to call him?"

"Who?" Lucille asked, staring off into space again.

"You know who!" Corrine waved a hand in front of Lucille's face. "Jeff! Mr. Business Card!"

Lucille's face registered shock.

"Oh, I couldn't possibly!" she gasped.

"Why not?" Corrine asked gently. "What do you have to lose? He sounds like a really nice guy. What does he do again?"

Lucille stared blankly at Corrine. "What does he do?"

"You know, besides ordering food at your diner. What does he do for a living?" Corrine was starting to get a little exasperated with Lucille.

"Oh, I don't know….." Lucille squeaked.

Corrine tapped her foot impatiently on the tile floor. "Um…..the business card? What does it say?"

"What does what say?" Robert boomed from the doorway.

"Hi honey!" Corrine gushed and ran over to him, showering him with kisses. Lucille tried to hide her disgust, but she may have let a small grunt slip out.

"Hello Luci!" Robert called out between kisses, as soon as his mouth was free.

"Hi Robert," Lucille said flatly.

"Well, you're a charmer tonight!" Robert walked over to Lucille and planted a kiss on her cheek. "What's the story? Why so glum?"

"A man asked her out." Corrine stated happily. "A man at the diner."

"A…….man asked you out!" Robert smiled broadly. "How did that happen?"

Corrine waited for Lucille to speak, but since she was as quiet as a closed book, Corrine decided to fill Robert in on the details.

"Luci got his order wrong....several times.....and then he left her his business card, a big tip, and asked her out at the end of his dinner!" Corrine replied, giggling.

"Let me get this straight....." Robert said, looking at Lucille, who wouldn't meet his eyes. "A man walks into the diner, you take his order wrong....several times......and before he leaves, he gives you a big tip, his business card, *and* asks you out?"

"YES!" Corrine answered for Lucille again.

"Well, Luci, I've got to say," Robert said sincerely. "That's a mighty pretty face you've got there. There's an innocence about you.....it probably took him in."

Corrine looked at Robert questioningly, with her lower lip sticking out in a pout.

"But of course, you're not as pretty as my Corrine here!" Robert was quick to respond. "But you are probably the second prettiest in line at this beauty contest!"

Corrine laughed while Robert leaned over and gently bit her pouty lip.

"So are you going to call him?" Robert asked, after he had finished kissing Corrine again.

"She doesn't know." Corrine said. "I think she's too chicken to call him."

"I am not chicken!" Lucille got up from her seat and shoved her cup of tea away. That seemed to wake her up out of her reverie. "I just don't feel that a woman should call a man, it should be the other way around."

"Well, did he ask for your phone number?" Robert asked.

"No." Lucille replied glumly.

"Well, then……" Robert spread his hands out, and waved them in front of her. "How is he supposed to call you without your number? You'll need to call him. He obviously wants you to call him or he wouldn't have given you his card. Call him tomorrow or the next night, so you don't seem too anxious."

"I am not anxious!" Lucille screeched. "I just don't want to call him. Not tonight, or tomorrow night, or ever!"

"But why?" Corrine asked. "Don't you want to be happy?"

Lucille searched Corrine's eyes deeply. "What makes you think going out on a date with this guy is going to make me happy?"

"Well, what if he turns out to be the man of your dreams?" Corrine asked her.

"Just one date won't hurt." Robert said. "You might like the guy."

"She already likes him!" Corrine stated proudly. "That's why she doesn't want to call him."

Robert turned to Corrine with a puzzled look on his face.

"She doesn't want to call him because she likes him?" Robert asked her. "That makes no sense. She should go out with a man whom she doesn't like?"

"No silly," Corrine laughed. "She likes him too much to call him. She would rather that he calls her instead. Catch her off guard, that sort of thing, sweep her off her feet. If she calls first, she has to come up with that first hello on the phone, and the first conversation ice breaker. It's like, I call you and what do I say that's going to pique your interest in wanting to talk to me more? She's nervous about being the opener. She'd rather be the closer."

Robert shook his head. "Please explain in English, or French preferably, what on earth you just said."

Corrine threw back her head and laughed.

"If he really liked me," Lucille cut in, "then he should have asked me for my phone number, not the other way around. He is the man, after all, he should be the one doing the courting, not me."

Robert tilted his head and listened to Lucille. He seemed enraptured. She went on.

"If I call him, it will go something like this: 'Hello, is this Jeff?' 'Yes, this is Jeff.' 'Hi, this is Lucille.' 'Who?' 'Lucille from the diner. I was your waitress the other night.' Then there will be silence on the other end of the phone. I will say, 'I'm Lucille, I served you a hot open roast beef sandwich and almost gave you soup and a salad with blue cheese dressing. I forgot you said you wanted fries with that. I tried to push a vegetable on you too.' Still there will be silence on the other end of the phone. At this point, I

158

will just say, 'I'm sorry, I have the wrong number.' Then I will hang up and never go back to work at the diner again, because I will be too embarrassed if he ever walks in again. Then again, maybe he won't come back. Or if he does come back, he won't remember me. But with my luck, I will get his order wrong again and he will remember me at that point. Or another scenario could be that I get his order wrong again and this time, he storms out of the diner, totally disgusted, tells all of his friends there's a flakey waitress working at that diner, no one will come back, and the diner will close down because of me."

Robert and Corrine burst out laughing. Finally, Robert gasped out between laughs, holding his stomach, "And how would it go if he called you instead?"

"It would go like this," Lucille continued. "It would go with me picking up the phone saying 'Hello?' 'Hello, is this Lucille?' 'Yes, this is she.' 'Hi Lucille, this is Jeff. Do you remember me from the diner? I was the one that confused you into taking my order wrong.' 'Oh, yes, of course I remember you, Jeff! Nice to speak to you again, thanks for calling.' Then the conversation will probably revolve around what my favorite color is, how old am I, where do I live, where do I want to go for dinner, that sort of thing."

"I like that scenario better too." Corrine tittered, and then cleared her throat, trying not to laugh again.

"And when he asks you where do you live, what will you say?" Robert asked. "That you live with your best friend and her boyfriend? Or will you just tell him that you have two roommates, and one of them is a man?"

"What difference does it make?" Lucille asked, alarmed. "Do you think who I live with really makes a difference?"

"Yes, absolutely!" Robert stated adamantly. "He will get jealous if he finds out you're living with another man, roommate or not. If you tell him you live with your best friend and her boyfriend, he will wonder why. He might think you're a waif."

Lucille gasped. "You invited me to live with you! I would have gotten my own place!"

"That's not what I'm saying!" Robert reached out and touched Lucille on her shoulder. "I'm happy you live with us, I am, really!"

Robert patted her on her shoulder and that seemed to placate her a bit.

"But some people don't understand that sort of thing." Robert explained. "He might wonder why you don't live on your own somewhere, and he may be uncomfortable coming to someone's house that lives with a couple. He might get the wrong idea."

Lucille started to visibly shake. "What wrong idea?"

Corrine interrupted Robert for a moment. "I don't see the problem in her telling him that she lives with us. What's the problem?"

"The problem," Robert replied patiently, "my dear ladies, is that some men don't understand why a woman isn't living on her own. He might think there's something wrong with her, that she's dependent on people or something like that."

The looks on Lucille's and Corrine's faces made Robert see that he was digging himself into a very large hole.

"Don't get me wrong!" Robert burst out. "I'm happy to be living here with the two most beautiful women in the world! But I know how men are. Jeff will probably be jealous that there's another man here. And if he is some successful businessman or something like that, he will wonder why Lucille's living with a couple instead of on her own somewhere. A man wants a woman to be dependent on him, but he wants to see if she's independent first."

Corrine and Lucille looked puzzled. Corrine finally spoke.

"Can you please stop speaking French and speak English this time?"

Robert laughed softly. "I guess now I am the one not making any sense. That's why women and men are from other planets. At least I gained some insight tonight as to why a woman should be called and not have her call the man. But now I'm taking it to the next level. A man wants to know that his woman is independent, and then he wants to try to make her dependent on him. He wants to feel like 'the man' when he does things for her, like picking up something at the market or pumping her gas. Do you know what I mean?"

"I guess that makes better sense now," Corrine said. "But if a woman is independent, then why should a man want her to be dependent? After all, if he's attracted to her independence, shouldn't she stay independent?"

"Like I said, a man wants to feel like a man and wants her to depend on him to do things for her." Robert said.

"I think that makes sense," Lucille said. "Which is why I would rather he call me first."

"How about if I call him?" Robert said.

"WHAT?" Lucille and Corrine both yelped. Robert laughed.

"What if I call him, I could say, I found his business card on the counter and needed his services as a……what does he do for a living?" Robert asked Lucille.

"I have no idea!" Lucille laughed. "I stared at his business card all night last night and all day today. Good thing I have the day off. Otherwise, I wouldn't be able to work. I would be worse than usual waiting on tables tonight. I would have been watching the door all night to see if he showed up."

Corrine and Robert waited expectantly while Lucille stared blankly at them.

"And?" Robert prompted.

"And what?" Lucille asked him.

"WHAT DOES HE DO FOR A LIVING?" Robert and Corrine both shouted at her.

Lucille let loose a belly laugh like she never laughed before. "Oh, my goodness, I am so silly, aren't I? Let me go get his card."

Lucille walked over to her purse and pulled the card out. She stared at it.

"I'm not sure what this means." Lucille finally said.

Robert made a "hand it over" gesture with his hand, and both he and Corrine studied the business card.

The card said simply, "Talent Director."

"I don't know about this." Robert said.

"What do you mean?" Lucille asked in a panic.

Robert realized he should not have spoken aloud, because now he made Lucille more paranoid than ever. But what the heck does "Talent Director" mean? What kind of talent was he looking for? Was he looking for a model? Lucille could definitely be a model. Was he looking for an actress or a singer? Or was he looking for the world's next porn star?

Robert decided he wouldn't say what he was thinking. He would just take matters into his own hands. He was very good at memorizing numbers, so he quickly placed Jeff's phone number into the file cabinet in his brain.

"Well, I'm not sure what a talent director does, that's all. I think you should go on a date with the guy and find out." Robert said, shrugging his shoulders and mentally repeating the telephone number in his brain.

"I'm not going anywhere unless he calls me." Lucille said stubbornly.

"Okay, suit yourself then!" Robert let out a sigh and walked over to the refrigerator. "What's for dinner?"

At that point, both Lucille and Corrine knew that the subject was now closed with Robert. Once he changed the subject, that was it. End of previous subject. Possibly forever.

The next day, Robert took out his cell phone and placed a call to Jeff.

"Hello." Jeff answered.

"Hello, is this Jeff?" Robert asked.

"Yes. Who am I speaking with?" Jeff asked.

"My name is Robert and I am Lucille's brother. Do you remember Lucille from the other night?"

"Of course I do. She was the beautiful waitress in the diner." Jeff's heart started to race when he thought of her.

"Yes, that's her. Can I please ask what your intentions are with my sister?" Robert asked bluntly.

Jeff sputtered, he didn't know what to say first. Finally, he said, "Well, I would just like to take her to dinner sometime. She is very charming."

"Well, she's not just charming. She's very intelligent, sweet and somewhat innocent. I just want to protect her from the wrong kind of man. Are you the wrong kind of man?"

Jeff was feeling really intimidated and wondered if he had made a mistake in giving a complete stranger his business card. He did that sort of thing all the time and he guessed that someday it would come back to bite him in the ass.

"Well, Robert," Jeff gulped. "I can't say for sure whether I'm the wrong kind of man or not. My intentions are just to take her to dinner and see what happens from there."

"Meaning?" Robert pressed.

"Meaning......whether or not we're compatible?"

"What line of work are you in? What exactly does a talent director do?" Robert abruptly changed the subject.

"I seek out musical and acting talent for theaters in Manhattan." Jeff answered.

"And how do you do that?" Robert asked, unrelentingly.

"I go to bars where they have karaoke singers, I go to church plays where I can see if anyone has talent, that sort of thing."

"And don't the people who are interested in music and singing already have the proper avenues to find work themselves?" Robert asked.

"Well, most of them do," Jeff answered. "But a lot of them are steered the wrong way, or they get discouraged and give up. I find really talented people and give them.....fresh hope."

Robert was silent for a moment; he was thinking to himself what to do. Finally he said, "Okay, that sounds good. Take down Lucille's number, she would rather that you call her. She's too shy to call you herself."

Jeff dared to laugh for a moment, if only in relief. "Yes, she did seem quite shy. That was part of her charm."

"She doesn't have any acting or singing talent, not that I know of." Robert added. "Unless she sings in the shower or something, when I'm not home."

"That's all right." Jeff said. "I'm not interested in her as a client."

"That's fine, then. Here's her phone number."

Robert gave him Lucille's phone number and abruptly hung up the phone. Jeff stared down at the piece of paper with Lucille's phone number on it and wondered what the hell he was getting himself into.

The phone rang. Corrine picked it up.

"Hello?"

"Is this Lucille?" Jeff asked, and when Corrine said no, he asked, "May I speak to Lucille please?"

"Sure," Corrine was dubious. Who was this man calling Lucille? "May I ask who's calling?"

"My name is Jeff." he stated. Corrine was shocked. How on earth did he get our phone number?

"Sure, I'll go get her."

Corrine ran into the living room, where they were watching television together.

"Luci, you have a call. It's Jeff!" Corrine couldn't contain herself.

"What?" Lucille said in an astonished whisper. She was shocked. "How did he get this number?"

"Where there's a will, there's a way, I guess!" Corrine said.

Lucille headed for the phone and then stopped.

"Wait a minute.......this is creepy." she said.

"What do you mean?" Corrine asked, her hand over the mouthpiece of the phone.

"He couldn't wait for me to call him? What the hell? Is he stalking me or something?" Lucille started to feel panic rising up inside of her.

Corrine hissed at her. "Just pick up the phone and ask him how he got your number!"

"What if he knows our address? What then?" Lucille was starting to hyperventilate.

"Look," Corrine said, "You wanted him to call you and somehow, by some miracle, here he is on the phone. Maybe someone at the diner gave him your number. Who knows? Things don't always have to be so sinister. Just ask him!"

Corrine held the phone out to her and Lucille weakly reached for it, feeling a bit nauseous.

"Hi Jeff," she said tentatively. "How….how are you?"

"I'm fine, Lucille, just fine. It's great to talk to you. I'm sure you're wondering how I got your number."

"Yes, actually, I am." Lucille tried to hide her churning emotions. Her knees were shaking.

"Well, your brother Robert found my business card and called me. I didn't know you were French. You don't have an accent like he does."

Lucille was really surprised. "Well……" she fished around for an explanation. "I was born here in America. He's a bit older than I am."

"Oh, I see. Well, I was wondering if you'd like to go out to dinner with me? You can pick the restaurant. Anywhere but the diner." Jeff joked.

168

"Why not the diner?" Lucille asked defensively. After all, she thought the food was pretty good there.

"Oh, there's nothing wrong with the diner. I just want to take you somewhere nicer." Jeff stammered hastily. "I mean, not nicer. Well, yes, I mean more elegant, I suppose. To make a good impression on you so you don't think I'm the wrong man. I mean, well, you don't want your co-workers watching you all night, do you? Not that we'll be out all night, of course, since we just met, but........." he trailed off.

Lucille thought his little awkward explanation was cute.

"I don't know too many restaurants in the area, Jeff, so can you select one for us? I'd be happy with whatever you chose." Lucille was surprised at how eloquent that sounded, unlike how nervous she was feeling.

"Great. What night do you have off from the diner?" he asked.

"Well, tonight I'm off. Then tomorrow I'm back on for five days." Lucille held her breath, wondering if she would have to wait a week before she could have dinner with him.

"Tonight is fine. Can I pick you up at 7:00?" Jeff asked in what Lucille thought was a "manly" tone of voice.

"Yes. I'll give you the address." Lucille said.

When she shakily hung up the phone, she walked over to Corrine, who was waiting for her in the living room.

"Well?" Corrine said expectantly.

"Tonight! At 7:00!" Lucille said, trying to keep from screaming.

It was no use. They both screamed, hugged each other, and jumped up and down together.

"I'll help you find something to wear!" Corrine said excitedly as they both ran up the stairs to Lucille's bedroom.

CHAPTER TEN – CORRINE

Corrine was seated in the middle on the bench seat of Danny's van because only someone her size was small enough to fit there.   Robert was riding shotgun.   Corrine was giggling uncontrollably. Robert couldn't tell if she was laughing or crying.

"I can't believe I'm out of the convent!" she laughed with tears in her eyes. "I've never done anything like this before!"

Robert was nervous, but Danny was beyond nervous.

"What is she doing here, man?" Danny asked Robert. "When those nuns find her gone, they're going to call the cops and think we kidnapped her!"

"Don't worry," Corrine said, "I will go back there in the morning. They won't even notice that I'm gone."

Corrine didn't realize that Lucille had been looking out the window and witnessed her escape.

Lucille was wringing her hands, not knowing what to do. She didn't know what was happening.

Lucille fell asleep like a ton of bricks while watching TV with Corrine. She was mentally exhausted from worry over Corrine professing her love for this Robert character. After she woke up on the couch, she discovered Corrine was gone, probably already in her room asleep. So she shut off the television and headed up to bed. Before she went to bed, she decided to open the window a little to get some fresh air. The heaters were not only practically fixed now, they were working overtime, and she felt very warm indeed. That's when she spotted Corrine, in her pajamas, running out of the building with Robert and the other guy. Lucille couldn't remember his name at all.

Lucille gasped as Corrine climbed into the van. The thought of Robert kidnapping her did not even occur to Lucille, since Corrine was smiling and holding Robert's hand. They looked almost like Bonnie and Clyde, two lovers on a journey of mayhem and mischief.

Lucille wondered if she should report this to the Mother Superior. She decided not to, because she didn't want to betray her friend. After all, she didn't know what Corrine's intentions were and she may very well sneak back into the convent sometime during the night. She didn't want to get Corrine in trouble.

But Lucille didn't sleep a wink the entire night. Meanwhile, Corrine was having the time of her life. She felt as if she had grown wings and was learning to fly.

"How will they *not* notice that you're gone?" Robert asked Corrine nervously. "Don't you have to get up early in the morning with the other sisters? Won't they miss you at breakfast?"

"Don't worry about that, Robert," Corrine said confidently. "When you both go back to work tomorrow, I'll just sneak back in.

172

One of you just needs to keep the door unlocked so I can sneak back in."

"Well," Robert said, lost in thought, "what happens if they catch you sneaking back in? What's the worst case scenario?"

"Robert, I don't want to worry about that right now." Corrine pouted. "I just would like to spend some time with you. Can I go home with you? Please?"

Robert didn't know quite what to say. He didn't really feel comfortable with the whole thing. He wasn't like his father; he didn't want to be like his father. His father would have been totally comfortable with stealing a nun out of a convent. His father was comfortable stealing anything or anyone.

"My darling Corrine, yes, you may come home with me." Robert said, and then fell silent for the rest of the drive home.

Danny dropped them off unceremoniously at Robert's house and then sped off. Corrine didn't understand why he was being so rude.

"He's not comfortable with what just happened." Robert explained.

"What do you mean?" Corrine asked. "What's the big deal? I'm just a woman who needs some freedom, that's all."

Robert turned the key and led her into his cozy little home. He reached around for the light switch and she practically waltzed into his living room. She threw herself on his leather couch and hugged a throw pillow.

"I can't believe I'm FREE!" she exclaimed, beaming.

"But my darling, you are not free." Robert said, a bit too sternly. "You are a nun!"

She gestured for him to sit next to her on the couch.

"Robert, I am free in my heart. I am going to leave the convent."

Robert was blown away. He didn't know what to say, didn't know what to do.

"Would you like some water?" he asked her nervously, and they both laughed. That was how the whole thing got started, after all, with Corrine offering Robert water at the convent.

"How can you leave the convent?" Robert asked her. "It's your life."

"No, it's not my life." Corrine stated firmly. "Now that I met you......I feel like..... you're my life."

Robert gulped. What did he get himself into? Yes, he was attracted to her. She was full of innocence and white light. He knew she would never hurt him. She was a very special woman and he was thrilled that she felt so strongly about him. But this was moving too fast. They barely knew each other! If she left the convent, where would she go? She would live here with him, he supposed. And what if something happened and they didn't get along? Love doesn't conquer everything, after all. Would she go back to the convent then? Would she slander him and get him in trouble once she went back? Hell hath no fury like a woman scorned. Robert knew that to be true, absolutely true. It was what finally did his father in. A woman scorned destroyed his father. But rightly so, Robert thought, because he needed something to destroy him.

"Corrine...." Robert started to speak, but suddenly was at a loss for words.

Corrine could practically read his mind.

"I know this is fast," she said. "But I won't ask anything of you other than to please just hold me tight and kiss me. Please."

She put her head on his shoulder and he drew her to him. They kissed deeply and strongly, and both of their heads were spinning. Before he knew what he was doing, he had drawn her body under him on the couch. Her body hungrily arched up to meet his.

Suddenly Robert jumped up.

"I can't do this!" he said, rubbing his eyes. "You're a NUN!"

"Please don't think of me as a nun anymore, Robert." Corrine sat up on the couch and her eyes were moist. She was startled at his abrupt change. One minute they were kissing, their bodies on fire, and the next, he was out of his mind with worry. "Robert, the convent was all I've ever known. But now.......since you......I know differently."

Robert crossed his arms and waited for her to say more. She beckoned him to sit on the couch next to her again.

"I promise to behave myself." Corrine said demurely, lowering her eyes. Robert sat next to her on the couch, but he kept a little distance between them.

"Robert, I don't know how I ended up in the convent," she explained. "It seems I was born there. They tell me someone dropped me off there as a newborn. I've always wondered what my life would have been like if my parents didn't drop me off there.

"It's not like I wasn't happy there, with all the sisters. I was. They all love me very much and they taught me many things. I didn't really miss the outside world; I didn't know what I was missing. I watched a little bit of television and saw how bad the outside world seemed to be, so I didn't care much if I spent the rest of my life in the convent.

"Was I curious about the outside world? Yes, I was. Who wouldn't be? But like I said, whenever I tried to go out, something bad would happen. There would be a car accident, or cars beeping angrily at each other, or someone would be out there yelling at someone else, that sort of thing. It wasn't pleasant. I felt like the whole world was crazy and the only sanity was within the convent walls. There was peace there, it was very peaceful.

"Then one night, Lucille came along. She was so broken, so battered, such a sad sight. My heart broke for her; she had been through so much. I watched her transformation, almost overnight, because of the love and peace that can be found at the convent. We all took care of her and she chose the convent life for herself. But don't you see? I never chose it. I never knew anything else. What little of the outside world I was exposed to seemed………. tumultuous. Dangerous. Until I met you."

She smiled at Robert then, and reached out to hold his hand. He covered the top of her hand with his, so he was holding her small hand between both of his large hands. This gesture made her feel nestled in his love, and happy tears started to fall from her eyes.

"I remember in an old classic movie, how a Mother Superior told a young soon-to-be nun that the love of a man and woman is holy too. That stayed with me. I didn't think I would ever meet anyone that I could fall in love with.......until you."

Robert was trying to fight back tears. On the one hand, he felt absolutely terrified that a complete stranger was telling him that she was falling in love with him. But on the other hand, he felt such a strong magnetic pull to Corrine that he felt like something magical was happening to him. Finally. For the first time in his life, maybe he could find happiness. He felt like he deserved happiness, in spite of what his father tried to do to him. His father tried to lead him down the wrong path. He wasn't like his father and he never would be.

Robert reached out and pulled her into his arms. They kissed passionately but Robert felt the need to hold himself back again after a few minutes.

"Robert, you don't have to stop." Corrine whispered into his ear. "Please make love to me."

He pulled away for a moment and looked down at her. She looked so beautiful, her eyes gazing up into his eyes, the innocence of her face, the desire showing through the innocence.....it was all too much for him to bear. He scooped her up off the couch and carried her into his bedroom. He laid her gently on the bed. He kissed her tenderly and caressed her body, but he didn't want to take her clothes off yet.

Corrine became impatient. Her body was on fire, she wanted – no, needed – to remove both her clothes and his. She wanted to feel his naked body against her naked body. She had never felt sensations like this ever before. She didn't know what to do with herself, she felt like she was soaring out of her body, almost like someone else had taken over and she was watching. She did not feel guilt, nor did she feel shame. She only felt desire. And love. Overwhelming love.

She didn't know who this man was, where he came from, or what kind of man he was. All she knew was that he was good, he was exactly what she needed, exactly what she was looking for her entire life. All her life's journey as a nun had been leading her to this moment. She was a woman. She had women's desires, women's needs. And she desperately wanted Robert.

She kissed him hungrily and pulled up his shirt to try to bring it up over his head. He gently placed his hands on hers to stop her. She let out a moan of frustration. He quickly covered her moan with his lips again. He kissed her whole face, her eyes, her chin, her forehead, her cheeks, then started working his way over to her ears. When she felt his tongue in her ear, she felt a bolt of electricity surge through her and she suddenly raked his back with her short, but sharp, nails. He winced for a moment in pain, until desire completely took over him and he reached out to undo the buttons on her night shirt.

Suddenly the two of them were pulling at each other's clothes and they didn't stop until they were naked. They pulled each other close, relishing in the feel of their bare skin against each other. There was a certain relief at that point for Corrine, because she ached to feel his body against hers. Robert nudged her to help him pull back the comforter so they could get under the soft flannel sheets. Those few seconds that her body was away from his was agonizing for her. She suddenly felt cold, almost shivering, and her anguish was relieved when he pulled her close to him again under the sheets.

She gave herself to him with total abandon. Robert himself could not believe the urgency of his feelings for her, his love for her. They made love several times during the night; neither of them could get enough of each other.

An hour before sunrise, Robert began to feel a wave of panic.

"We must get you back to the convent before they realize you're gone!" he said frantically. "I'm so sorry you didn't get any sleep, my love."

"I'm not sorry," Corrine said gently, stretching her naked body on the bed. "I'm not sorry at all. But.......I will get dressed, if only for you, so you don't panic."

They got out of bed and began to put their clothes on. In half an hour, Danny was at the door to bring them back to the convent.

Lucille was still pacing the floor. She hadn't slept all night. The other sisters were at Mass while Sister Celia remained in the kitchen to cook breakfast for everyone. Lucille didn't know what to do, where to go. She watched out of her window for Corrine's return. She heaved a sigh of relief when she finally spotted the familiar van heading down the street. She put on her robe and ran downstairs to open the door for them before they could ring the doorbell and Sister Celia would find them.

"Get in here, now!" Lucille hissed at Corrine.

Corrine was startled for a moment by the sudden opening of the door, but she danced toward Lucille, smiling brightly at her.

"Are you insane??" Lucille asked her. "Where have you been all night?"

Corrine blew a kiss to Robert, who got back in the van so they could drive around to the front entrance and ring the doorbell.

"Where do you think I've been all night, Luci?" Corrine said playfully, putting one arm around Lucille's shoulders. "I've been in Robert's arms all night. And I've never been happier in my life!"

"You're crazy! You've gone completely mad!" Lucille whispered harshly as she shoved Corrine up the stairs in front of her. When they arrived at Lucille's bedroom, she hurriedly pushed Corrine in there and closed the door.

"I have been worried sick about you all night!" Lucille said, her knees shaking with the relief of having Corrine back.

"You didn't have to worry about me." Corrine said in a small voice. "I was not in any danger."

"You..........SLEPT with him?" Lucille asked, fearful of Corrine's answer.

"No, we didn't sleep at all." Corrine giggled.

"OH MY GOD!" Lucille cried out. "Oh my God, how could you?"

Corrine stuck her chin out defiantly. "Very easily. I love him, Luci."

"WHAT?" Lucille almost screamed out, but caught herself. She didn't want Sister Celia in the kitchen to hear them. "Are you nuts? You just met the guy! And what kind of man has sex with a nun? He's no good, I tell you, he's no good. He's using you! He's a slime ball!"

"Don't talk that way about my Robert!" Corrine interrupted her. "He is not a slime ball! He was the one who kept pushing me away. I was the one who begged him to make love to me."

"Oh, yeah, right! You little fool! You were just playing right into his hands! You expect me to believe he – a man – didn't want to make love to you – a woman – an easy target?" Lucille laughed bitterly. "Come on, get real!"

"I am being real, Luci. For the first time in my life, I am being and feeling very real." Corrine said confidently but quietly.

"So, what now?" Lucille asked her, trying to stare her down. "Are you going to be sneaking out with him every night and coming back every morning? Do you expect me to open the door for you every morning so you could sneak back in here? No way. I won't

181

do it, I tell you. When I saw you leave with them last night, I was going to go straight to Mother Superior and tell her what you'd done."

"No, Luci!" Corrine cried.

"But I didn't." Lucille said, squaring her shoulders and walking away from Corrine for a moment. "You're my best friend. I couldn't do that to you."

Corrine sighed with relief. "Thank you."

"But that doesn't mean I'm not going to try to talk you out of this nonsense you've gotten yourself into! Okay, so you lost your virginity. Big deal. No one else needs to know about it, right? You can still be a nun, you could still —"

"No." Corrine said firmly. "I'm leaving here tonight, Luci. I'm leaving with Robert. I can't be a nun anymore. I love him."

Lucille heard those words and started shaking. She was still turned away from Corrine, and Corrine could see her shoulders shaking. Lucille began to sob violently, almost as violently as the first night she showed up at the convent. Lucille got down on her hands and knees and crawled to her bed. She started punching the mattress.

"How could you?" Lucille cried. "How could you?"

Corrine padded quietly over to Lucille and got down on the floor next to her.

"I love him. Please understand, Luci. I love him. I can't be a nun anymore. I have to be with him." Corrine said, stroking Lucille's hair.

Lucille and Corrine fell into silence for a few moments. Lucille finally stopped sobbing after a while and started to breathe almost normally.

"How are you going to do it?" Lucille asked. "Are you going to pack your stuff and say goodbye to all of us, or are you going to slip away like a thief in the night again, and this time never come back?"

"I'm going to say goodbye to everyone." Corrine answered. "I will not sneak away again and risk them calling the police. I will own up to what I did, own up to my decision. I want to walk out of here, the only home I've ever known, with my head held high. I don't want to be on the run, I want to be able to love and be loved in return, and live my life in peace with Robert."

Lucille felt like the rug was being pulled out from under her. Corrine was leaving her. The convent would not be the same without Corrine.

"When are you going to tell everyone?" Lucille asked, brushing away her tears.

"After breakfast." Corrine said confidently, like she had been planning this for a long time. "I'm going to go down there and sit with everyone and eat my breakfast and then I'll tell them. Okay?"

"What exactly are you going to tell them? That you slept with Robert? Mother Superior will go down to the basement and kill him. There will be a nun massacre."

Suddenly, Corrine began to giggle. "A nun massacre?"

"I know it's stupid what I just said, but I really think all of us are going to storm the basement and kill him. I know I will be leading the way!" Lucille said flatly.

"Well, then I won't tell everyone that I slept with him. I will just tell them that I love him and I'm leaving the convent with him. Okay?"

Lucille pondered that for a very long moment. Lucille was being really quiet and Corrine could see that her mind was racing a mile a minute. Could she possibly ask her? Lucille thought. Would it work?

"Can I come too?" Lucille finally said.

Corrine stared at Lucille in astonishment. "You want to leave the convent too?" Corrine asked, shocked. "Why?"

"I know it sounds stupid, but I'll miss you. I don't think I could be here without you." Lucille said, tears falling down her cheeks again. "I love the convent, I love the peace, I love being away from the outside world. But......you're my best friend. I love you more than the peace of the convent. I can't be here without you."

Corrine didn't know what to say. It would be difficult to ask Robert to take both of them out of the convent and have both of them live with him. But Lucille knew what she was thinking.

"I would only ask to stay with you for a little while, only until I can get my own place and a job. Okay?" Lucille said.

"Well," Corrine said slowly, "I'll ask Robert what he thinks, what the best plan of action would be."

"Okay, thanks."

They suddenly felt very awkward together. They've been friends for so many years, and yet they felt awkward at that very moment. They decided to go down to the kitchen and help Sister Celia with breakfast.

When the sisters piled into the kitchen after Mass, Corrine and Lucille sat down with everyone and ate breakfast. Even though no one knew anything yet, you could still cut the tension with a knife. Mother Superior finally broke the ice.

"Sister Corrine? Sister Lucille?" she asked. "Neither of you were at Mass this morning. I can see both of you have something on your minds that's bothering you. Please feel free to share, if you like, we're all family here."

Corrine and Lucille exchanged glances. Finally Corrine decided to speak. She squared her shoulders and got up from the table, looking like she was about to make an announcement. She even cleared her throat. Everyone stared at her expectantly.

Suddenly she burst into tears and ran from the room. Lucille and Mother Superior hastily got up and followed her. Sister Celia rose from her chair and was about to follow too, but Mother Superior waved a warning hand at her. Sister Celia felt extremely peeved over that. She couldn't run after her own daughter and see what was troubling her? She was getting tired of having to keep her secret. So very, very tired.

Sister Celia decided to follow them anyway, at a discreet distance. When they all entered Corrine's room, they shut the door behind them. Sister Celia resolved to eavesdrop outside the door of her daughter's room.

Once inside the room, Corrine ran to face the window, Lucille sat on Corrine's bed, and Mother Superior approached Corrine's back and placed a hand on her shoulder.

"I can see you are burdened, child." Mother Superior said. "Please unburden yourself. If you've committed a sin, we can pray together and ask God for forgiveness."

"It is not a sin I've committed," Corrine said with steely conviction, turning to face Mother Superior. "It's something that's made me very happy."

Mother Superior was taken aback. She began to get a sick feeling in her stomach, remembering the vision she had after Sister Celia told her about her pregnancy. Mother Superior pretty much knew what was coming next. Though she was trembling, she spoke in a strong voice which didn't betray her nerves.

"What has made you so happy, child? So happy that you can't face the rest of us, bursting into tears and running from the room?" she asked gently.

"Mother," Corrine began. "I fell in love."

Before Mother Superior could interrupt, Corrine went on.

"Mother, I can't live here anymore. I'm not going to continue being a sister any longer. I fell in love with a man whose name is Robert, the man downstairs fixing the heating system."

Mother Superior put up a hand to stop Corrine from saying anything further, so she could tell her how foolish she is, how young she is, how she doesn't know the ways of the world, etc., but Corrine ignored her hand and kept right on speaking.

"Mother, I know this is sudden, but I know it with all my heart and soul. I feel it in my bones. I love him, Mother, and he loves me. I'm going to leave here and be with him."

"And I'm going with her." Lucille spoke up. "I'm sorry, Mother, but she's my best friend."

Mother Superior didn't say anything for a moment. She was choosing her words carefully. Meanwhile, on the other side of the closed door, Sister Celia felt like she was going to have a heart attack. She couldn't lose her daughter. All these years keeping silent, having to stay away from her, not being able to give her any special treatment, was all for nothing. Corrine was going to leave, and Sister Celia, her mother, would never see her again. Sister Celia began to drop to the floor, her heart heavy. She grasped the doorknob for support and it turned, opening the door.

The three sisters inside the room all turned when they heard the door opening. They were shocked to see Sister Celia crouched down outside the door, toppling into the room. They rushed to her side and were alarmed to see that she was pale as a ghost.

"Sister Celia, are you all right?" Mother Superior asked nervously, feeling her forehead and grabbing her wrist to feel a pulse. "Lucille, please call an ambulance!"

As Lucille raced out of the room, Sister Celia cried out, "NO!"

Lucille stopped in her tracks and went back to Sister Celia's side.

"Corrine….." Sister Celia croaked out.

"Sister Celia……" Mother Superior said in a warning tone, a fearful tone.

"Corrine, my daughter," Sister Celia continued. "Please give me your hand."

Corrine grasped Sister Celia's hand. Again Mother Superior used a warning tone with Sister Celia.

"Sister, you are frightening the girls." Mother Superior said. "Please let us call an ambulance so we can get you some help."

Sister Celia's vision was beginning to dim and she wanted to say what she had to say before she passed out. She filled her field of vision only with Corrine's face.

"I'm sorry child, they told me I couldn't tell you." Sister Celia began. "I am your real mother. Father Harris and I fell in love and consummated our love. You were the gift of my life. The best gift of all my life. I wanted to raise you on my own but our Mother promised as long as I never told you I was your real mother, we could all raise you here in the convent. I'm so sorry I never told you. I love you so much. I'm so proud of you."

Corrine was so shocked, she didn't know what to do. So much was happening to her all at once. Sister Celia was her mother? Father Harris was her father? She had virtually no time to digest this assault of information. Corrine felt like her chest was going to burst open. Meanwhile, Sister Celia was squeezing her hand, but her grip was fading fast. Corrine couldn't lose her mother now!

Sister Celia started to cough. Mother Superior felt like all of her own air supply was being cut off. She couldn't speak a single word and she was rooted to her spot, frozen in place.

"Follow your heart, my child." Sister Celia said to Corrine as both women's eyes filled with tears. "If this man loves you, follow your heart. I wish I did. I wish my love had the courage to do the same. Your father loves you, and he wants to be in your life. Please don't hate us. We love you, we always will."

Sister Celia's eyes started to show signs of lifelessness. Suddenly she wasn't staring at Corrine anymore, even though her gaze was fixed on her. Sister Celia was no longer in her body.

Corrine unleashed a primal scream and grabbed Sister Celia's body, shaking her.

"Mother, don't go!" she screamed. "Mother! Don't leave me!"

Sister Celia's body was limp. Mother Superior, sick in her heart, leaned down and closed Sister Celia's eyelids. Suddenly Corrine pushed her.

"YOU!" Corrine cried. "It's all your fault, isn't it? You told her not to tell me she was my mother!"

"Corrine, please......" Mother Superior started, but Corrine put a hand in her face.

"NO!" Corrine yelled at her. "All these years, I didn't know I had a mother and a father! I thought I was nobody! I thought I was a baby no one wanted, so they dropped me off at a convent!"

Corrine began to pace back and forth, her face so red it looked like it was about to burst.

"She fell in love and she paid the price, didn't she?" Corrine cried. "Didn't she!"

Corrine tried to wipe away at the endless tears that were streaming down her face, but it was no use.

"Father Harris wouldn't leave the priesthood." Mother Superior said quietly. "He left for a few years, joined another church, but then he returned when you were a young child."

"Father Harris left my mother?" Corrine screamed. "How could he? Didn't he love her? If he loved her, they should have gotten married and raised me themselves!"

"Their love was an abomination!" Mother Superior finally raised her voice and let loose her emotions. "They had pledged their lives to the Lord, they couldn't just forsake their commitment to Him, just to raise a child born in sin. Don't you understand that?"

"A child born in sin." Corrine repeated, shaking her head in disbelief. "A child born in sin. Was that all I was to you, Mother?"

Lucille got up and tried to comfort Corrine but Corrine lashed out at her blindly, without warning. She didn't want anyone near her at that particular moment.

"I was nothing but a burden to you all, wasn't I? No wonder Sister Celia was so cold to Father Harris. It was because he didn't have a set of BALLS!" Corrine yelled those words in Mother Superior's face. "He didn't have THE BALLS to do the right thing! He and my mother should have gotten married and we would have been a family! We would have had a normal life! I wouldn't have been kept like a dark, dirty little secret in this convent! I would have been out there –" Corrine pointed at the window, "having a life for myself. Instead, here I am locked up like a prisoner."

"Come on, Corrine, you didn't always feel like that, did you?" Lucille finally found her voice. "You said you found it peaceful here and you didn't care about the outside world."

"I WAS A FOOL!" she screamed at Lucille. "And now that I met Robert, I won't let any of you stop me anymore! I'm going to leave here and be with him!"

"If you leave here with him, something terrible will happen." Mother Superior said quietly but powerfully.

Corrine turned to look at her. "Don't try to scare me. I love him. Nothing terrible will happen to me."

"Corrine," Mother Superior took her face in her hands and held it so tightly that Corrine couldn't get out of her grip. She forced Corrine to look into her eyes. "Listen to me, child. Listen to me carefully. You will die if you go with this man."

Mother Superior let Corrine go so that her words could sink in properly.

"Why are you trying to scare me?" Corrine lashed out. "This is a pathetic scare tactic you're trying to lay on me, isn't it? Stop it! I won't die if I go with Robert! That's preposterous! He makes me happy, happier than I've ever been! On the contrary, I will LIVE! I will finally be free to live my life!"

Mother Superior shook her head. "This Robert you speak of.....he's a very bad man."

Corrine stopped in her tracks. "No, he isn't." Corrine raised her head defiantly.

"I've seen him in a vision, before you were born, Corrine." Mother Superior said. "Yes, he is charming now, but he is going to turn into......... one of the biggest criminals this world has ever known. And you will get sucked into that criminal world. And you will die."

Corrine began to back away from Mother Superior.

"No," Corrine said defiantly. "You're lying."

"I wish I was, child. But I know this is true."

"HOW!" Corrine spat out. "How do you know this is true? What are you, a fortune teller or something?"

"I saw him in a vision," Mother Superior said again. "I saw the whole vision, from beginning to end. You.....will.....die."

Corrine put her hand over her heart and started to sob violently. Her fierce cries racked her whole body. Lucille was afraid to go near her, afraid that Corrine would lash out at her again. After a few minutes, her sobbing began to subside. She looked up at Mother Superior and walked over to her slowly. When she was about three inches away from her, she locked eyes with her. Mother Superior was suddenly powerless to look away.

"If I am going to die, then......" Corrine said gravely, "then I will die happy."

Then Corrine left the room running. Mother Superior and Lucille heard her running down the basement stairs.

"May God's Will be done." Mother Superior said in a shaky voice when she heard Corrine's voice calling for Robert. "And may God forgive me and have mercy on all of us."

Lucille took one look at Mother Superior's face, and then she looked down at Sister Celia's body on the floor. She couldn't believe what had just happened here. Her life was over. Sister Celia's life was over. She had lost all respect for Mother Superior.

There was nothing left for her to say, nothing left for her to do. She left the room in search of Corrine.

CHAPTER ELEVEN – DEREK AND BEN

Gloria watched helplessly as the two men devoured their porterhouse steaks, which she had been forced to cook for them. She had to give them everything they asked for or they said they would kill them both.

Derek hadn't arrived yet – where on earth was he?

Ben was sitting in a chair at the table, watching the two men eating their steaks. The poor kid was probably wondering why he couldn't have one too, Gloria thought to herself. There were three in the fridge, one each for Gloria, Ben and Derek -- until these derelicts came along and stole the steaks, along with Lee's life.

Not to mention they were stealing her life too, as well as the lives of her sons. If Derek didn't get here soon, something had to be done. The police couldn't be called. How could she know for sure that once they got the money, that they wouldn't kill them all anyway?

Derek knew where the money was hidden. Their father kept a large sum of money in a safe at their summer home for emergency purposes. Sure, they all knew it was illegal to keep money out of bank circulation, but times were tough and banks were shutting down left and right in this terrible economy. How would they know their money would be safe unless they put it somewhere safe?

Sure they had their stocks and bonds in the safe too, which she was sure these criminals wanted as well. Once they finally get what they wanted, Gloria and her sons would be close to destitute (if left alive as promised). They would have to sell their home to recoup some of the money they had lost. Gloria's pension wouldn't be enough to support her and her sons. Sure her sons were both working, but neither of them earned enough money to continue the lifestyle they were all used to. She would have to go back to work. They would all have to start over.

Gloria just didn't have it in her. She was retired now. She and her husband were supposed to retire and travel the world with all of their money. She and her husband had even put aside a nest egg for their sons' inheritance. When her husband was killed right in front of her eyes, she wished she had died that night too, right along with him. She couldn't handle life without him. Especially not with Lee coming around all the time, threatening her and blackmailing her.

Well, Gloria thought as she looked down at Lee's dead body on the floor, he certainly got what he deserved, didn't he? He was lying in a pool of blood next to the refrigerator, staring up at the ceiling. He could no longer threaten her. He was dead.

And she was alive, wasn't she? Again, she was alive and spared death. Twice. First her husband dies in a car accident with her, and then Lee gets killed a few feet away from her. But would her life be spared once more? These two men may just decide to kill her and Ben (and Derek, if he ever got here), once they got the money.

She had to do something. If she had to die, she didn't care. But she didn't want Ben to die. Ben was young and he had his whole life ahead of him. Derek would take good care of him, he always did. Derek loved his brother fiercely, that she was sure of.

While she watched in disgust the men eating their steaks with such gusto, an idea began to formulate in her mind. She noticed that one of the men had his gun still in the holster in the belt on his pants. The other man had the gun on the table. If she could just distract them both, then maybe.......maybe Ben could make a run for it.

"That certainly was delicious, Gloria!" one of the men said, the one with the gun in the holster. She decided to just call him "Holster."

"It most certainly was!" the other man said, the one with the gun on the table next to him. He was rubbing his belly and licking his fingers. He had literally chewed the meat right off the bone. She decided to call him "Bonehead."

Gloria did not say anything to them. She simply got up and collected the plates.

"Would you mind if Ben helps me do the dishes?" Gloria asked. "We always do the dishes together."

Ben looked up questioningly. Since when did he ever do dishes?

Holster let out a belly laugh. "What a mama's boy! He does the dishes!"

Bonehead laughed too, still rubbing his fat belly. "Better him than me!"

They both laughed and Gloria motioned for Ben to join her at the sink. She leaned over and whispered to Ben, "Run when you get the chance. Don't ask questions, no matter what happens, just run. Okay? Got it? Nod your head once if you got it."

He nodded once.

Gloria went over to the trash compactor and was about to scrape the bones into the can. She picked up the clean picked bone and surveyed it briefly. She flicked her finger against the bottom edge, at the bottom of the "T" shape. It seemed sharp enough.

Bonehead was sitting in the perfect place, right near the garbage can.

Gloria asked Ben to go to the table and pick up the empty glass that was a couple of inches away from Bonehead's gun.

Gloria calmly threw one set of bones in the trash and picked the other one up, positioning it in her hand properly. She was thinking "brass knuckles" only with a protruding spear coming out of those brass knuckles. She casually glanced over at Bonehead, surveying his neck.

With her heart pounding wildly, she let out a primal scream and plunged the sharp edge of the bone right into Bonehead's jugular. Then she dived for Bonehead's gun, dodging the blood squirting out of his neck. Holster jumped up immediately, just as Gloria pointed the gun at him. He swung the gun out of his holster as Gloria squeezed the trigger. Her gun didn't fire. The safety was on. While she fumbled with the safety switch, Holster fired two shots at her. Gloria took both bullets in the chest, and the gun slid out of her hands and back onto the table as she dropped down at Bonehead's feet. Bonehead was clutching his neck, trying futilely to get the bone out. In a matter of seconds, he was dead.

Ben's hand was three inches away from the gun. He had been about to pick up the glass his mother asked him to pick up, but he stopped dead in his tracks when he saw his mother stab one guy in the neck and then try to shoot the other guy. When that guy shot his mama down, Ben let out a piercing howl that conveyed all of his anguish. Seeing nothing but red in his fury, Ben grabbed the gun that fell from his mother's hands and quickly shot his mother's murderer with it.

Holster fell to the floor, dead. Bonehead was already dead.

Ben ran to his mother's side. She was still alive, but just barely.

"Mommy!" he cried, trying to pick her up.

"No, son," Gloria whispered. "You need to leave me be. I can't get up."

"But why, momma, WHY?" Ben wailed.

"Benny boy, I was just trying to look out for you. You need to run as fast as you can away from here. Wait for Derek and then you boys need to run. Don't call the cops, because they might arrest you for shooting and killing. Just get out of here, run as fast as you can."

Ben just sat there on his knees with his butt on his feet and rocked back and forth. He started pulling his hair.

"MAMA!!! MAMA!!" he cried. "Please don't die!"

Gloria was so relieved she was able to turn the safety switch off the gun before she got shot. At least her boys were safe now.

"Hush, now!" Gloria said. "Your father's here, he's come to get me!"

Suddenly, she smiled peacefully and stretched out one arm to the ceiling. In the next moment, her arm dropped to the floor and she was gone.

Ben looked around. "Daddy?" He looked up at the ceiling. He looked behind him. "Daddy, where are you?"

Derek walked in at that moment. He was stunned. He had never seen so much blood, so many dead bodies in all his life. He didn't realize that Ben was still alive, since he was hunched over on the floor next to his mother. Derek felt so weak that he almost passed out, until………

"DADDY!!! MOMMY!!!" Ben screamed and Derek was shaken out of his shock.

He ran to Ben's side and saw his dead mother on the floor. Derek's voice caught in his throat, he couldn't speak. He started to sob quietly while Ben watched him.

"She said Daddy was here." Ben told him. "She said Daddy came to get her. But I didn't see him. Do you see him, Derry?"

"Mom and Pop are together now, Benny." Derek said, wiping away tears. "We've got to get out of here. Now. We have to call the cops."

"NO!" Ben said quickly. "Mama said to run! She said don't call the cops because I killed this guy here and she's afraid they'll arrest me. That's what she said. What does 'arrest' mean? Does it mean I'll go to jail?"

"You shot him?" Derek raised his eyebrows in disbelief. "Who else did you shoot?"

"Mama stabbed this guy in the neck with a steak bone and then the other guy shot her. I picked up the gun that was on the table and shot the man that shot Mama. That's when she told me to run and then she said that Daddy was here for her."

Derek noticed Lee's body in the corner.

"How did Lee die?" Derek asked quietly.

"One of these guys shot him. Lee took me home and while I was hugging Mama and telling her all about the horses, these two men busted in the door and shot Lee."

So they apparently followed Lee here. Did Lee know they were coming? Was it all part of some plan that the three of them had cooked up and then Lee got caught in the crossfire? There is no honor among thieves. Maybe they decided they didn't need Lee anymore once he led them to the money. The money would be

200

better split in half than in thirds. Or perhaps Lee was innocent in all of this?

Regardless, innocent or guilty, it was all his fault, Derek thought angrily. Lee was a dirty slime ball. Why did he bring these men to our home? Why did he even have to be in our lives? It was all his fault!

"Let's get out of here!" Derek said. He grabbed Ben's hand and they raced out the door. Derek was about to start the engine of his car when he realized that perhaps it might be better to take the thugs' vehicle instead. The police may be looking for Derek's car, since they would be on the run. But they wouldn't know what the thugs' vehicle looked like. Lee's car was still parked in the driveway. The cops could surmise that the three dead bad guys all came here in Lee's car.

Derek's car should remain in the driveway so the cops would have a nice puzzle to sort out. While they were busy sorting out the puzzle, he and Ben would just keep running, get as far away as they could, and start a new life. The cops would think they're missing and possibly dead too.

That was a good idea. That was the only idea. Derek asked Ben to get out of their car and he walked toward the thugs' vehicle. The key was in the ignition.

Derek and Ben drove until they were out of the state. After several hours, Derek thought it would be safe to stop at a diner because they were both starving.

"Can you believe they wouldn't let me eat the steak? There were three of them!" Ben said. "One for you, one for me, one for Mommy. They could have at least let me eat one!"

Derek told Ben to pipe down and not talk about it while they were in the diner. He didn't want anyone to overhear them.

Suddenly, at the counter, there was a very familiar face. It was a very wonderful familiar face. That face happened to belong to Derek's teacher from his security guard training. Luciano Piccardo's face lit up when he saw Derek, and he quickly got up from the counter and walked over to their table.

"Derek!" Luciano said with a slight Italian accent. He put his hand out and shook Derek's hand warmly. "So good to see you! How's my favorite student?"

Derek was so happy to see Luciano. He was more than just a teacher to him, he was his friend and confidant. He felt like seeing Luciano at this time was divine intervention.

"Well, to tell you the truth, Luciano, things aren't so great right now." Derek said.

"What is it?" Luciano asked, concerned. "What is it? Tell Luciano. I'll help you any way I can, you know that, right, Derek, my friend?"

"Well, it's really complicated," Derek began. Luciano settled back in the booth and crossed his arms, waiting expectantly. Derek told him the whole story of what happened, and Ben was finally able to put all the pieces of the puzzle together for himself. Ben didn't understand that Lee was trying to extort money by using

202

Ben as a pawn in his little game, which ultimately backfired on Lee anyway.

Ben was very close to his mother. Gloria and Derek did give him a lot of love and support while Derek's father didn't. That's why when Lee came along, Ben was able to have a little fun with his real father to some extent. But Lee's intentions were not just to get to know his son. He was using Ben as bait to get to the really big fish.

Lee apparently knew that their family had money in a safe somewhere. He must have found out through Ben. Poor innocent Ben was always unnoticeable, all the while listening and absorbing conversations that people thought they were having in private. No one paid attention to his presence because they thought he didn't understand what was being said. So apparently, at some point in his life, he overheard talk of the money in the safe at the summer home. Somehow Lee had gotten this out of him. Lee must have owed these goons some money, so he figured he'd dangle Ben in front of them and use him as a pawn in their game to get their money back from Lee. Lee figured he'd be free at that point and maybe even get a third of the money, if there was enough. He cared nothing about his son or he would have never put him in danger.

But Lee lost that game first. Lee was the first one to go. The goons just needed Lee long enough to get to their destination and then he was no longer needed. Lee may have thought they were all "thick as thieves", but as we know, there is no honor among thieves. Eventually, all bad people, no matter how deep their friendships seem, will turn on each other.

When Derek was done telling Luciano everything, they all just sat back and looked at each other. Derek felt like he was out of breath and Luciano was stunned.

"Don't you think it would be better to call the police?" Luciano asked. "After all, your brother here......" he smiled and gestured to Ben, "would not be put in jail. Anyone can see what a simple, kind, innocent person he is. Anyone would see that what happened was in self defense."

"I'm not so sure about that," Derek said. "And there's the small matter of the two of us running away from the scene of the crime. And also, if anyone finds out about the money in the safe at the summer home, it will be taken away from us, since it's illegal to keep money that way."

"Do you have a key, Derek?" Luciano asked. "Were you able to get the key?"

"I threw the key away," Derek said.

Luciano and Ben both gasped.

"Why did you throw away the key?" Ben asked. "Mama and I were waiting for you to come home with the money!"

Ben started to weep then. Derek tried to shush him before he got too loud. Ben sometimes got very loud when he cried and sometimes crying sent him into major tantrums.

"Benny Boy, don't worry about the key anymore," Derek said. "I already went to the summer home, opened the safe, and took all the money and the stocks. Then I threw away the key!"

A sigh of relief went around the table.

"Okay, this is what we need to do then," Luciano said. "I can get you both new identities, but it will cost you, unfortunately. New birth certificates, passports, driver's licenses, etc. Does Ben drive?"

"No, but he would need some kind of non-driver identification card." Derek said.

"I can get you both jobs," Luciano said. "Derek, I can get you a security guard position in a very prestigious office building. Benny, there is also a job opening at the newsstand there in the lobby, they need a cashier. I know you used to work as a cashier, right?"

Ben nodded. This was definitely fate, running into Luciano at a diner.

"You leave everything to me," Luciano said assuredly. "Do you need a place to stay tonight? You're probably better off coming home with me rather than staying at a hotel or motel. The cops might already be looking for you."

"Thank you, Luciano," Derek said, "for your generosity and all of your help. We don't want to inconvenience you."

"Forget about it!" Luciano waved his hand at them. "My wife would love to have you stay with us for a while! We have plenty of room, you can stay as long as you like. We'll help you get new clothes and help you find a new place to live. I've also got people on the inside who can check to see how the police search is going."

"Luciano, I don't know how to thank you." Derek said.

Luciano smiled at him. "You can thank me by staying safe, starting new lives and…. paying me!"

Derek chuckled. "I know you have your expenses in order to get us new identities. I'll be happy to pay you whatever you need, and then some!"

CHAPTER TWELVE – LUCILLE

Jeff had picked a really fancy restaurant indeed. Lucille was actually afraid to pick up her glass of water for fear she might drop it and break it, thus incurring more expense for dinner. She didn't know why she worried so much, since he seemed to have plenty of money. She just wanted to make a good impression, but she couldn't pinpoint exactly why.

This was the first man she had ever been interested in. Any other men she had ever encountered were always leeches and slime bags. Of course, all the men she had encountered previously were her mother's boyfriends.

She wondered then, for a fleeting moment, where her mother was, what she was doing, and did she miss her daughter at all? Did her mother ever wonder where she disappeared to? She didn't usually think about her mother anymore, so it was surprising to her that her mother popped into her mind just then.

"What are you thinking about, Lucille?" Jeff asked. "Are you usually this quiet?"

Lucille giggled nervously. "I'm sorry, but I guess I'm just not used to this."

"Used to what?" Jeff asked. "Going out to dinner?"

"That, and........" Lucille fumbled for the words. "Being out on a date."

"Surely you've dated before?" Jeff raised his eyebrows.

"Not really," Lucille said. "I used to be a nun."

Lucille was instantly sorry that she had blurted that out. Corrine warned her not to say anything about being a nun. That was an instant mood killer.

Jeff, on the other hand, was wildly delighted that she had just said that. He laughed and clapped his hands.

"You used to be a nun? Are you serious?" he asked her, his hands in a mock prayer position.

"Yes, I'm serious."

"Wow!" Jeff said, and reached for her hand. Lucille wouldn't give it to him. Jeff cleared his throat and pulled his hand back nonchalantly. "Well, I guess I'm flattered that I'm your first date."

They both reached nervously for their water glasses. Jeff was nervous about not wanting to offend her, and Lucille was just plain nervous. Thankfully, their appetizers arrived just then. Lucille wondered to herself how she was going to eat all of the food she ordered. Jeff was insistent that she have an appetizer to start with. She was also sure that he was planning to order dessert as well.

As she picked up her fork to jab a piece of fried calamari, a short, slim man with light brown hair and glasses walked over to their table.

"Jeff? Is that you?" he asked.

Jeff looked up and just about spit out his calamari in shock. Lucille wondered why he was so upset about this nerdy looking man walking over and standing at their table. Was this his boss or something?

"Oh, hi Dick, how are you?" Jeff fumbled, wiping his hands on his napkin and shaking Dick's hand.

"Oh, pretty good, thanks." Dick answered. "My mom and I are having dinner right over there." Dick motioned to where his mother was sitting. He really is a Momma's boy, then, isn't he? Jeff thought to himself. The grapevine at work was right!

Lucille found it endearing that this nice man was having dinner with his mother. She caught herself smiling at him. Dick smiled back at her while waiting for Jeff to introduce them.

"This is Lucille." Jeff finally said, waving a hand in her direction.

"Nice to meet you," she said softly, still smiling at him.

"Nice to meet you too!" Dick said. In fact, the only reason he got up from his chair was to come over and meet this beautiful woman. When he first laid eyes on her, he thought, Wow! She had the face of an angel! He had to come over and meet her, to see if she was really that beautiful up close. Now that they were actually speaking to each other, and smiling at each other, Dick knew he was smitten. But of course, it was hopeless. She was on a date with the biggest Casanova in their company, who worked in the mailroom.

"Well, Jeff, I must say I'm impressed seeing you in such a dapper suit, since you're always in jeans at work." Dick said, winking at him.

Jeff cleared his throat nervously, coughing a few times. He looked directly at Lucille.

"Yes, there's no reason to wear anything else but jeans there, when I'm busy working." Jeff said, nervously. "So many people, so little time to get everything done. Jeans are the most comfortable clothes to wear when you're constantly on the move."

"Oh, you two work together?" Lucille asked while Jeff coughed louder.

"Yes, we do!" Dick said, smiling at her. "He's our....."

Jeff coughed so loud, they both thought he was going to hack up half a lung.

"Are you all right, Jeff?" Dick asked, hitting him on the back. Dick was worried he would have to attempt the Heimlich maneuver.

"I'm fine, Dick. It was so nice to see you." Jeff said, attempting to dismiss him.

"You too." Dick said, then turned to look at Lucille again. "It was really nice to meet you."

"Nice to meet you too!" she said, still smiling that genuine beautiful smile that made Dick want to bang his head on the table, wondering how in the world Jeff gets all these beautiful women. It must be some kind of overconfidence or something.

As Dick walked back to his table, Jeff wiped his forehead.

"Are you all right?" Lucille asked him.

"Yes, yes, I'm fine." Jeff said, relieved that Dick was gone.

"So, you two work together?" Lucille asked. "He's a talent agent too?"

"No, he's a computer geek." Jeff blurted out, then caught himself.

"A computer geek? How do talent agents work together with computer geeks?" Lucille asked, genuinely curious. She wanted to know more about his line of work.

"Well, we don't actually work together, per se." Jeff said, wiping his mouth. "He does the computer work when we need to airbrush the pictures of the models and stuff like that."

"Does he know how to set up computers for people?" Lucille asked.

"I would imagine so," Jeff said, shrugging his shoulders. Enough talk about Dick.

Lucille shot up from her chair. Jeff caught her hand before she could get too far.

"Where are you going?" he asked, nervously.

"Oh, I just want to get his card because my friend..... my brother.....Robert wants to get a computer but he doesn't know the first thing about one. So maybe Dick can help him?" Lucille answered, breaking free of Jeff's grip and heading boldly over to Dick's table.

Jeff held his head in his hands while Lucille marched over to see Dick. This evening wasn't going very well, he thought.

Dick looked up from his meal when he noticed, in his peripheral vision, a person heading toward them. It was Lucille! What on earth was she doing heading over here? Nonetheless, he was thoroughly pleased.

"Hi," Lucille said, a bit shyly considering the fact she charged right over to him so quickly. "Jeff told me you know about computers."

"Yes," Dick said, beaming at her. "What would you like to know?"

"Well, actually, it's for my .... brother Robert. He wants to buy a home computer and needs some help. I was wondering if you could help him?" Lucille asked, shyness completely taking over her to the point that she shifted her gaze from his face to her own feet.

Dick exchanged glances with his mother, who smiled encouragingly at him. When Dick had first gotten back to their table after meeting Lucille for the first time, he told his mother how he couldn't understand how slime balls like Jeff got all the nice girls. Dick told his mother that if he had a chance with a girl like that, he would move heaven and earth for her.

"Of course, I'd be happy to help your brother Robert!" Dick said, smiling from ear to ear.

Then suddenly there was an awkward silence. Neither one knew what to say at that point. They smiled at each other and then Lucille looked down at her feet again.

"Do you have your card with you, Richard, so you can give it to this pretty girl?" his mother offered.

"Oh!" Dick said, as if a light had turned on in his head. "My card! Of course!" He took out his wallet and shuffled through it. Then he looked up again, startled. "Gee, I forgot. Where are my manners? Lucille, this is my mother. Mom, this is Lucille."

"Nice to meet you!" both women said and smiled at each other.

Dick pulled the card out of his wallet and handed it eagerly to her. "Please call me anytime, I'm available."

As the words were leaving his lips, he thought, oh no! I'm available? That sounds way too anxious; he hoped she didn't see what a desperate nerd he was.

"Okay, thanks!" Lucille said, reaching out to shake his hand, then his mother's hand. "I'll have my brother Robert give you a call!"

As she walked back to her table, she heard him mutter to his mother, "Of course! Her brother Robert will call me!"

She wondered why Dick suddenly seemed disappointed when she promised that Robert would be calling him. Wasn't that the whole purpose of why she asked for his card, so he can get some business?

As she walked back to their table, Jeff got up nervously from his chair. Lucille thought to herself, wow, this guy is really polite! He actually stands up when a woman, his date, is approaching him! Such manners!

"So," Jeff said, fumbling for words to not sound obvious of what he was fishing for. "What did you guys talk about?"

"Oh, I got his card so Robert could call him and get his computer set up." Lucille answered casually.

"Okay." Jeff said. "Did you guys talk about anything else? Like our work together?"

"No, not at all." Lucille casually picked up her fork and stabbed another piece of calamari. Jeff let out a huge sigh of relief, which made Lucille glance curiously at him.

"Good calamari, huh?" Jeff said, smiling at her, his confidence returning.

"Yes, really good." Lucille said, suddenly developing a ravenous appetite.

After dinner, Jeff asked Lucille if she'd like to go to his place and watch a movie.

"No thanks," Lucille said. "It's getting kind of late. I guess I'd better head back."

"It's only 9:00!" Jeff protested and then caught himself. "Well, instead of a movie, how about a cocktail?"

"I don't drink," Lucille reminded him. She had already told him that at dinner when he offered to buy an expensive bottle of red wine.

All Jeff could think of at this point was getting Lucille drunk and in bed. So he was very disappointed with her answer.

"How about some coffee or tea?" Jeff asked.

"Well, we just had some with our dessert," Lucille reminded him again. And again, Jeff was sorely disappointed. Suddenly, he had an idea.

"Okay, how about you come over to my place and I'll take some pictures of you?"

Lucille stared at him questioningly and she was starting to get a bad feeling.

"Oh, I didn't mean it to sound like that," Jeff added hastily. "I just meant that you're so beautiful, I thought maybe I could take some headshots of you and let one of my clients see your picture. Have you ever considered modeling?"

Lucille thought of the hard work she did at the diner. It would be so nice to have an exciting job in modeling. What the heck, it couldn't hurt to try, right?

"Well, I've never really considered that, but......." Lucille trailed off.

"Well, let's consider it tonight!" Jeff said triumphantly and linked her arm through his. "Come on, m'lady, our chariot awaits!"

He drove Lucille to his apartment while he created the game plan in his head. Lucille had a strange feeling, perhaps instinct, that she was doing the wrong thing. You're being too paranoid! Lucille told herself. Come on, do something daring and exciting for once in your life!

When he opened the door to his apartment, she was struck by how small it was. It was decorated purely as a single bachelor would decorate it – the bare minimum, with some throw pillows and candles strewn about as if he had power outages constantly.

"Have a seat," he said, gesturing to the brown leather couch with the leopard pillows. "I'll be right back."

Lucille looked around the room. There was a large screen television, some magazines on the coffee table, and a couple of empty bottles of beer on one side table next to a recliner. She just couldn't get over the amount of candles he had in the apartment.

Suddenly her eyes focused on a yellow legal sized pad on the table. There were women's names on it. She looked down the list of perhaps twenty women's names and saw her name was next to last on the list. She wondered what this list was about. Some of the names had been crossed off, but her name was still uncrossed. Was this a list of models he had lined up?

He came into the room at that moment, not realizing she had seen the yellow pad. He was holding a camera and a hairbrush. He put the camera down on the coffee table, then noticed the yellow pad and hastily threw it across the room so it landed on the recliner.

"What's that?" she asked him. "The list of all the models you work with?"

A huge grin spread across his face as the light dawned on him. It was so nice of her to give him an easy answer to her question.

"Yes!" he nodded animatedly. "That's it, exactly!"

He was relieved he didn't have to think on the spot and make something up to cover up the fact that was his score pad – a "wish" list of women he wanted to score with. All the names that were crossed off were the women he already scored with. He made a mental note to remember to buy more condoms, he was probably down to his last box.

"Well, why is my name on that list?" she asked. "I'm not a model."

"Not yet, you're not!" Jeff said, raising one fist in the air excitedly. "But we'll see what happens after I take these pictures!"

He asked her to turn around so her back was facing him. Then he leaned over and whispered seductively to her, "I'm going to brush your hair."

She whipped away from him suddenly. "My hair looks bad?" she asked, running her fingers through it.

"No, no! Not at all!" he said quickly. "I just want to get your hair right for the picture."

"Oh, I could do that. Where's your restroom, I'll go fix my hair and my makeup right now." Lucille said, and got up off the couch. Jeff weakly pointed in the direction of the restroom.

This night was not going as planned at all, Jeff thought. But there's still hope. If I can't get her drunk, maybe I can get her feeling sexy some other way. Women usually loved it when I brushed their hair. Oh well! That attempt has been shot to hell. Once I start clicking those pictures, she'll loosen up. Women love having their pictures taken, and being told they're beautiful. Jeff smiled assuredly to himself while he waited for her to return.

When Lucille came back out of the bathroom, she meekly sat back down on the couch.

"Okay, I'm ready!" she said, and posed in a silly manner. She tilted her head back and looked up at the ceiling. Jeff thought to himself, are you kidding me?

"All right," Jeff said, reaching out to touch the sides of her face, touching her hair. "I just want to make one modification."

Jeff reached out to unbutton her blouse. She automatically slapped his hands away and got up.

"What the hell are you doing?" she asked angrily.

"Nothing, nothing!" Jeff said, trying to calm her down. "You're buttoned up tight all the way up to your chin, so I thought for the picture, we could go with something softer."

"Oh," Lucille said, and sat back down again. "Okay, but I'll undo the buttons, if you don't mind."

The photo session did not go well. Lucille was stiff as a statue in all the pictures. Her genuine smile was completely gone and replaced with crazy, uptight, frozen, phony, forced smiles. These were some of the worst pictures he'd ever taken. Most of his subjects (or victims) were already loosened up from some wine and their blouses revealed a lot more cleavage. These pictures were horrible and he began to regret the time and money that he wasted on Lucille. He began to mentally count how much money he lost at dinner, the dry cleaning bill for this name-brand suit he bought at the used clothing store, the gas for his car……..

When he realized that she was not going to sleep with him, he decided to put a merciful end to the evening.

"Okay, that's it." Jeff said. "I'll get the pictures printed out and I'll give you a call when I hear something from my clients."

It was such an abrupt end to their evening. Lucille got up, confused by his change in attitude, and headed awkwardly for the door. He followed behind her and opened the door for her.

"Thank you for a lovely evening," she said, not knowing whether or not to kiss him. He didn't look like he wanted to be kissed.

"Thank you too!" he said, looking at the doorframe and at the wall, at the floor and anywhere else but her face. He just wanted her to get the hell out of there and maybe he still had enough time to call one of the other girls on his yellow pad list. The night was still young, it was only 10:30.

"Wait," Lucille said. "Aren't you going to drive me home?"

"Oh," Jeff said, groaning inwardly. "Where are my manners? Let me call you a cab."

When Lucille got home, Robert and Corrine were watching television in the living room. Corrine jumped up when she arrived.

"So?" Corrine asked excitedly. "How did it go?"

Lucille didn't know what to say. "It was......okay, I guess."

Robert got up and headed to the window. He saw the cab leaving.

"He didn't drive you home?" he asked.

"No, he called me a cab." Lucille said meekly.

Corrine and Robert exchanged glances.

"Is he going to call you again?" Corrine asked her.

"I guess so. I don't know." Lucille shrugged her shoulders, but she knew deep down inside that he wouldn't. She also wondered why she wasn't terribly disappointed. Her mind kept floating back to that yellow pad list on his table.

"Do you want some tea?" Corrine asked her, not knowing what else to say. She didn't want to ask too many questions in front of Robert, she thought it would be better to girl-talk about it later on or tomorrow, when Robert was at work. Maybe Lucille would open up about her date at that point.

"No thanks," Lucille said. "I'm just going to go to bed."

Corrine and Robert exchanged glances again while they watched her leave the room. Lucille stopped suddenly and reached into her purse for something. She turned back around and held out a card to Robert.

"Here's the number of a guy that can help you set up your computer." Lucille said. "Good night!"

CHAPTER THIRTEEN – CORRINE

Corrine was shaking with anger and grief as she ran down the basement stairs.

"ROBERT!" she screamed when she saw him. Robert was squatting on the floor with his back to her. Upon hearing her scream, he leapt up in one motion and dropped the wrench that he had been holding. The tool hit the cement floor with a loud clang. Corrine ran to him, and he opened his arms and swept her up into a tight hug.

"What is it, my darling?" he asked, bewildered.

Robert knew it would be difficult for her to leave the convent, knew the other sisters would take it hard. That morning, Corrine was filled with so much determination that she was fierce with courage. He was surprised now to see her so hysterical.

"What happened?" he asked her, gently rubbing the back of her head, trying to soothe her sob-wracked shuddering body.

"My mother is dead!" she cried into his chest. "My mother is dead! And I never knew she was my mother!"

"WHAT?!" Robert shrieked.

Robert never lost his cool. He was shocked to hear that Corrine's mother was dead. Who was her mother in the first place?

Robert led Corrine over to a chair and he cradled her in his lap. Through her sobs, she told Robert the story.

"Father Harris is your father?" he asked, shocked. "The same Father Harris that was here last night and ate dinner with Danny and me?"

"The very same," Corrine said, wiping the tears from her eyes, though it was useless to do so. The wiped-away tears were quickly replaced with fresh tears.

"I can't believe they never told you!" Robert said, suddenly angry.

"I can't believe it either!" Corrine said, heaving a heavy sigh. "What damage would it have done to tell me? I would still have respected them the same. In fact, I would have respected them even more, treasured them even more, knowing they were my parents."

Lucille came into the room just then. She walked over to Corrine and gave her a gentle hug.

"Corrine, I'm so sorry. I don't know what to say." Lucille choked out. She was heartbroken for Corrine.

"What's going on upstairs?" Corrine asked. "Have they taken Sister Celia's...... I mean...... my mother's body out yet?"

"The ambulance is on its way." Lucille said. "Mother Superior didn't call 911 right away. She gathered up the sisters and we all prayed over Sister Celia, I mean, your mother's body. Father Harris is upstairs now. He's waiting to talk to you."

Corrine looked at Robert, as if to ask him what she should do. Robert nodded to her and she got up from his lap. Corrine straightened her clothes and took Lucille's hand in hers. They went up the stairs together. Lucille tried to keep Corrine steady as she climbed the stairs, since she was shaking like a leaf and her legs seemed to be very weak. She could feel Corrine's body shuddering with sobs. But she also felt Corrine's determination.

The ambulance had just arrived. They were getting the stretcher ready to carry out Sister Celia's body. Corrine asked them to please wait a few moments because she wanted to have a private moment with her mother.

Corrine approached the doorway of her bedroom and saw that Father Harris was in there, alone with Sister Celia. He was having a private moment with her as well.

"Celia, my love, I'm so sorry for what I've done." Father Harris said, stroking Celia's hair. He had tears in his eyes and his voice was very shaky. "Celia, more than that, I'm so sorry for what I haven't done. I wasn't there for you when you needed me. Please don't ever doubt my love, I've always loved you. But......I was a coward. I should have taken on my responsibilities to you and to our daughter. I handled everything so badly. I was so young back then, we both were. I thought being a priest was my calling and that nothing could keep me from that, or should keep me from that. I didn't realize that it was more important to be a husband to you and a father to Corrine. Our lives would have still been

224

dedicated to God, just in a different way. I'm so sorry I didn't see that."

Father Harris paused to wipe away his tears with the back of his hand. He openly sobbed for a few moments. Corrine just stood silently in the doorway, watching him. Her heart was aching to be there next to him, to hold him, but she knew she should stay back and let him have his private time.

"Celia, my love," he said, "If I could do it all over again, I would have married you. But we can't go back, can we? That is the one thing I will regret for the rest of my life."

He leaned down and gave her a kiss on the lips. As he got up, he looked up and saw Corrine standing in the doorway. He inhaled his breath sharply and then fresh tears sprung from his eyes.

"Corrine....." he choked out.

Corrine ran to him and hugged him tight. They both wept silently. Any anger that she felt toward her father for leaving had melted away. She could see how sorry he was, she could see all the regret in his eyes when he looked down at her.

"Corrine," he said, breaking their embrace for a moment. His eyes searched hers. "Could you ever forgive me?"

Corrine looked up at him with eyes filled with tears and love. "Yes, I forgive you."

He pulled her into another tight embrace and they silently held each other for what seemed like eons. Finally, she broke away

225

from him to lean down and talk to her mother. Father Harris was about to leave the room to give her privacy, but she held him back.

"Please don't leave. What I have to say, I need to say to both of you." Corrine said resolutely.

She turned back to Celia.

"Mother," she said softly. "My mother." Corrine wiped more tears from her eyes. She felt as if the tears would never, ever stop. "I always knew you as Sister Celia. We didn't get to spend much time together. Now I remember how Mother Superior would always walk into the room whenever you and I were alone. It was like she was afraid of our mother-daughter bond; she was afraid you would betray your promise and tell me you were my mother."

Corrine shook her head at the memories. "How could I have been so stupid? How could I have not known?"

Corrine felt a small rise of anger toward Mother Superior, but she tried to squelch it. What use was it now to be angry at Mother Superior? No amount of anger could bring back all of those lost years.

"I should have sensed our bond somehow, Mother. I should have. I always knew you were special. I never got to get close to you, but then again, the only one I was close to was Lucille. And before she came, everyone here treated me with so much love that I felt I had many mothers. But only you were my real mother, and I wish I had known that. I would have treasured you. We could have had many long talks together. We could have had a lot of fun together."

Corrine turned to look at Father Harris.

"You were special to me," she said tenderly, "even though I didn't know you were my father. You always made time for me and we did spend a lot of time together. I will always treasure that, and I'm thankful for that. Even though I didn't know you were my father, I still felt that love from you. Thank you."

He nodded to her, tears in his eyes. He couldn't speak, he was too choked up. Corrine turned back to her mother. She stroked her face, and really took a good look at her. She wanted to study all of her features so that she would always remember her. She didn't have any pictures of her mother to take with her, so she had to memorize her face.

"I love you, Mother," Corrine said fiercely. "I will always love you. I will always treasure you in my heart. And I will miss you terribly."

Corrine gave her mother a kiss on her forehead. As she rose, Father Harris came over and offered his hand to her. He then put his arm around her, and father and daughter left the room together.

Mother Superior was in the kitchen with all of the other sisters gathered together in mourning, as the paramedics prepared Sister Celia's body for transport. Father Harris and Corrine entered together. Mother Superior got up out of her chair when they entered.

Corrine and Mother Superior locked eyes as intensely as two rams would lock horns. There were tears in the Mother's eyes as she held out one hand to Corrine. Corrine walked over to her,

227

but she didn't embrace her. She stood an arm's length away and just looked into her eyes.

"I forgive you," Corrine said. "I realize you felt you were doing what you thought was best. The past can't be undone, and there's no sense in being angry with you."

Corrine took Mother Superior's still outstretched hand and shook it in an impersonal, stiff way.

"Thank you for everything you've done for me." Corrine said. "You've given me a good home and a lot of love. All of you have." Corrine looked around the room at all of the other nuns. "I just want to say thank you to everyone."

"Are you still leaving us, child?" Mother Superior asked.

"Yes," Corrine said. "I'm leaving. Robert and I are going to be together, regardless of whatever premonition you've had about us. We all have to die sometime. At least, knowing I'll be with Robert, I'll die happy."

"You will not die happy, I assure you," Mother Superior whispered hoarsely. "You will die very violently."

Mother Superior's sharp words cut through Corrine like a knife. Corrine felt a sharp pain in her chest at those words. Corrine tried to keep calm. She looked down at the floor, swallowing, wondering what to say next.

She would die violently? What kind of crazy visions did the Mother Superior have? Or was this just a scare tactic to keep her here in the convent?

Corrine finally looked up at Mother Superior.

"Violently or not," she said, "I will accept my fate. I love Robert. He is the man that I am meant to be with for the rest of my life."

Father Harris glanced at Mother Superior. What was she talking about? he wondered to himself. My daughter will die violently? He knew that the Mother had visions and that they usually came true. But what was this about his daughter dying violently?

Suddenly, everyone in that room felt a peace settle over them. The peace was palpable and it was like everyone was told, "Don't worry," by God Himself.

"God's Will be done." Mother Superior said softly. It was as if everyone had made peace with whatever fate had in store for them.

Even Lucille felt it. She had never experienced anything like that before. It was like an invisible embrace from God. Suddenly, her heart was at peace and she knew her entire life, her destiny, lay before her.

Lucille and Corrine went upstairs to pack while Robert and Danny finished the heating job. Mother Superior asked Father Harris to stay while she collected the money to pay them. Corrine and Lucille came downstairs with their suitcases. Father Harris looked at them both with a heavy heart.

"Will we ever see you again?" Father Harris asked them both. "Will you come to visit?"

Corrine looked at Mother Superior and then back at her father.

"I don't think so," she said.

Father Harris hugged Lucille first, and then hugged Corrine so tightly and fiercely, she could barely breathe.

"I finally am able to share time with you as my daughter and now you're leaving." Father Harris said sadly. "But God's Will be done. You have your own life now and your destiny is before you."

Mother Superior gave a choked sob but didn't try to embrace Corrine or Lucille because she had a feeling they wouldn't have wanted her to. She said a quiet prayer in her heart for them and sent them some love through her heart. She hoped they could feel her love, would feel her love, in their future.

After Robert and Danny had packed up their van with their tools and remaining supplies and equipment, they went back in the house to get paid. There was an awkward silence that fell on all of them as they stood in a circle looking at each other. Finally Mother Superior handed Danny an envelope.

"Thank you for a job well done," Mother Superior said. "It looks like everything is working well and we should be comfortable for the remainder of the winter."

"You're welcome," Danny said.

Mother Superior's eyes rested on Robert. "Please take care of her."

"I will." Robert replied solemnly.

"If there is any way to change destiny," Mother Superior said to him, "I need you to ignore what your father told you."

Robert looked at her, puzzled. An uneasy feeling swept over him.

"What did my father tell me?" he asked slowly, staring at her.

"That you have a criminal spirit." Mother Superior answered matter-of-factly.

"MOTHER!" Corrine cried out! "How could you say such a thing?"

Robert was rooted to his spot, his eyes never wavering from Mother Superior's eyes. How did she know? How could she know that?

"Your father had the criminal spirit and you do, indeed, have it in you as well," she continued in a steely voice. "No matter how much you fight it, or think you can fight it, you have it in you."

Robert swallowed hard.

"Please pledge your life to God and all of that can change," Mother Superior said. "Money is not your friend, God is your friend. Remember that."

Robert felt very uncomfortable. How am I supposed to pledge my life to God, he asked himself. Should I join the priesthood and leave Corrine?

"You are probably asking yourself questions about how to pledge your life to God." Mother Superior said gently.

"Stop it, Mother!" Corrine shouted at her. She knew how Mother Superior could get inside a person's head.

"I will not stop it," Mother Superior said, shaking her head. "I am trying to warn you both, for your future's sake, for your souls' sake. Robert knows what I'm talking about."

Robert was quiet for a moment, still shaken from what Mother Superior told him. Finally, he nodded to her. He reached out to take Corrine's hand.

"Good-bye." Robert said to Mother Superior. He nodded to Father Harris, who reached out a hand. Robert shook his hand.

"Please take care of my daughter," Father Harris told him.

"I promise you," Robert said firmly, "I will protect her with every ounce of life in me."

"I believe you." Father Harris said.

Corrine hugged her father goodbye and then raced out the door. She couldn't handle knowing that she would never see him again.

It was her choice, after all. She could come back here and see him any time she wanted to.   But……the memories of her mother dying here were too painful. She knew she would never be able to return.

Robert gave her a good life, Corrine thought to herself as she busied herself looking for the money. And Corrine didn't feel that he was a criminal at all. They all made a decision together; they were all in it together. Robert was the mastermind behind all of the jobs and no one ever got hurt, after all. Robert wasn't a violent man. Robert cared about people. Robert loved her.

They were all a family now. These were not criminal activities, these were jobs. People worked at jobs so they could be paid, right? Corrine reasoned. It wasn't a crime to make money. Those banks and convenience stores recouped the money back very quickly. She was almost completely sure that if the bank personnel had a chance, they would probably take the money and run too. If they had a good plan to get away with it successfully, they would do the same thing.

Lucille tried to earn what people called "an honest living" through waitressing and customer service. She wasn't good at it. What did Robert say about her? He said she "had a face that attracted predators."

Robert always said that he thought Corrine was the most beautiful girl in the world. But Lucille, he said, had such an innocent face that she could get away with murder. It would be hard for her to date because there were a lot of predators out there that would just want to take advantage of her and steal her innocence away. But Lucille could use that innocent face to everyone's advantage -- and she finally learned to.

That innocent face was their ace up the sleeve when it came to a successful job.

No one could ever suspect that face of any wrong-doing.

It was fun to see how puzzled everyone was when Lucille handed over a "Stick 'Em Up" note. They were still bewildered as they loaded the money into the bags. How could an innocent face like that rob a bank or convenience store?

Well, they certainly couldn't do it alone, individually. But as a group, as a well-rehearsed unit, they created money magic. And what's wrong with making money?

Corrine always felt sorry for those people in their dead-end "honest" jobs. Those people usually died of a heart attack or stroke before they could ever retire. All those good pensions that they paid into for thirty-plus years working for the same company..... they never saw a cent of it if they dropped dead, did they?

How could the Mother Superior have seen a vision of them dying violently in some act of crime? So far, they've been doing this pretty steadily and they worked out such great plans for successful heists. What could possibly go wrong?

Nothing! Corrine shook her head. Mother Superior was just using scare tactics. All of her bogus inspiration was just used on all of the nuns for inducing guilt. And guilt was an emerging angel, as she said. Then they were all angels there, she supposed. All of them filled with guilt for craving chocolate or wanting to watch some late night television instead of sleeping, eating and praying 24 hours a day.

This was an exciting life, Corrine thought. New faces, new places. All that money to spend leisurely, doing whatever they wanted to do. Robert didn't come home exhausted from work every night. Robert had a Joie De Vivre everyday now! They laughed more than ever, had more fun than ever, since he quit his job and decided to organize a team of the best equipped people to score the largest amounts of cash.

Robert didn't keep all the money, Robert always shared the money. Robert cared about all of his people. Robert would never put anyone in any danger.

As if he knew she was thinking about him, he entered the room.

"How's everything going, my darling?" he asked her, giving her a kiss.

"Well, these guys have hidden the money away quite ingeniously!" Corrine said, sounding as cheerful as she could. "But it is kind of fun going through all of these paintings looking for it. The warehouse is big, we'll all be busy for a long time, I guess!"

"That's the spirit!" Robert smiled at her. "That's my girl!"

"When we finally do get out of here with the money," Corrine asked, "what do we plan to do with it? Are we going on vacation, maybe?"

Robert smiled at her. "We can do anything you want with the money!" he said jubilantly. "It's our money! There's plenty to go around! We should all go on vacation! Where would you like to go, my darling?"

"How about Hawaii?" she asked shyly. "I've always wanted to go there."

"Hawaii it is!" Robert chuckled. "Though we should stay away from the volcanoes, lest we 'die violently' near one of them! Can you pick something less dangerous?"

Robert planted an affectionate kiss on Corrine's nose.

"Less dangerous?" she asked. "What about Switzerland?"

"Too many mountains!" he said. "We're bound to fall down and kill ourselves!"

"What about a tropical island? We could scuba-dive!" Corrine said excitedly.

"My dear girl, we could drown that way!" Robert laughed. "Or get eaten by a shark! Pick someplace safer!"

Corrine thought for a few moments. "There is no place in the world that's ever going to be one hundred percent safe!" she finally said, laughing.

"Exactly, my love!" he boomed. "So this is why we must enjoy every second that we have together. Everything in life, that's worthwhile, has its risks. Right? Life is for living! Let's live it up to the fullest!"

236

"Sounds good to me!" she sang out and hugged him fiercely. Their bodies rocked back and forth in an intimate, playful dance.

Corrine always felt light as a feather around Robert. She was so happy with him, they were so happy together.

"Where is everyone, by the way?" Robert asked. "I haven't seen anyone for a while. I've walked around, but they must have hidden themselves pretty well."

"I just saw Lucille a few minutes ago," Corrine said. "And Derek and Ben were just around the corner, the last time I saw them. But Dick......I haven't seen him lately."

"Tricky Dicky!" Robert laughed. "I just saw him a little while ago and complimented him on his work. He's been very valuable to us."

"Do you think he and Lucille will ever get together?" Corrine asked him.

"If Lucille would just open her heart, they will. She's too scared, she's like a mouse that's been caught in too many glue traps." Robert said softly. "To her credit, she has been through a lot. But Dick is a nice guy, they would be happy together, I think."

"I think so too." Corrine said.

Suddenly, Corrine heard a female voice in the distance. It sounded like......Sister Celia? Her mother?

Corrine whipped her head around and saw a bright light shining in the hallway.

"Robert?" she asked. "Where's that light coming from? I hear someone calling me....."

Robert turned casually around to see where Corrine was looking. He gasped.

"Corrine!" the voice called. Corrine thought perhaps it was Lucille, but her memory banks were telling her it was her mother's voice. She started walking towards the doorway.

"NO!" Robert called out and ran to stop her. "You mustn't go that way!"

Corrine stopped suddenly when he grabbed her hand and pulled her back.

"Why not?" she asked. "Someone's out there calling me and they're holding a bright light of some kind........maybe it's Lucille and she found something?"

"NO!" Robert cried out. "I've seen that light before! Don't go. It's too risky. I don't know what will be waiting for us on the other side of that doorway. Come here and hide behind this large painting until the light fades away."

Corrine stared at him, puzzled. "But it sounds like......I'm not sure, but it sounds like....a voice I've heard a long time ago. I know it can't be my mother, but I just want to see......"

"NO!" Robert beseeched her, getting on his knees and holding her legs. "It could be cops! It could be a trick! Please don't go! HIDE! NOW!"

"Okay!" Corrine said, laughing at his panic. What was he so scared of? "I'll just stay here and keep looking, then!"

The light in the hallway suddenly faded away. Corrine no longer heard that voice. Robert breathed an audible sigh of relief and reached out and hugged her tightly.

"Stay with me, always." Robert said. "I will keep you safe."

Corrine was suddenly filled with such a huge surge of love, even more love than usual, for Robert.

"I will protect you till the end of time." Robert said fiercely.

CHAPTER FOURTEEN – DEREK AND BEN

"I miss Mom." Ben said.

Derek was standing up on a platform going through some old crates while Ben was a few feet away looking out of one of the warehouse's many large windows.

"I miss her too, Benny." Derek said, tossing one of the crates aside.

Still nothing. How long have they been in here, anyway? Maybe Robert didn't hear those men right. It seems like they have all been through every square inch of this warehouse and still no money.

Or maybe it only *seems* like they've all been through every square inch of this extremely large warehouse. There were so many rooms and rooms within rooms.....how can they be sure they've covered all of the territory?

Derek was wondering to himself why he wasn't getting hungry yet. Even more strange was why Ben wasn't complaining about being hungry or tired yet. Ben's been extremely patient during this whole ordeal, in fact. Maybe he's finally grown up? Ben has been handing this warehouse experience like a mini adventure, finding rats and moths and all kinds of other creatures that he could play with. Derek certainly wished he had Ben's attitude about life sometimes.

Life was pretty good for them since Luciano got them new identities. They moved a few states away and as promised, Luciano got them both jobs. Derek was working as a security guard in a very prestigious office building and Ben was working at the coffee shop / newsstand in the same building.

Everyone loved Ben. How could anyone not love Ben? He greeted everyone in the morning with a cheery voice and a bright smile. He was very helpful if they couldn't find something in the store. When he made their coffee, he always put a smiley face on the cup for them, and wrote their name on it. In case, he said, someone at work tries to steal their coffee. Sometimes, he even gave tea drinkers an extra tea bag on the side. He felt that people in the office worked really hard and sometimes couldn't get away from their desks to come down to the shop to get more tea. And he was told that most places had hot and cold water coolers, so they could just re-use the cup and use a fresh bag for more tea.

The owner of the store knew Ben was giving away free tea, but he didn't mind at all. If he got extra people coming to the shop because of how much they liked Ben, then it was a win-win situation for him. Ben had a way of endearing himself to everyone.

"Good morning, Dick!" Ben said cheerfully. "I know, the usual. Extra light coffee, no sugar, extra cinnamon, coming right up!"

"How are you doing, Ben?" Dick asked him.

241

"Every day is a good day!" Ben said, bustling around preparing his coffee.

What a good attitude that kid has! Dick thought to himself.

"Hey, Ben!" Derek came around the corner and yelled to him from the doorway. "Do you want to go to that place across the street for lunch?"

Ben returned to Dick carrying his coffee in a large cup with a smiley face on it. He had written "D-I-C-K" on the cup, in bright orange letters.

"The Italian place?" Ben asked, smiling from ear to ear. "Chicken Parmigiana!"

"MEATBALLS!!" Derek laughed at him. "It's a plan, Stan!"

Derek nodded a polite hello to Dick, a man he sees everyday but never speaks to, and then turned and walked back to his post.

Ben handed the coffee cup to Dick and rang up his order. As Dick was handing him the money, he asked, "Is that security guard a good friend of yours?"

"He's my brother!" Ben said proudly.

"Your brother! Really!" Dick said. They didn't look much alike at all.

"Yup!" Ben said. "The best brother ever, Derry is."

"Terry?" Dick asked.

"No, Derry!" Ben said. "His name is really Derek, but I've been calling him Derry since I was a kid."

"Oh," Dick said. "I guess I'll call him Derek."

"You want to come to lunch with us, Dickie?" Ben asked. "Their food is the best in the world!"

Dick smiled at him. Ben was such a nice guy.

"Thanks, Ben, I appreciate the offer, but I might be working through lunch today."

"Well, you shouldn't do that too much. You're too skinny already." Ben said.

Dick couldn't help but laugh. Coming out of Ben, it didn't seem like an insult. In fact, Dick knew Ben didn't have an insulting bone in his body; he was just being downright honest with him.

Dick patted his flat belly and smiled at Ben. "I might just take you up on your offer, then. I'll talk to you later. Have a great day!"

"You too, Dick!" Ben said and turned smiling to his next customer.

As Dick walked back to the elevators, he saw Derek at his post. Dick walked over to Derek to say hello. He put out his hand and Derek shook it firmly.

"Your brother just invited me to lunch with you two." Dick said, laughing. "He told me I'm too skinny and shouldn't work through lunch."

"That's Ben, all right!" Derek laughed too. "Well, of course you're welcome to join us. My name's Derek."

"I'm Dick, nice to meet you. Thanks for the invitation, what time do you guys go to lunch?"

"At 1:00. It's a great place, a genuine Mom and Pop operation." Derek said. "The meatballs are the best I've ever had!"

"Well, I'm always on a quest for great meatballs!" Dick said cheerfully. "I'll see you both at 1:00 then!"

"I'll be right here!" Derek said smiling, mock-straightening his shoulders and standing at attention like a good soldier. Dick saluted him with a chuckle as he turned to get onto one of the elevators.

There are a lot of nice people here, Derek thought. A friend of Benny's is a friend of mine too. That Dick guy seemed like good people.

At 1:00, Derek and Ben waited as Dick got off the elevator.

"I'm glad you're coming!" Ben said to him. "Get ready for the best Eye-Talian food in the world!"

"I'm ready!" Dick said with a grin. "I need to put some meat on my bones, huh?"

"Yeah," Ben said, poking him in the stomach. "You're too skinny."

"I'll work on it." Dick laughed. "Let's eat!"

Dick ended up trying the baked lasagna and he had to admit it was the best lasagna he ever had in his life. It was the beginning of a beautiful friendship: Dick, two brothers and Eye-Talian food!

When lunch was over, Ben waved goodbye enthusiastically to Dick as he got back on the elevator. Dick waved back to them, smiling to himself. Dick was happy to have made some friends, since everyone in the office upstairs always made fun of him, calling him a Mama's Boy.

"What a great guy!" Ben said to Derek. "I'm glad we made a new friend, Derry!"

"Me too, Benny, me too." Derek said. "Now you'd better get back to work before everyone misses you too much!"

"Okay," Ben said resignedly, tongue-in-cheek. "Back to the old coal mine!"

Ben slumped his shoulders and walked slowly back to the newsstand, dragging his feet in a mock fashion.

Derek laughed at the way Ben sometimes pretends he hates his job, especially since Derek knows how much Ben loves his job. Ben is the only person he knows that can spring up out of bed every morning singing a song. In fact, whatever song happens to be playing on the alarm clock radio when it went off each morning is the song that Ben sings for the rest of the day. Even Derek admits to having that song in his head all day as well. Probably because Ben doesn't give him a chance to forget it!

Derek was happy with their new lives, very happy. He sometimes thought of what they had been through and shuddered. For his brother's sake, he never brought it up. He knew Ben sometimes had nightmares about what happened. I suppose it's not possible to see your mother die in cold blood and not have nightmares. Also, Ben innocently killed a man and he's very worried about that.

"When I die, am I going to hell?" Ben would ask him all the time.

"No, you're not going to hell." Derek would tell him.

"But I killed someone," Ben would say. "If you kill someone, you instantly go to hell, right?"

"Ben," Derek would patiently tell him, "God knows you're not a murderer. You were just doing what you had to do under the circumstances. And you may not have been able to save Mom's life, but you certainly saved mine. If you hadn't killed that guy, he might have killed me when I got home."

"Mom saved my life." Ben would repeat over and over again, sometimes like a broken record. "Mom saved my life."

Whenever they would watch a television program that portrayed some kind of selfless act which led to a miracle, Ben would always say, "Mom saved my life."

Sometimes Ben would come to Derek's room in the middle of the night to tell him he had a bad dream. Ben's dreams were the usual flights of fancy, filled with spaceships, or very tall cornfields, or big monsters chasing him. But sometimes, Ben's dreams were very specific flashbacks to that horrible day that caused them to leave their home forever.

One night Ben had a dream that a porterhouse steak was chasing him and trying to stab him in the neck. Another night he had a dream that Mom was flying around the kitchen, saying "Catch me! Catch me!" laughing hysterically, and flying further away whenever he got close enough to catch her. Sometimes he dreamed of Lee trying to shove him in front of a bunch of running horses. Ben always woke up screaming before the stampede crushed him.

Other than that, life was pretty normal for them.

Derek met all kinds of attractive women while he was at his post. He didn't think he was much to look at, himself; he thought he was just a big muscle head. But the ladies seemed to like muscle heads, or at least perhaps just his muscle head in particular. He didn't see women flirting with any of the other security guards, only him.

One woman, who was at least ten years older than he, was very persistent at trying to ask him out. He wasn't interested and was trying to be as polite as he possibly could to let her off easy. She didn't want to give up, she was still trying.

There was another girl who was at least ten years younger than he, very immature and always asking him if he wanted to go out to party with her. She really did look like a real party girl and he just wanted to tell her she was going to lose her good looks really quickly if she didn't stop partying. She might even lose her job if she didn't stop partying. Sometimes he could swear she was wearing the same clothes from the day before.

And there were all kinds of other women, all ages, all different hair colors, eye colors, pretty, not pretty, sexy, not sexy, that would flirt with him as they entered the building and when they left for the day.

There was no one that really interested Derek enough to take out on a date and leave Ben at home alone. Of course Ben was quite capable of being home by himself, since he was in his thirties now. But his maturity level was still that of a child.

One night, Derek had to work late and Ben kept calling him on the cell phone every half hour. Ben would hear things in the apartment building and think burglars were coming to get him. Or he dropped a glass and was afraid to pick up the shards for fear of cutting himself. Sometimes he overcooked dinner in the microwave and got so upset he couldn't think of anything else to eat. Or perhaps a light bulb burned out and he panicked so much about being in the dark that he couldn't remember where the light sources were in the other rooms. Ben was still very much a child, maybe worse than a child sometimes.

But he did have that child-like way to brighten people's days, including Derek's own days. Ben was his best friend.

Robert came into their part of the warehouse just then.

"How's it going, gentlemen?" Robert asked them. "How much closer are we to financial freedom?"

"Well, I feel like I've been through every inch of this warehouse," Derek said, trying to sound patient, "but I'm still looking."

"What about you, Ben?" Robert turned to look at Ben, who was under a table shining a flashlight on something. "Have you found anything yet?"

"There's a big spider down here, a white one." Ben said. "I've never seen a white spider before. Do you want to see it, Robert?"

Robert looked at Derek and they both shrugged their shoulders.

"Well," Robert said to them, "keep up the good work. I'm sure we'll find it soon."

It seemed to Derek that Robert felt badly about the last outburst he had over Ben when he called everyone over to see the rat. Robert seemed much nicer just now. Maybe he's starting to mellow out a little bit about this whole fiasco? Either that, or maybe he was just getting as tired as everyone else was.

In fact, Derek was surprised he wasn't actually tired. He wasn't hungry, either. He was just – existing -- to look for the money.

"I had another bad dream," Ben said, rubbing his eyes.

"When?" Derek asked. "Just now?" Derek didn't realize that Ben had fallen asleep.

"No, a little while ago....." Ben said cryptically. It wasn't like Ben to not say something that was on his mind immediately. Ben always spoke about events and things going through his mind right when they happened.

"When, a little while ago?" Derek pushed. "Did you fall asleep?"

"No," Ben said and got quiet. It seemed like he was trying to hide something.

"Out with it, Ben." Derek jumped down off the platform he had literally just climbed up on, and walked over to Ben and put his hands on his shoulders. "Tell me what's on your mind."

"Well, Derry," Ben said, avoiding Derek's eyes. "There's something weird about us being here."

"What do you mean?" Derek asked, trying to get Ben to look at him.

"I don't remember walking in here." Ben said.

Derek was perplexed. What does he mean, he doesn't remember walking in here?

"You don't remember walking......into the warehouse?" Derek asked him. Sometimes it was like pulling teeth trying to get something out of Ben when he didn't want to talk.

"I don't remember how we got here." Ben shrugged his shoulders and walked away toward the window. "That's all."

"You don't remember us following those guys?" Derek asked him. "Remember we were at the bar and then we left in our cars and were following those guys?"

"Yeah, I remember that." Ben said quietly.

"So then, that's how we got here." Derek said.

"I don't remember walking in here." Ben said stubbornly but quietly.

"What do you mean, Ben? We did walk in here at some point. We're here, aren't we?"

"Yeah, but......." Ben trailed off. "I don't remember how we got in the warehouse."

"Ben," Derek asked patiently. "What's the last thing you do remember?"

"We got shot." Ben blurted out quickly, and then stuffed his fist into his mouth and started nervously biting his hand.

Derek was bewildered. Was he talking about a dream he had? Ben was obviously confused. But then why did Derek suddenly have a funny feeling in his stomach when Ben said that they got shot? It was almost a feeling of........denial. Derek was suffering from.......denial of trying to remember something?

"What do you mean, we got shot?" Derek stormed over to where Ben was standing by the window and turned him around to face him.

"I don't want to talk about it anymore." Ben said, and made a zipper motion across his mouth.

"By golly, we're talking about this!" Derek said insistently. Derek's stomach was starting to feel really funny. But it wasn't like the usual weird stomach feeling he has. This was more of a *heart sick* feeling he was getting.

"What do you mean, we got shot?" Derek asked Ben again, trying to calm himself down and sound patient. He didn't want to scare Ben anymore than he was already scared.

"We got shot, Derry, don't you remember?" Ben said and started to cry.

"Where did we get shot, Benny? Tell me. What happened? Tell me the whole dream."

"It wasn't a dream, Derry," Ben said, looking at him frightfully. "It was real. Then I woke up in the warehouse."

When Ben said that he woke up in the warehouse, it confirmed to Derek that it was just a dream. But still that weird feeling Derek felt inside persisted. He couldn't yet heave that giant sigh of relief that was just waiting to be heaved.

"Okay, Benny," Derek said patiently, even cracking a smile for him. "If you woke up in the warehouse, then it was just a dream. It wasn't real. If you wake up from something, then it was a dream, right?"

Ben walked away from Derek and started singing an old song that had the words, "Bang, Bang, you shot me down."

Derek walked over to Ben and turned him around to face him again.

"Look at me, Ben." Derek said forcefully. "Tell me what you saw."

"We got shot," Ben said simply, "and then we woke up in the warehouse."

"When did we get shot?" Derek was just about at the end of his patience. He felt like he was going to explode from whatever this crazy feeling was that he was experiencing.

"Outside the warehouse." Ben said, starting to sing again.

"We got shot outside of the warehouse." Derek was trying to piece the dream events together, and he felt like Ben was giving him the teeniest tiniest pieces of a puzzle one at a time.

"Who shot us?" Derek asked fearfully.

"The cops." Ben said matter-of-factly.

"What cops?" Derek asked, feeling himself break out in a sweat. To his surprise, his forehead was not wet yet.

"The cops that shot us." Ben looked at Derek like he was a little kid that didn't understand. Derek felt like banging his own head against the wall.

"Okay," Derek said, feeling a little faint now. "Where did the cops that shot us come from?"

"Out of their cars." Ben said. "Don't you remember, Derry?"

"No, Benny, I don't remember. This is your dream that you woke up from."

"No, Derry, this isn't a dream. I told you that. It's real." Ben was adamant and started to stamp his feet.

"It's not real, Benny, it's your dream!" Derek said, but deep down inside, he felt denial rising up in his gut like bile. "I just want you to tell me your dream so you can get it out of your system and not be scared about it anymore!"

"We're not allowed to talk about things like that," Ben said. "We can't talk about the time Mama got shot, right?"

"No, Benny, this is different." Derek wanted to pull his own hair out. "Right now, we're talking about a dream you had. Remember you said you woke up in the warehouse?"

"IT WASN'T A DREAM!!!" Ben screamed at him and started running around the room in circles. "IT -- WAS -- REAL!!!"

"If it was real, then why don't I remember it?" Derek tried not to yell but he had to raise his voice in order to be heard over Ben's thundering running footsteps.

"YOU WERE RIGHT THERE NEXT TO ME!!!" Ben shouted.

Derek slowly shook his head from side to side. He got down on his knees and an overwhelming feeling of sadness came over him. He didn't know what to think anymore, what to believe. Was Ben cracking up? Was he, Derek, himself, cracking up?

Suddenly they both heard a voice coming from the hallway. It sounded like their mother's voice. There was a bright light in the hallway.

"BOYS!" the voice said. "Stop fighting and come over here this instant! I've been calling you long enough!"

Derek froze with fear and stayed in place. Ben jumped up and started running for the doorway. He stopped short just as he got there.

"Mama?" Ben asked, and cocked his head. Ben turned to look at Derek and he put out his hand. A huge smile spread across Ben's face. Derek was afraid of that smile.

It was a smile of peace.

Derek never saw Ben smile like that before.

"Come on, Derry! Let's get out of here!" Ben said, laughing.

Derek got up from his kneeling position and followed Ben to the door. He took Ben's hand and they stepped through the doorway together.

CHAPTER FIFTEEN – ROBERT

I am NOT like my father, Robert thought to himself. I am nothing like him.

Robert blew through those paintings as if they were brush standing in the way of a pleasant hike in the woods. He had expected this to be easy. It wasn't.

He heard those men talking about the money. They said the money was in the warehouse. They said they had hidden the money so expertly that no one would find it except them. HA! Robert could find the money, he WOULD find the money. If there was money to be found, then Robert was THE ONE to find it.

The one useful thing that Robert's father did teach him was to believe in himself.

Robert grew tired of constantly moving from place to place. They had to, because of his father's occupation. His father was a professional thief.

"I have a criminal spirit," he used to tell Robert all the time. "And you will wake up one day and find that you have it too."

Robert would shake his head whenever he heard these words. He was not like his father; he would never be like his father.

His father used to laugh at what he called the "Average Joe" who would go to work every day, come home, watch some television and go to bed, then start the same cycle over again the next day. What kind of Joie De Vivre was that?

There was excitement in being a thief: danger lurking around corners, and plenty of money to be had, as long as you played your cards right. And play his cards right, he did -- until the day someone else stole those cards away from him.

Robert used to think they had to move whenever the wind would blow. In fact, they would settle in a town for a least a year and then they would move on. For all the money his father made, what good was it to them if they couldn't have some stability, a nice house, nice cars, things like that? The only material item consistent in Robert's life was his suitcase.

After his father had leeched the town free of all their worldly goods, they would move into a new town. And so on. This way, they would never get caught. Robert felt it was like a vampire draining all the people in the town and when there was no one left to bleed dry, they would move on to a nice, new fresh town with new, unfamiliar faces that were totally unsuspecting of what his father was going to do.

Nothing was off limits for his father. He gambled. He shoplifted. He mugged people. Sometimes he even pick-pocketed his own friends. No one would suspect him. He was too charming, and he was too handsome.

His father used to say that he was so handsome, that he could steal the chickens out from under a rooster. Robert used to wonder what kind of interest his father had in chickens anyway? Besides money, his father was interested in anyone of the female species. And most of his money was begotten from rich women whom he'd beguiled and then disposed of. And all of these women were none the wiser. Where did all my money go? They would ask themselves. I must have spent it without realizing it, they would think. They would never, ever suspect that Robert stole it from them.

Oh, he had many skills, his father did. He could cheat the pants off the biggest cheat. He could buy a car from a man for dirt cheap and then sell it back to him at the highest price possible. He could buy a old, broken down house from a man at the lowest possible price, then hire that same man to toil his blood and sweat away fixing up that same house, and then sell it back to that same man for a huge profit.

But he finally met a woman, one woman, who outsmarted him.

Robert could never make any friends because they moved around so much. One day, when he was twelve, they moved into an apartment in a small village in France. There was a beautiful young girl of 13 who lived next door. Her name was Helena. Robert fell madly in love with her.

But he had to leave before the romance could blossom. Damn, his father was always ruining his life (and those of others). What he couldn't forgive his father for the most, was ruining Helena's mother's life.

Robert used to watch Helena outside in the garden while he was tending to his chores. She used to sing to herself and dance around the flowers in the garden. He thought she was the most beautiful girl he had ever seen. Little did he know, she knew full well he was watching her, but she made sure he didn't catch on to the fact he was being watched himself. She was secretly watching him watch her. She knew how badly he liked her, how badly he wanted to be with her.

One day, she pretended she caught him watching her and coyly walked over to him. He remembered she was wearing a flowing transparent yellow dress, which left little to the imagination. Her body was fully developed for a girl of 13 years old.

Her mother wasn't home and his father wasn't home.

His heart was hammering in his chest as she approached him.

"Hi there," she said, smiling softly at him.

"Hello," Robert said nervously. He was worried she was going to slap him for watching her dance in her garden.

"My name is Helena," she said, twirling a strand of hair around. "I think you're a very handsome boy."

"I'm Robert," he said, wiping the sweat off his hands and offering his right hand to her.

She shook his hand playfully and then pulled him close to her.

"Would you like to kiss me?" she asked, whispering in his ear, which brought shivers all the way up and down his spine.

"Yes," he answered boldly, looking right into her eyes.

She kissed him deeply, using her tongue. He had never kissed a girl before and he didn't think kissing involved tongues. But he went with it and found himself getting extremely aroused.

Helena pushed herself against him and laughed softly when she felt the bulge in his pants. She teased him by moving her hips against him and moaning softly.

Robert didn't know what to do with himself. He grabbed her head and kissed her fiercely. Suddenly, there was the sound of a car beeping. His father was home.

Robert didn't want his father to find him out here in the garden with Helena. If his father knew he had made a friend, he would do everything to try to destroy it. But it was too late. His father was already at the door. Robert pulled away from Helena suddenly and crouched down with his back to his father so that he wouldn't see his arousal.

"Hello, Robert!" his father said cheerfully. "Who is your beautiful friend?"

"I'm Helena," she said and extended her hand demurely to his father. Robert's father kissed her hand and looked deeply into her eyes.

"Nice to meet you, Helena. Are your parents home?" he asked.

"No, it's only my mother. My father passed away a few years ago, God rest his soul." Helena made the sign of the cross. "I saw Robert out here doing his chores and thought I would come over to say hello."

"Well, that's wonderful!" he said. "It's always nice when Robert can make friends. Would you and your mother like to come over for dinner this evening? I'm an excellent cook!"

Robert's heart sank, knowing that his father would put the moves on Helena's mother and then they would have to move again and he would never see Helena again.

Helena and her mother came to dinner, as expected. Also as expected, Helena's mother was a beautiful woman and Robert's father literally charmed the pants off her. The two adults spent quite a lot of time together, which also left Helena and Robert alone for the same amount of time. But Robert was afraid to get close to Helena because he knew they would be leaving soon. Helena was completely perplexed by Robert's sudden and persistent coldness, which was in stark contrast to the first day that they met.

But such was Robert's life. Once they moved again, after he had literally taken almost every dime from Helena's mother's inheritance from her husband, Robert vowed to himself that he would never become a criminal like his father. Robert vowed to learn a trade and stick with it, earning an honest living. Robert wanted to meet a woman, get married and have a normal family. That was his goal in life.

When Robert was eighteen years old, he moved away from his father. He worked various jobs to make enough money to rent a small apartment in France. He went to trade school in the evening and learned everything to do with plumbing, heating and air conditioning. When he was twenty five years old, his father was arrested for rape.

It seems that one of the women he was trying to "drain dry" was smarter than he was. She falsely accused him of rape and he went to jail. Robert never went to visit him, not even one day. Robert felt his father deserved to go to jail.

After his father was in jail for three months, apparently he couldn't take the pressure of prison life, so he hung himself. Robert didn't know where all of his father's money was, and he didn't want it anyway. It was dirty, filthy money. Robert decided instead to move to America and start his life over again.

Robert didn't have a criminal spirit like his father. Robert wanted to go to the United States of America and put his honest working skills to good use, and make some good honest money.

Robert worked for several companies before he met Danny. Danny owned his own plumbing business and they got along very well. Within five years, Robert bought his own home. It was a modest home and Robert was very proud that he had bought it with his own hard-earned, honest money.

I will never be like you, Father, Robert said to himself every single day. I do not have a criminal spirit like you do.

Robert's entire life was turned upside down when he met Corrine. Not only did he suddenly have love in his life, which he was truly grateful for, now he had a second mouth to feed, and someone else's needs to take care of. In addition, there was another mouth to feed named Lucille, who was her best friend.

He used to call them both "Nun Refugees." He was proud to support both of them. He was happy to finally have found love in his life. Corrine was everything he ever dreamed a woman could be. She was so innocent, so beautiful, and so very honest. All of her emotions were pure. She was not a manipulating woman, like some women that he had met in his life.

Robert had made friends with some of his co-workers and they used to go out to bars and pick up women. None of the women that Robert hooked up with were like Corrine. The other women were just looking to score, looking for a rich man to take care of them. Robert wanted something deeper. Robert wanted someone who would love him for himself, his personality, his soul. Corrine was that woman. She was the most pure, genuine woman he ever met. She was his soul mate. He fell in love with her almost immediately.

He was empathetic to what she had gone through. The poor girl was born without ever knowing who her mother was. Robert wasn't sure if that was better or worse than knowing your parent and knowing what a bad person he was. Robert never knew his mother, though, since she died giving birth to him. Robert often wondered what his mother had been like, and what she would think if she knew that her husband was a professional thief.

Robert wondered if his father was a thief all of his life or if he had just become a thief after his wife died. That was a question that would remain unanswered for the rest of his life.

When Corrine and Lucille moved in, Robert was happy. Lucille tried to stay out of their way as much as possible. She took several jobs, trying to make ends meet so she could move out and get her own apartment. No matter what job she took, she just couldn't make it work.

Robert used to tell her that she could make money with that face of hers. He didn't know how, he thought perhaps modeling at first. He never imagined it would be by robbing people of their money, by taking them by surprise at how an innocent face like that could want to steal your money.

Corrine offered to get a job but Robert insisted that she didn't. After a short while, Robert and Corrine decided to get married. Robert felt strongly that his wife shouldn't work, especially once they started having children.

Corrine got pregnant twice during their marriage. Unfortunately, both pregnancies ended in miscarriage. They were heartbroken about it. But they didn't let that get them down. Corrine was a very healthy woman and she was sure she would get pregnant again someday, and be able to carry the child to term. That's what the doctor told her, anyway. He told her she was still young, there was plenty of time.

There was a lot of pressure on Robert to support all of the people living in his household. Lucille did work for a while, which took some of the pressure off, but mostly he wanted to provide Corrine with all the luxuries she missed out on while she was in the convent.

One day, Lucille came home with Dick's number, a computer expert who would help Robert set up a computer. This was the computer age, after all, everyone should have a computer at home, right?

Robert was very impressed by Dick's knowledge and expertise. Dick also had other skills, since he studied electronics and engineering as well. Robert suddenly had an idea, almost a vision, of setting up some kind of business with Dick that would make them both rich.

When Dick came over, Lucille happened to have the evening off from work. Corrine and Lucille left the men alone, for the most part, but stayed close enough by them to be able to talk about them.

"So Jeff never called you, huh?" Corrine asked her.

"Nope." Lucille said. "But I'm not disappointed at all."

"Really? Why?" Corrine asked.

"Well, he wasn't really my type, I guess." Lucille shrugged her shoulders.

"Then what is your type?" Corrine asked.

"Darned if I know!" Lucille said, laughing. "I don't think I even have a type. I don't think I'm even meant to be with anyone."

"That's silly!" Corrine scoffed. "You are so beautiful and you're a wonderful woman! Any man would be lucky to have you!"

"Yes, that would be correct," Lucille said, "but what man would make *me* feel lucky to have *him*?"

266

Corrine thought for a moment. "That's a good one," she finally said. "You want a man that's worthy of you, too, right?"

"Exactly," Lucille said, looking down at her nails. "I don't want some asshole in my life that's going to suck me dry of my life's existence. Like my mother, for instance. I think she was attracted to anything that wore pants and a tie." Lucille thought for a moment. "No, scratch that. They didn't have to wear ties, they could wear anything they wanted. She brought home any low life that walked or crawled. And those low-lives always hit on me."

Lucille shook her head at the memory, tears starting to form in her eyes.

"After having those shining examples of men, plus this latest disappointment with Jeff, how am I supposed to trust anyone?" Lucille asked her best friend.

Corrine was quiet for a moment, then looked over at Dick.

"What about that guy?" Corrine asked her.

"That skinny, nerdy guy?" Lucille asked. "I'm not really attracted to him."

Corrine slapped her forehead with her hand. "What's wrong with him? He seems like a nice guy."

"What's so nice about him?" Lucille asked. "We know nothing about him. The only thing I know about him is that Jeff works with him. And I don't know Jeff very well, especially since he never called me."

"Why don't we ask him why Jeff didn't call you?" Corrine suggested.

"Are you kidding me?" Lucille said, starting to feel panicky. "That would be crazy! I don't know how well they know each other! I think that would be totally inappropriate!"

"Okay, okay!" Corrine said, holding up her hands. "Don't kill the person, just the idea, okay? Sorrrreeee!"

"I'm sorry," Lucille apologized. "You have nothing to be sorry for. I guess I'm just....on edge from being disappointed all the time."

"What do you mean, all the time?" Corrine cocked her head at her friend. "It was only one date. What else are you disappointed about, all the time?"

"Well," Lucille began, "you and Robert are so happy. And I'm in the way. I'm a third wheel. I just want to earn enough money to get out of here and give you guys your privacy."

"Robert doesn't mind!" Corrine assured her. "He loves you like his own sister!"

"I know he cares about me," Lucille quickly put in. "But I shouldn't be here in the middle of your relationship. You and he are newlyweds. You're trying to have a baby. I'm just in the way."

"No, you're not!" Corrine shook her head. "If I ever do have a baby, you can help me take care of it!"

Lucille smiled at her wryly. "Yeah, that would be fun. Changing poopie diapers and all that. Fun!"

"Oh, come on!" Corrine said, play-punching her in the arm. "Babies aren't just about poopie diapers. They're wonderful little creatures!"

Lucille wrinkled her nose at her. "You can keep them!"

"What, you don't like children?" Corrine asked, miffed.

"I like children just fine!" Lucille shot back quickly, hoping she didn't offend her. "I'm just not ready for them. Myself. That's all I'm saying."

"So you want to move out once we have children?" Corrine asked, almost sullenly.

"No, you silly goose!" Lucille said, laughing. "I'm trying to get out of here NOW so I can leave you free to TRY as much as you like to have children! After all, you can't be too uninhibited with me in the same house, now can you?"

"Our love life is just fine!" Corrine said. "I'm not inhibited at all."

"Yeah," Lucille smiled at her, shaking her head. "I can tell. Thin walls."

"Oh!" Corrine put her hand over her mouth and they both laughed out loud.

Dick and Robert walked over to them just then.

"This man is a genius!" Robert said, patting Dick on the shoulder. "I'm so glad you went out with that Jeff character, if only to meet Dick."

Lucille snorted at Robert, shaking her head.

"Dick tells me that Jeff works in the mailroom." Robert said slyly.

•   "WHAT?" Lucille turned to Dick. "I thought he was a talent director?"

"Talent director??" Dick laughed out loud. "Is that what he told you?"

"Yes! In fact, look......." Lucille ran to get her purse and took out his card to show Dick. "See? Talent director. Who makes up fake business cards?"

"People like Jeff!" Dick said. "Oh, this is so rich! It all makes sense now!"

"What makes sense?" Robert and Lucille asked at the same time.

"The way he acts at work." Dick said. "He's the biggest Casanova going. He's got all the hot women all the time hanging all over him. That must be his game, telling them he's a talent director."

"But how do you know that he isn't?" Lucille asked petulantly. "Maybe he works two jobs."

"Listen," Dick said, "the guy's a con artist. He's a nothing. The women like him because of the way he fakes his way through life. Then I hear stories from other women who've dated him, complaining that he cheated on them with other women. The guy is bad news. I can't believe someone like you went out with him."

Lucille stiffened. "I didn't know he was like that or I would not have gone out with him."

Dick looked at her thoughtfully. "No doubt."

Lucille didn't know what to make of Dick. Robert put his arm around Dick's shoulders.

"Would you like something to drink?" he offered.

"Sure, thanks." Dick just wanted to be around Lucille a little longer.

An hour passed while they shared good wine and good conversation. Lucille didn't drink the wine, she had her usual seltzer and cranberry juice. Dick was very impressed with her.

Dick was telling them stories from work, about how people called him a Mama's Boy because he lived with his mother. He told them about his past, about his brothers, about how his father died. They all sympathized with him. It seemed all of them had some tragic happenings in their past. Then Dick mentioned Derek and Ben to them.

"I've got to tell you," Dick said, "I've never seen two brothers more devoted to each other. They're best friends. It's really refreshing."

Lucille thought it refreshing that Dick had such a good relationship with his mother. She didn't think he was a Mama's Boy at all. She was impressed with any man that treated his mother so well. She was a little envious of their relationship, since her relationship with her own mother was so strained. Her mother never looked for her after she left home, and she never contacted her once she was in the convent. She knew she would never see her mother again.

"Are there any openings at your firm that would hire someone like me?" Lucille asked suddenly, not sure why.

"Are you kidding? Who wouldn't want to hire you?" Dick said. "What are your skills? Not that it matters, probably. One look at your face and you'd be hired. Geez, you can rob banks with that face of yours."

Everyone laughed. No one noticed that Robert suddenly got very quiet. It was like a light went on in his head. The wheels were beginning to turn. Rob banks with that face?

Robert tried to mingle in with the rest of the conversation for the night, but Corrine could tell he was very distracted by something. He didn't seem distracted in a bad way, but Corrine could tell he was excited about something, had an idea that he wanted to pursue. At some point soon after, Dick looked at his watch and got up, saying it was time for him to get home. He had an early day the next day.

"Well, Dick, thank you so much for all of your help," Robert said. "I hope you'd like to come over sometime and have dinner with us?"

Dick looked directly at Lucille with intense eyes when he gave his answer. "I'd love to. Thanks!"

"I'll give you a call tomorrow and we'll plan it." Robert said, putting his hand on his shoulder and ushering him towards the door.

"Goodbye, Dick, talk to you soon!" Corrine said, waving.

"Bye Dick!" Lucille said shyly. She always felt shy, for some reason, when people were leaving. It was like she was afraid she had to start all over again, breaking the ice, for the next time she saw him.

After he left, Robert turned to the girls and said, "What a nice guy that is!"

Lucille nodded her head in agreement while Corrine let out an emphatic "Yes!"

Robert looked at Corrine curiously and Corrine nudged her head in Lucille's direction. Robert got the hint.

"Do you like Dick?" he asked Lucille.

"Sure I like Dick!" she said.

"But not in 'that way' right?" Corrine asked her. "That's what she told me."

"I like Dick just fine!" Lucille said, throwing up her hands and suddenly turning red when Robert and Corrine burst out laughing. "He's a nice enough guy."

273

"But you said he was a skinny nerd, or something like that." Corrine said, trying to hold down her giggles.

"He's fine just the way he is!" Lucille said, and stomped out of the room.

"She likes Dick just fine!" Robert whispered conspiratorially to Corrine and they both burst out laughing again. Lucille heard them and shook her head, continuing in the direction of her bedroom. I can't believe I just said "I like Dick just fine." Lucille thought to herself. What kind of nun am I?

Robert couldn't sleep a wink all night. He kept thinking and putting together a plan in his head. He loves Corrine and wants to provide for her and their future children. He's making decent money in Danny's business, but he feels he can make more money, do more with his life. The words of his father kept coming back to haunt him, as well as the words of Mother Superior. If he put his plan into action, wouldn't that make him a criminal, just like his father?

No.

His father hurt people. Actually, his father destroyed people's lives. Robert wouldn't do that. What Robert was planning was to just take a little bit of money from convenience stores and banks which could easily recoup their money back within a few days. That doesn't count as hurting anyone. That's not a crime. That's just a......setback. Yes, a temporary business setback.

He could consider himself like a modern day Robin Hood, stealing from the rich and giving to the poor.

Except that he wasn't really poor.

But then again........they could use a little more money if Corrine is going to be a stay-at-home mother. Plus, even with Lucille living there, she wasn't contributing enough money as a waitress in order to help in the grand scheme of things. But......that face of hers could make some money, couldn't it? That face of hers could rob banks, couldn't it? No one would ever suspect that face of anything mischievous. By the time they robbed the place, people would still be shaking their heads in bewilderment, thinking, that sweet young face just robbed me?

But of course, he had to put together his team first. He would call Dick in the morning.

Dick, Derek and Ben came over the following evening to discuss Robert's plan. Robert had asked Dick if he could come to dinner and invite the "muscle" and his brother. Robert told them he had a great plan to discuss with them.

"I want to put together a team of people who could pull off some jobs." Robert said, after they had finished their dessert. Corrine and Lucille were starting to clear the dishes away but Robert asked them to please sit and he could help them with the dishes later. Dick also offered to help with the dishes.

"Now, I know how this is going to sound to all of you, but it's really not as bad as it sounds and it would benefit all of us greatly. What I'm asking from all of you is a challenging experience that could lead to very prosperous lives for all of us. There is minimal danger involved. I've thought the whole thing through from beginning to end, and there is little risk as well. The profits could be very great if we all work together, like a well-oiled machine. We can rehearse it as much as possible before we actually do the job, until we're completely comfortable with it." Robert began.

Everyone exchanged glances. No one was worried, so far everyone was intrigued. They were all relaxed, everyone had a little bit of wine (except for Lucille), but she had enjoyed so many laughs at dinner that she was very relaxed and feeling just as mellow as everyone else.

"What I'm proposing," Robert went on, "is a very well-organized small heist."

Lucille completely abandoned her relaxed state. "WHAT??" she screeched.

Robert just held out his hand to Lucille and made a 'calm down' gesture.

"Please let me finish." Robert continued, while Corrine and Lucille stared at each other in disbelief. "It's not what it sounds like. We are not going to become major criminals. I think it might be.......fun......and very profitable.......if we just take a store's profits for just one evening and split it among us. We have all of the tools needed to do this."

Everyone was staring at Robert, waiting expectantly for his next words.

"Everyone sitting here has the skills needed to achieve this. How many of us are completely satisfied with our jobs?" Robert asked. No one except Ben raised their hands.

"How many of us would like to make more money? Actually, NEED to make more money?" Robert asked while everyone raised their hands.

"Robert, I told you I would be willing to get a job," Corrine put in.

"Corrine, we discussed that. We both want you to stay home and raise our children." Robert said firmly, and then he softened a little. "That's what you want too, isn't it?"

"Well, yes, but......" Corrine started, but then decided not to say anything else.

"All I'm saying is for us to stretch our skills and have a little adventure. Will it be challenging? Yes. Will it be risky? Yes. But if we play our cards right, the risk will be minimal and the challenge will be routine. Does everyone understand what I'm saying so far?" Robert looked at everyone and everyone nodded their heads. "So here we have me, to start with." Robert put a finger to his chest and Lucille wondered why he did that, since everyone knew what "me" meant.

Suddenly, Robert was starting to get on Lucille's nerves. She was remembering what the Mother Superior said. The heat in Lucille's body was rising due to the panic of the memory. Mother Superior's prediction was coming true. Robert was going to become a criminal and Corrine would die. But since everyone was sitting there enraptured with what Robert was telling them, she kept her mouth shut.

"My father was a master criminal," Robert said. "He taught me everything there is to know about robbing banks. But my father used to also cheat women – widows -- out of their husbands' money, leaving them destitute. My father was a criminal that was to be despised. I don't think taking some money from a few convenience stores and banks is such a crime, really, since the money can be recouped back for them very easily. Don't you all think so?"

Everyone exchanged glances and shrugged their shoulders. No one spoke.

"Think about it, people!" Robert went on, starting to sound like a motivational speaker. "Dick, the people at your job think you're a Mama's Boy. You've been earning the same salary for..... how long now?"

Dick simply nodded. Robert continued. "And Derek, you and Ben both work jobs that you seem to be happy with. Are you happy with your level of income?"

Derek shrugged his shoulders. "It could be worse," he said.

"Of course it could be worse!" Robert shot back, beaming like a preacher that got a sinner to admit his sins. "It could always be worse! But my question to you is.....are you happy with your level of income? Don't you want to buy a nice fancy car to drive around in? Don't you want Ben to have everything he's ever dreamed of?"

"I can't argue with that, Robert," Derek said. "You're right about that. Yes, I have thought of those things."

"I'm happy with my life," Ben said. "I like my job, I like the people, and my brother Derry takes good care of me. We have a nice apartment, don't we Derry?"

"Yes, we do Ben." Derek said and looked back at Robert.

"Ben, do you have any dreams of your own?" Robert asked him. "Don't you want some adventure in your life?"

"I watch a lot of television," Ben said. "There's a lot of adventure on TV."

"I think I speak for Ben when I say that we've already been through enough adventure and just want to lay low now." Derek said nervously, hoping Robert wouldn't probe into that.

"I'm not trying to put you at risk," Robert said. "I respect how you feel, but what I'm proposing has minimal risk. It is practically fool-proof. We will never get caught if we all work together seamlessly. And we will never do this until our plan is seamless."

Everyone glanced at each other, more nervously now. Lucille could see that Robert was starting to scare everyone a little. Except for Corrine. She was gazing dreamily at Robert. Nothing he can do or say ever sounded wrong to her, did it?

"How would this plan of yours not be risky?" Dick asked.

"Here's how," Robert said, smiling like the Cheshire cat. "In this room, we have a computer and electronics specialist, a security guard trained in how to subdue people, if necessary – but it won't be necessary, so we'll just say we have a very large man that looks quite formidable; we have a nice young man who is filled with innocence, we have a woman that is filled with logic and reason," Robert looked proudly at Corrine when he said this, and then his eyes settled on Lucille. "And we have a woman with the face of an angel that no one would suspect is actually asking for the money."

Everyone was silent for a moment. Finally Dick spoke.

"There have been plenty of movies out there about groups of people, such as you speak of, robbing banks, casinos, hotels, you name it. And all the plans always go awry at some point." Dick said flatly. "I'm not trying to burst your bubble, I'm just trying to be realistic."

Robert smiled peacefully at him. "And I appreciate your input. But this is not a movie. This is real life. And the plan that I have going through my head is foolproof."

"Well, then," Dick said, "I think we all are curious to hear your plan, then."

Everyone nodded in agreement.

CHAPTER SIXTEEN – LUCILLE

This is my life now, Lucille thought. I'm working for a madman trying to find money in an old warehouse.

Lucille was starting to get frustrated. She thought back on her life and realized she hadn't accomplished much. She was a drifter now. She had friends, but she was truly alone in her heart. She couldn't give her heart to anyone, not even sweet, genuine Dick.

Jeepers, she wished he would let her call him Richard. His mother called him Richard. What was the deal there? No other person in the world could call him Richard except for his mother? Maybe he was a Mama's Boy after all.

Lucille looked at Corrine and Robert. Yes, they loved each other very much. But somewhere along the way, Robert lost sight of his good senses. He was too worried about money all the time. Corrine wasn't getting pregnant any time soon, Lucille could see that after all the talks they've had on the subject. Corrine went to the doctor and though there was nothing physically wrong, Corrine said she felt in her heart they would never have children.

Corrine even said she felt it stemmed from her guilt due to leaving the convent. Corrine said she felt God was punishing her for abandoning her vows.

Lucille argued that Corrine was born into the convent and everyone lied to her about her parents. Corrine knew no other life and that should have been enough for her guilt to be alleviated. After all, shouldn't a person have a right to choose what kind of life they want for themselves?

Corrine chose Robert. Corrine never looked back.......until now. Suddenly, she was feeling like God was punishing her by making her "barren" and she felt she could not be a complete woman until she gave Robert children.

Lucille herself felt like a lost soul. Her life with her mother had been truly unhappy and filled with the dangers of lecherous men lurking at every corner. Her life at the convent was filled with peace but......still she yearned for something more. She escaped by watching television and lived dangerously through her favorite science fiction shows. She treasured her friendship with Corrine, and when Corrine decided to leave the convent, she followed her like a puppy dog.

What would Lucille's life be like if she had stayed behind after all, in the convent?

Lonely. Why lonely, when she had all of the other sisters there, who loved her?

Because being a nun was not her true calling. She had not received "the calling" like all of the other sisters: a call from God asking them to devote themselves to His Will. No, she had *escaped* to the convent. The convent was her refuge from the risk of possible rape everyday from living with her crazy, insecure, lazy mother who had unscrupulous boyfriends.

Lucille heaved a heavy sigh. She reached out for another crate of paintings.

Suddenly, she realized that in her search for the money, she had not looked at any of the paintings. She had looked behind them, inside of the frames, inside the crates......but she had not looked at any of the actual pictures.

Isn't that what life was about? Wasn't life about the journey, not about the destination? She was so worried about finding the money that she missed out on the joy of looking at the pictures. Of course, Robert would kill her for wasting time looking at the pictures when she should be looking for the money. The pictures were unimportant. They weren't planning to open a gallery, Robert would say. His life was about the destination, not the journey.

Lucille looked at the first picture in the crate. It was a picture of a woman and a man on a beach looking lovingly into each other's eyes. Maybe it was her imagination, but that woman and man strangely resembled her parents. They both looked so young, so much in love.

The next picture showed a little girl in school wearing a uniform. She was sitting alone, eating her lunch. The little girl looked strangely like she did when she was about that age. She remembers having a uniform that looked like that.

The next picture showed a young woman running through streets. It was done in heavy watercolor and it was painted in a very blurry style in order to portray the fast movement.

The picture that followed showed two women smiling at each other, as if they were sharing a secret. Those women strangely resembled Lucille and Corrine.

Lucille got up and shook her head. She was imagining things. She decided to take a short break and look out the window. She walked over and tried to open the large, heavy window to get some air. She managed to open it from the top because pushing down was easier than pushing up.

She breathed in the fresh air. There were sounds of traffic in the street, people driving back and forth from work, all living their normal lives. There was a faint metallic smell in the air, but she didn't mind. She felt she had been breathing the old smell of the warehouse for way too long now.

Where was everyone? Suddenly, she realized she hadn't heard anyone's voice in a while. She started walking towards the doorway and walked into another room. No one in there.

The warehouse was so large, and Lucille kept getting lost. She felt like she was walking in circles sometimes. Or was she walking in squares or triangles? This warehouse was like a very large box with lots of little boxes inside of it.

Suddenly, she started to panic. Where was everyone? Should she call out? She didn't want to alarm anyone, but she knew they would all come running if they heard her call out.

No, she decided. Let's grow up here and put on our big girl panties, she said to herself. Don't panic. Just keep walking in one direction, she counseled herself. You're bound to run into someone at some point, right?

Lucille walked from room to room until she finally found Robert and Corrine.

"Luci!" Corrine called out and put her arms out. "Where have you been?"

"I've been looking for you guys too!" Lucille said. "Have you seen anyone else yet?"

"We haven't seen anyone for quite a while," Robert said. "I'm wondering if they left us."

"Well, wouldn't they say something if they were going out?" Lucille said. "Like, if they were going out to get food for us or something?"

"I don't think they went out to get food," Robert said sullenly. "I think they just got disgusted and left us."

"Now, Robert," Corrine consoled him soothingly, "they didn't leave us. This warehouse is huge. It's hard to stay together. Didn't you tell them to look in every inch of the warehouse?"

Robert nodded silently and Lucille thought he resembled a little boy just then.

"Well, then, we know they're here somewhere." Corrine said calmly, rubbing his back. "And just as soon as they find something, they'll yell out and we'll run and find them."

"This place is huge," Lucille said. "I was starting to get a panic attack while I was looking for you guys."

"You and your panic attacks!" Robert said, shaking his head and laughing. "I hope one day you grow out of these panic attacks!"

Lucille felt a bit defensive, but she didn't react to him that way. She looked Robert square in the eyes and said, "I hope I grow out of them too."

Robert smiled at her and nodded. Then he walked away from the girls and let them have a little privacy. But to Lucille's surprise, instead of looking through more crates, Robert simply walked over to the window and looked out. That was the first time she ever saw him doing nothing. He wasn't barking orders at people. He wasn't acting all anxious. He wasn't being paranoid. He was……just looking out the window.

Why should that be so unusual? Lucille wondered.

"So……" Corrine linked her arm through Lucille's. "Do you miss Dick? Were you looking for him just now?"

"NO, I wasn't looking for Dick!" Lucille said in a mock disgusted tone of voice. "I was looking for you!"

"We're fine, we're right here." Corrine said and glanced over at Robert. Lucille sensed a sadness come over Corrine.

"What's wrong?" Lucille asked her dear friend.

"I don't know," Corrine replied, her eyes filling with tears. "Something's changed, I can't explain it. Robert seems……afraid."

"Afraid of what?"

"I'm not sure." Corrine said, wiping away a tear.

"Afraid of not finding the money?" Lucille pressed.

"No," Corrine said. "I think.........I think he's afraid of moving on."

Lucille looked at Corrine, puzzled.

"Moving on from........where? Here? The warehouse? You mean, if he doesn't find the money? He'll feel like he failed all of us, won't he?" Lucille asked. "Most of all, he'll feel like he failed himself. And you know how he is; he's the big strong he-man that has to take care of his women!"

Corrine looked at her and more tears spilled out of her eyes.

"No, Luci, I think he's afraid of.......moving on with his life."

Lucille waited for her to continue. Corrine kept wiping away tears and she couldn't speak for several moments.

"I don't think we're ever going to leave this warehouse," Corrine finally said.

"What?" Lucille said, completely confused. "That's silly. Of course you're going to leave this warehouse! We will leave with or without the money. We can't stay here forever."

"Yes, we can." Corrine said. "Some of us will be staying here forever."

Lucille looked at her, completely perplexed. For some reason, a small feeling of fear started in her gut. But it wasn't fear for herself, it was fear for Corrine. And fear for Robert. But it became more than fear.....was it......sympathy?

"Come on," Lucille said assuredly. "Robert will come to his senses and the two of you will leave this warehouse eventually."

"I'm sure the others already have," Corrine said gravely. "And you need to go too."

"Don't be silly," Lucille said. "I'm not leaving here without you guys."

"Luci," Corrine said, urgently, taking both of Lucille's hands in hers. "You have your own life to live. You can't depend on us anymore."

Lucille took in a sharp intake of breath. "What do you mean? I don't depend on you. I have my own job, my own money......"

"You depend on our friendship," Corrine continued, "and there is nothing wrong with that, except it's keeping you from living your own life. It's keeping you from finding a man to love and share your life with. Don't be afraid of love, Luci. It's out there waiting for you. Not all men are like those men your mother brought home, or like Jeff."

Lucille's eyes started filling with tears.

"I won't even bring up Dick because I know that whole situation just annoys you," Corrine joked through her own tears.

288

"But he does love you, I'm certain of it. Your decision is your own. You have your life ahead of you."

"You have your life ahead of you, too!" Lucille said forcefully. "You and Robert! Someday you'll have children and you'll be a family! Why are you so sad?"

"Because we're never leaving this warehouse. I know it." Corrine said miserably.

"Oh, come on!" Lucille said, shocked that Corrine was saying things like this. This wasn't her friend speaking at all. Her friend Corrine was filled with courage and determination. This Corrine in front of her had.....given up on life.

"Robert will not leave this warehouse, with or without the money." Corrine said sadly. "We will be here forever."

Lucille got scared then, chilled to her bone. "How can you say such a thing?"

"We had a chance to leave, but Robert wouldn't go." Corrine said, not meeting Lucille's eyes.

"What do you mean?" Lucille asked frightened. She felt an ominous premonition of some kind, coming on like a dark cloud.

"It's not important," Corrine said, shaking her head and gazing at her friend sadly. "The important thing is that you go. Go and live your life. Fill it with love. Fill it with your dreams and make your dreams a reality. Go. You deserve better than this."

Lucille started to cry openly. She reached out and hugged Corrine tightly.

"I won't leave you," Lucille said fiercely. "I won't leave you alone to live the rest of your life in this stupid warehouse."

Corrine laughed bitterly. "The rest of my life? I didn't say the rest of my life. I said FOREVER."

Lucille looked at her perplexed. Suddenly, Corrine started moving away from her. It was like Lucille was gliding backwards on a carpet being pulled slowly on a smooth floor.

Lucille reached out her hands to Corrine but Corrine turned away from her.

Suddenly Lucille heard Dick's voice calling her. She turned around in the direction of the doorway and it was filled with light. She turned back to Corrine and called out, "You see? Dick didn't leave! He's right here!"

Corrine turned around and looked at Lucille one last time. "Goodbye Luci. I love you."

"I love you too!" Lucille cried. "Come with me! Dick is here, come with me!"

"I have to stay with Robert," Corrine said. "I love him."

Robert turned away from the window and watched Lucille leave the room. He had tears in his eyes. Corrine walked over to him and they hugged. That was the last thing Lucille saw before she passed through the doorway.

A light was shining in Lucille's eyes. It was annoying her. She felt like she had just woken up out of a sound sleep that she desperately wanted to get back to. The lights were too bright. What was happening? There were people's heads above her, grabbing her hands and touching her face.

Dick? Was that Dick? Yes, it was. He was off to the side, pacing the room. Why was he wearing a hospital gown? Finally, the people backed away from her and Dick approached her swiftly.

"Oh, Lucille!" he cried out. "I thought you'd never wake up!"

Wake up? Lucille looked around. She was lying in bed, in a hospital room. There were doctors and nurses all around her.

"Dick?" she asked panicking, trying to get up. She was too weak, and her elbows kept slipping on the sheets. "Where am I?"

"You're in a hospital. You've been in a coma for two weeks."

Lucille gasped and it hurt to breathe. A coma? How did she get into a coma?

Dick gently placed his hand over her hand. "I know you have a lot of questions," he said gently. "I'll tell you everything you want to know. But first, just try to take it easy. I can see you're starting to panic and that's not good. Just try to relax and breathe normally."

"You're a very lucky woman," a female doctor said from the other side of the bed. She was listening to Lucille's heart with a stethoscope. "We were all very worried there for a while."

"I told you she's a fighter," Dick said.

"She's a lot like you," the doctor smiled at him.

Lucille looked questioningly from the doctor to Dick. Suddenly she noticed that Dick's face was bruised.

"What she means is," Dick said, reading her mind, "is that... I've been in a coma too. I woke up out of my coma a couple of days ago."

Lucille stared at him agape. What was going on here? Her mind was so jumbled and fuzzy, she could hardly think. Last thing she remembered was being in the warehouse with Corrine and Robert.

"What happened?" Lucille asked him frantically. She reached up and grabbed his arms. "Tell me everything.......now."

"I'll leave you two alone," the doctor said, and the two nurses left with her.

Lucille looked at Dick and Dick looked at Lucille, wondering how much he should tell her at this point. She had just woken up, he didn't want to give her too much information or she would go into shock. He probably wouldn't tell her everything. After all, mercy was more important than the truth sometimes.

"Lucille," Dick began, "do you remember anything about going to that warehouse, following those men in the cars from the bar that night?"

Lucille thought back, licking her dry lips. Dick instantly reached over and poured her a glass of water and put a straw in it. He put it up to her lips and she sipped the water thirstily.

"Yes," she said, "I do remember that. We got out of your car and walked to the back of the warehouse. But........that's all I remember."

Dick tried to sigh with relief but he didn't want Lucille to see his relief. He didn't want to tell her what happened to them behind the warehouse, which is what put them in their comas.

"Well," Dick said, "things didn't go well. You remember the men we were following that night? The men that Robert said had hidden the money in the warehouse? They were cops, Lucille."

Lucille tried to sit up in bed again while Dick reached over and pushed the button so the back of the bed would rise a little more.

"The cops had been watching Robert for a while but couldn't find a way to bust him. So they pretended they were crooks who had hidden some money in a warehouse, knowing Robert was listening. So the cops lured us all to that warehouse."

"There was no money?" Lucille asked in a raspy voice. She was not used to talking, it seemed, due to being asleep for two weeks. She tried to clear her throat. "It was a set-up?"

"Yes," Dick said, "it was a set-up. When we got there, the place was surrounded with cops. Only we didn't know that. Our job was to go to the back of the warehouse and sneak in that way. But………something happened."

Dick cleared his throat nervously while Lucille watched him warily.

"The others were in front of the warehouse and the cops jumped out of the cars and surrounded them. Robert and Derek both pulled out their guns and………" Dick couldn't finish.

"What happened?" Lucille asked him. "You need to tell me. I can handle it."

"I'm not sure you could right now," Dick said. "Maybe you should just get something to eat and then rest a little. Let's watch some TV. I think your favorite sci-fi show is on."

Dick reached over to get the remote control and Lucille slapped his hand before he reached the item.

"Finish the story." Lucille said through her teeth. "Now. Please."

"Oh, Lucille, I don't know how to tell you this." Dick shook his head, starting to cry. "When my mother told me what happened, I couldn't believe it. I remember some of it, but only bits and pieces."

"Tell me what you remember."

Dick took a long, heavy sigh and went on.

"Robert pulled out a gun and the cops immediately fired on him. Corrine ran in front of him before the bullets started, but it was too late. They were both shot down."

Lucille screamed. Dick reached out and tried to soothe her, but she had burst into tears. She was gasping, and every breath she took was an extreme effort.

Dick decided to just blurt the rest of the story out. At this point, she was already hysterical, so he might as well finish telling her.

"Derek pulled out a gun and Ben grabbed it out of his hands and started firing on the cops. Derek tried to get the gun back from him, but......the cops fired on them too. They're gone too."

"OH MY GOD!" Lucille cried. Dick sat on the bed and pulled her into his arms. They both sobbed together for quite some time.

After they quieted down, Lucille settled back against the pillows, completely drained.

"So, then, what happened to us?" she asked. "What happened to us, to put us in comas?"

Dick heaved another heavy sigh. "My brothers happened to us."

"What?" Lucille asked, not knowing what he was talking about.

"My brothers are all cops. They had been listening to their police scanners. They were not on duty that night. They heard that there would be some action down at the warehouse so they all got dressed up and headed out there. My brothers did that sort of thing all the time; they got off on the action. They're all a bunch of assholes."

Dick's hands were in fists. "They spotted us going to the back of the warehouse and followed us. When they saw it was me, they………"

Dick stopped speaking. Suddenly, he couldn't speak.

"Would you like some water?" Lucille asked, handing him her water glass.

He accepted it and took a sip out of her straw. She didn't even mind that he just got his saliva and lip germs on her straw.

"Lucille," he said, trying to figure out a way to tell her some of the story without telling her the complete story. Some things were best left unsaid, especially out of mercy. If she found out the truth of what happened to her, she would never live a normal life. As it was, she already hated men. The best thing, Dick decided, was not to tell her the whole truth. Hopefully, she will never remember those events on her own.

"Lucille, my brothers always hated me. When they saw it was me, they started beating me with clubs. They knew you were with me, so they………beat you with clubs too. They beat us into comas."

"Those bastards!" Lucille gasped.

296

Dick refrained from telling her that they all took turns raping her before they beat her into a coma. Dick prayed sincerely to God to please not bring back her memory of that night. She would never be the same if she remembered the brutal rape and beating. Dick remembered how helpless he felt, not being able to save her, even feeling relief at being knocked out finally so he didn't have to watch anymore. But his memory of the event was pretty vivid and he would have to live with that the rest of his life.

"They're in jail now," Dick said. "Since they weren't part of the operation that night, the cops found them after they had taken the bodies.....our friends.......away in the ambulances. The cops found out what they had done and they were all arrested. They'll be in jail for a long time."

Lucille was in total shock, she didn't know what to say.

Her best friend was dead. The others were dead. Her family was gone.

Mother Superior was right.

Then Lucille remembered Corrine's last words to her. Corrine told her she had to go on with her life.

"Dick?" she asked meekly. "Do you remember anything else? Like......being in the warehouse?"

He remembered only too well being in the warehouse. But.....they never actually made it into the warehouse, none of them did. So why......? What was that dream he had during his coma?

"Dick," Lucille went on, "I had a dream that I was in the warehouse and we were all looking for the money."

Dick stared at her in shock. Did they have the same dream?

"I had a dream like that too," he said. "But how is it possible that we both had the same dream?"

Lucille felt a sense of something unrecognizable wash over her. She knew Dick was there too, that he had the same dream.

Except it wasn't a dream.

"Dick, do you remember Ben finding a rat?"

Dick just looked at her. They both stared at each other. They both knew the truth.

"We were.......there?" Dick asked her.

"I.......think so." Lucille said.

"How is that possible?" Dick asked. "It can't be!"

"Dick," Lucille reached out a hand to him as chills filled her body. "We were there. Well, at least, our spirits were there. Our bodies were here. We were with them."

Dick let go of Lucille's hand and paced the room slowly. He stopped to look out the window.

Lucille watched him walk away from her. She knew he was thinking about that possibility.

"I think that warehouse was like a sort of, holding pen for us so we could reflect on what we did." Lucille continued. "Did you notice the paintings? The ones I looked at were about my life. I didn't notice that until the end.....just before I woke up."

Dick turned to look at her as she continued speaking.

"When I was a nun, we were told that we all have souls and that our souls would go to heaven, or hell, depending on how we lived our lives here on earth."

Then Lucille suddenly had a revelation about why Robert didn't want to leave the warehouse. He was afraid of going to hell.

It sickened Lucille to realize that Corrine and Robert would haunt that warehouse forever with their lost souls.

"I don't really believe in hell," Dick said, "but I do believe in heaven. I don't think a loving God would create a place like hell."

"I don't either," Lucille said, growing even sadder. "I think our souls were lost there in the warehouse with......their souls. I think Derek and Ben moved on, but Corrine and Robert told me they were staying. Forever."

Dick ran back to her bedside. "What do you mean?"

Lucille related the story to Dick as she remembered it. It was quite clear in her head. Dick was shocked.

"We are really lucky, then," Dick said and squeezed Lucille's hand. "Aren't we?"

"I think so." Lucille said shyly, looking away.

They both sat in silence for a few moments, holding hands.

"So……where do we go from here?" Lucille asked him.

"Hopefully, not to jail." Dick tried to joke, but he was serious. "We are criminals, you know."

"But we got beaten within the edge of our lives!" Lucille said. "How can they put us in jail after that?"

"Maybe we'll get community service, then." Dick said, trying to reassure her. "Whatever it is, we have to pay our debt to society."

Lucille looked at him shyly. "What about after that?"

"After jail? Or after our debt to society?"

Lucille nodded.

"Then," Dick said thoughtfully, rubbing his chin, "I'd like to take you out to dinner."

Lucille giggled and then stopped laughing because it hurt her ribs. She reached out and pulled Dick close to her.

For the first time in her life, Lucille planted a kiss on a man's lips. It felt good. She could get used to that.

THE END

ABOUT THE AUTHOR

Lucia T. Chiarelli lives in scenic Orange County, NY with her fiancé Michael and their dog child Pipi. Lucia is a Reiki Master who also provides angel card readings, as well as animal communication and stress management tips. She is also a musician who has played in several bands (such as Cowhouse), as a singer, guitarist, keyboardist and drummer.

Lucia has been writing stories since she was a child and is extremely happy to have finally published her first novel, *Criminal Spirit*.

Please be on the alert for Lucia's next book, "*Advice From A Sicilian Rebel*," which is a series of funny memories from growing up in a Sicilian family, as well as snippets of her own unique view on life as it has presented itself to her thus far. The book will provide advice on several topics such as internet dating, Facebook, food shopping, health challenges, driving, menopause, the fear of having your appendix removed (as well as other fears and phobias), and other day-to-day things in life we take for granted. This book should be ready by the end of 2013 / beginning of 2014.

If you'd like to reach Lucia, she can be found on LinkedIn or you could send her an email at luciachiarelli14@gmail.com (please reference "Criminal Spirit").

Made in the USA
Charleston, SC
11 June 2013